Enjoy the
adventures
Lindsay
Schepfer

THE ADVENTURES OF KELTIN MOORE

The Beast Hunter
Into the North
Dangerous Territory

ALSO FROM LINDSAY SCHOPFER

Lost Under Two Moons
Magic, Mystery and Mirth

Dangerous Territory

A Keltin Moore Adventure

LINDSAY SCHOPFER

to Laura Schopfer
For all the good memories and years of
playing make-believe together

ACKNOWLEDGMENTS

Thanks to all of the fans of *The Adventures of Keltin Moore* for their ongoing shared love of these stories. We've come a long way since the first Keltin Moore short story was posted on my otherwise empty website.

Jerry Bowman and the Northwest Carriage Museum for their generosity and fantastic information.

Gordon Frye for his knowledge of firearms and infectious passion for history.

My creative writing students for helping me to see the craft of storytelling through new eyes.

All of my beta readers for their enthusiasm and tenacity.

My friends and family for their love and support.

Kathryn and Elizabeth for giving the best grins, giggles, and hugs a daddy can get.

And my beautiful wife Elicia, my dearest friend, biggest fan, and beloved eternal companion.

PROLOGUE –DANGEROUS WORK

Keltin paused to wipe away the sweat that had dripped down under the band of his wide-brimmed hat. The late summer sun beat down on him relentlessly, forcing him to question whether he'd made a mistake by wearing his familiar, long hunting coat, even with the inner lining removed. He'd had the coat since his first beast hunt, and it had done wonders at keeping him dry and warm in Riltvin's long rainy seasons, and had even saved his life more than once from an attacking beast. But as he walked forward carefully, searching the forest floor for any signs of the beast he was tracking, he couldn't help wondering whether the added safety was worth the discomfort in the oppressive heat.

Looking down, Keltin noticed a single leaf turned over to show its silver underside against the carpet of green around it. Searching the area, he found the slightest indentation in the dusty dry forest floor. A track. Keltin straightened up and continued onward, searching the ground for more signs of his quarry's passing. Head down, he made his way forward, trying to ignore the sensation of sweat pouring from his body and trickling down his face, sides and legs. He paused as the trail disappeared once again. Turning, he searched for a broken twig or another footprint, anything that would indicate the passing of the beast. Too late, he heard the gentle rush of wind from somewhere above him.

A weight slammed into his back and drove him to the forest floor. He tasted bitter earth in his mouth, his nose smarting as it came into sharp contact with the bark of a dead tree. The razorleg's sharp forelimbs tore at his coat and the pack on his back. Keltin tried to roll away to freedom but was hampered by the closely growing brush and bracken all around him. The beast savaged his back, ripping and shredding the fabric with terrible intensity.

Keltin knew it was only a matter of seconds before the beast's bladed feet would reach his flesh. His rifle useless, he fumbled for the revolver in his belt. Finding the handle, he pulled it free, aimed it behind himself, and fired the entire chamber through his own coat and pack, hoping he would hit the beast's body. The Matlik rounds in the pistol lacked the deep penetration of a Reltac Spinner, but they were still powerful enough to penetrate the tattered fabric and the contents of his pack to strike the body of the razorleg. He felt the beast spasm on top of him, and Keltin used its pain as a distraction to allow himself to remove the Lawrie hunting knife from its sheath on his side and stab awkwardly upward while turning and rolling. He almost ended up on top of the beast but managed to come to a stop lying on his side.

Keltin rolled away to safety and rose up onto unsteady legs, knife held out in front of him. The razorleg thrashed around as it struggled to its feet and tried to regain its balance on spindly legs. Keltin tried to gauge just how wounded the beast was as he considered his next move. With his revolver empty and his rifle lying on the ground where he'd dropped it, Keltin tightened his grip on his knife. On his back, he could still feel the tattered remains of his pack and coat. Somewhere amidst the wreckage was his Ripper, a savage short polearm designed specifically for finishing wounded beasts.

Keeping one hand on the knife and both eyes on the beast, he began to slowly extricate himself from his coat and the straps of his pack. A distant part of his brain registered relief as he pulled his coat loose, exposing his sweat-soaked shirt to the dry forest air. Meanwhile, the beast had fully regained its balance. Turning towards him, it hissed and lunged, stopping short less than a yard from his feet. Keltin slashed the air with his knife in a warning gesture. The razorleg lunged again, forcing Keltin to take a step back while still working furiously to free himself from his coat and pack.

Finally the coat and pack fell to the ground. He risked a look at the tattered heap and spied the Ripper lying among the sad remains of his belongings. He dove for the weapon, grabbed it, and came up ready to face the beast. The razorleg surged forward again but this time Keltin met its lunge with an attack of his own. He drove the spiked point of the Ripper into the thorax of the beast, knocking it completely off its feet and onto its back. Throwing his weight against the haft of the weapon, he drove the point deep into the creature like a naturalist pinning a flutterby to a display board. The razorleg kicked out desperately and Keltin staggered back, watching as the beast thrashed in its death throes. When it was finally still he dropped to his knees and said a brief, grateful prayer.

Opening his eyes again, he looked down and was surprised to see blood running down his tattered shirt sleeve. Apparently the beast had gotten closer than he thought. Quickly he stripped off his shirt and checked himself as best he could for injuries. Inspecting his clothing first, he found that while his coat had been badly torn, the back of his shirt was still intact. He was grateful, as it would have been next to impossible to treat an open wound on his back by himself. As it was, he had several scratches on his neck and arms with one long shallow gash in his left forearm. Quickly retrieving clean wrappings from his pack, he dressed his wound as best he could.

That done, he put his shirt back on before rolling up his tattered coat and tying his pack back together as best he could. Returning to the dead beast, he used the broad blade of the Ripper to cut off its vile head with a single blow before retrieving his rifle and the last of his gear. Bending down, he picked up his hat before turning to slowly… painfully… make his way back to town.

CHAPTER 1 – TRUE COURAGE

Keltin's boots crunched on the gravel path as he slowly walked towards the large manor house. The surrounding grounds were well-kept if somewhat wild. It seemed that the burgeoning upper class of Riltvin lacked the old world aesthetic that their Eastern neighbors enjoyed. Still, the mark of wealth was all around him, causing him to feel mildly uncomfortable in the plain, somewhat humble clean change of clothes he kept for Days of Rest and making appearances in town while on a hunt. Shouldering his rifle and his poorly repaired pack, he climbed the steps to the pair of front doors framed by pillars of stone that had no doubt added considerably to the final price of the manor house. Keltin gave a sharp rap on the door with the impressive brass knocker, waited a few moments, and then knocked again.

The door opened to reveal a man in his middling years dressed in a uniform that was nicer than any clothing that Keltin had ever owned. Keltin resisted the urge to self-consciously tug at the cuffs of his shirt as the doorman addressed him.

"May I help you, sir?"

"Yes. My name is Keltin Moore. My sister Mary works here. She sent a letter inviting me to come visit her once I got to town."

"Ah," said the main with just the slightest nod. "I see. Mary told us that we should have expected you several days ago."

"There were some complications with a beast hunt on the way here."

Keltin wasn't sure how much more he should say about it, but it seemed that the doorman accepted his story without question or interest.

"I see. Please step inside."

Keltin entered the front doors into the largest, most ornate reception area he'd ever seen. The ceiling stretched away to an ornate chandelier high above his head. A staircase spiraled around to a second-floor far above him as a hallway passed by the bottom stair, leading off to multiple rooms. Keltin felt his insecurity grow as even the shine of the marble floors made him feel inadequate. He hoped that he had shaken all the dust of the road off of his boots before stepping inside. The doorman cleared his throat.

"May I take your... ah... accoutrements, sir?"

The doorman reached for Keltin's rifle, pack and gear, stopping just short of touching the haft of the Ripper. Keltin dutifully handed each to the man, who took it all and carried it gingerly through a doorway and out of Keltin's sight. After several moments of waiting, the doorman returned.

"Just wait here. Please don't touch anything."

He turned and ascended the stairs up and out of Keltin's sight again.

Keltin fidgeted in the entryway. Resisting the urge to wander around staring with his mouth open like a country yokel, he opted instead to admire the incredible craftsmanship of the chandelier and brass candle holders on the walls. He was examining a tasteful bunch of cut flowers arranged in a copper vase when he heard a soft gasp from the top of the stairs.

"Keltin!"

He looked up and felt all the uncertainty in his heart melt away at the sight of his younger sister. Mary wore the modest dress of a governess, her hair up in a tight bun, the same familiar shade of brown she had inherited from their father, so unlike the ruddy tones that Keltin shared with their mother. Mary raced down the stairs and threw her arms around him.

"It feels like I haven't seen you in years!" she said, burying her face in his shoulder.

Keltin returned the hug fiercely while favoring his injured left arm.

"I've missed you Mary," he said. "You don't know how much."

Mary trembled slightly in what might have been a chuckle, a restrained sob, or something in between. "I was so worried when you didn't arrive days ago. I thought something had happened."

"It nearly did. I had a bad run-in with a razorleg, but I'm all right."

"Good."

Mary pulled back to smile up at him her eyes glistening slightly. "It seems like so much has happened since I saw you last. Krendaria, the gold rush... You've been through so much."

Keltin shrugged. "You've seen a fair share of changes yourself. The last time I saw you, you were just getting your start as a maid. Now look at you. A governess in a great mansion. I'm sure that father would be proud."

Mary nodded and gave a little sigh.

"I wish you could tell me all about your adventures, but I can't leave the children for long. Would you like to meet them?"

Keltin gave the answer that he was sure Mary was hoping for, though it was not necessarily the one that he was feeling.

"Of course. You've told me so much about them. I'd love to meet these children I've heard such glowing praise of."

Mary smiled sheepishly. "They are good children, for the most part, and very well behaved. I'm sure they'd be interested to meet you."

Mary turned and led him up the stairs, keeping one hand firmly clasped around his good wrist. Keltin dutifully followed her, trying to remember all those things that he had meant to tell her while elegant paintings and immaculately cleaned rooms blurred by them. Mary stopped at one of the doors and ushered him inside. The room's interior reminded him of the one-room school building that he and Mary had attended as children, except that this room was much nicer and only slightly smaller. Two children sat side by side in desks that had never seen as much wear and tear as the ones that Keltin had once sat in. The two children, a boy and a girl somewhere between eight and twelve, sat busily copying sentences from a large book laying open between them. Mary released his hand and went to stand in front of the two children who looked up at her with mild curiosity.

"Josiah, Madelynne, I want you to meet a very special guest," she said. "This is my brother. He's a beast hunter."

Keltin gave the children a somewhat awkward smile. He didn't consider himself uncomfortable around children, only inexperienced. He rarely saw the young children of his Uncle Olphe, and there was little call to interact with children in the business of hunting monsters. For their part, Josiah and Madelynne seemed just as unsure of him as he was of them. They both gave him a soft, polite 'hello' before turning back to their governess as if to ask whether they should return to their school work. Mary seemed oblivious to the awkwardness of the situation, beaming with pride, though Keltin wasn't sure whether she was proud of her brother or her students. Perhaps it was a little of both. He struggled to think of something to say, but was grateful when Mary broke the silence.

"Alright, I'm sure that my brother is very tired from the road. Perhaps we can talk to him later about some of his adventures." She checked a small pendant watch on her dress. "Continue your penmanship practice for another ten minutes. I'll be back after that to check on your progress."

Mary turned and led Keltin out of the room, closing the doors quietly behind them.

"Aren't they wonderful?" she asked as they walked away.

"They seem very well behaved," said Keltin.

"Oh they are. I have no complaints about them. I'm sure

they'll be very excited to talk with you later. They are always asking me about you."

Mary led him back downstairs and through another winding corridor to a doorway that led outside to a beautiful walkthrough garden. The day's heat was beginning to wan and Keltin admired the mix of native Riltvinian flowers along with other hardy imports that could survive the sometimes harsh weather of his home country. Mary led him to a patio with elegant rattan furniture and a lovely view of the flowing green grass of the grounds out beyond. In the distance, Keltin could see a small lake and a stand of trees farther away. Mary followed his gaze.

"All of this is part of the Whitt's estate," she said. "Mr. Whitt keeps the lake stocked with fish, and he'll often have guests fish it, or go hunting in the woods for pheasant and small game in the fall."

Keltin nodded, trying to imagine what life would be like with so much wealth. Mary took his arm and led him to a bench in the shade where they sat down together.

"So," she said, "tell me how you are doing. Are you still working with Mr. Jaylocke and Bor've'tai? I had half-expected them to be with you."

"They stayed back in Gillentown while I came along here ahead of them. We didn't want to bother hauling all of our gold down here only to find out that the rates aren't as good in Maplewood as we thought."

Mary's eyes lit up. "Did you really get a lot of gold up in Drutchland?"

Keltin nodded. "More than I've ever seen at once before, that's for certain."

"Have you given any thought to what you'll do with it?"

"Some. Though I'd always thought that if I ever got enough money, I'd see to it that you and mother were provided for—"

"No," Mary said with gentle firmness. "You don't need to be concerned about providing for us like you used to. The Whitts are very good to me, and mother is with Uncle Olphe's family now."

"Yes... how is mother doing?"

"Well enough. She's taking it upon herself to be the unofficial tutor to all of her nieces and nephews there. I suppose once a teacher, always a teacher."

Keltin nodded absently. After a moment, he looked up to see his sister watching him.

"Have you considered trying to write to her again?" she asked.

"No. I stopped trying a long time ago."

"Maybe you should try. It has been a long time."

"I wasn't the one who cut it off in the first place and kept it that way all this time."

"I just don't like seeing you two so unhappy. None of us have forever."

" I know." Keltin looked out at the grounds. "I do wish things could have been different," he said. "I've tried to do the best I could, ever since father..."

Keltin trailed off. Mary gently patted his arm.

"He'd be proud of you. I know it. You've continued the family trade and taken care of mother and I all this time on top of it. But you don't need to worry about us anymore. We're all right. Maybe it's time for you to start thinking of yourself, and what the rest of your life will be like."

A face suddenly flashed in Keltin's mind as a name followed close behind that pierced his heart completely. Elaine Destov. Keltin had not seen Elaine since the end of the Krendaria Campaign the previous year. The campaign had been organized by the nobility of Krendaria in a desperate gamble to save their autumn harvest from an unseasonably large infestation of beasts. The hope had been that by assembling the best hunters available and placing them under military direction, the campaign would succeed in driving back the beasts, providing food for the starving lower class and staving off an angry revolution. But revolution came nonetheless, while Keltin and his companions barely survived the horrific experience.

It was in the late days of the campaign that Keltin had met

Elaine for the first time. Along with a few others, the two of them had endured weeks of depredation together, trapped in a farmhouse surrounded by deadly monsters. Despite the desperate conditions, Elaine had remained stalwart and steadfast, demonstrating both courage and determination in the darkest of moments. Eventually the beasts were defeated, and the crops, if not the nation, were saved. Elaine had bidden Keltin a tender farewell and returned home to her family in Kerrtow, the capital city of faraway Malpin on Krendaria's northern border.

Since then, they had maintained a steady correspondence, and over time Elaine had slowly revealed more and more of her true feelings for Keltin, eventually confessing to emotions that went far beyond an admiration for his character and courage. For his part, Keltin knew that he had strong feelings for Elaine, but as yet he'd still been unable to express them. He had little experience baring his soul, and what little experience he did have still pained him to think about. The best he had managed was begging for her patience as he tried to sort out his feelings. As a result, the letters between them had become fewer and more distant until they had both stopped writing altogether, leaving a void that was as painful to Keltin as it was seemingly impossible to fix.

Forcing himself back into the moment, Keltin wondered if Mary might have intended for him to think of Elaine. While she and Elaine had never met, they had become fast friends through correspondence in the last year. Could Elaine have confided her feelings about Keltin to his sister? He wasn't sure, but he did know for certain that he did not want to discuss Elaine with Mary right at that moment. He searched about for a subject that was somehow related to their conversation.

"Actually, Jaylocke, Bor've'tai and I have done a lot of talking about starting up a beast hunting business together."

"Really? In Gillentown?"

"I'm not sure. Maybe, though there isn't a lot of business around Gillentown. Maybe we should set up shop further into the hill country where beasts are more common."

"It'll be hard for Mrs. Galloway to see you go. You've boarded with her ever since you left home."

"I've hardly been there at all for the last year, and before that I rarely spent more than a week at a time with her. Besides, it's not as if she doesn't have other customers. Grel'zi'tael and the rest of the Loopi have moved in already and have become good friends with Mr. Renlowah. They're even talking about working together with him. Apparently, Grel'zi'tael has shown great interest in tending gardens with Mr. Renlowah, and Shar'le'vah and Val'ta'lir would be strong, sturdy hands helping with the local crops and orchards."

"They must be very impressive. I've only ever known Mr. Renlowah, and even he intimidated me."

Keltin nodded again. The Loopi people were large and ape-like, each one of them standing well over six feet tall. Far from dumb brutes however, all of the Loopi that Keltin had met seemed equal parts stoic, wise and kind. He was proud to consider Bor've'tai and his fellow Loopi among his very best friends.

Mary looked down at the watch pinned to her dress and stood up quickly.

"I need to get back to the children. Feel free to enjoy the garden and grounds. Mr. Whitt has said that you're welcome to be their guest tonight if you don't have other accommodations."

"That's very generous of them, although I wish I could spend the time with you instead of them."

"I know. Mrs. Whitt says that I may join you for dinner, and we can speak again after the children have gone to bed. In the meantime, you may want to have a look around. There's someone here that you might be interested to meet."

"Oh? Who?"

Mary's eyes twinkled. "I'll leave that as a surprise for you. I'll see you at dinner."

With that she rose to her feet and quickly made her way back inside. Keltin sat on the bench looking out over the expansive grounds for a while before getting up to wander among the roses and other neatly spaced flower bushes. He walked up and down the rows, seeing the flowers without really looking at them. Eventually he grew tired of the blossoms, and decided that he would try walking down to the lake when his finely-tuned senses detected footsteps on the rocky path behind him. Turning, he saw a man walking towards him. He was in his middle years, robust and a little wide in the middle, dressed in a fine suit that glistened with gold from the shoe buckles to the pen in his lapel.

"Mr. Moore?" he called, his bassoon voice firm and strong. "I hope that you're enjoying my garden."

"Yes sir. Are you Mr. Whitt?"

"Indeed I am. Pleased to meet you. Your sister has told us quite a lot about you."

Keltin nodded, completely at a loss for what he should say or do. Of course, he had interacted with men and women of a higher social standing than himself multiple times. Often, it was the wealthy owner of a mining company or lumber mill that had hired his services. During his time in Krendaria, he'd even had some limited interactions with a duke, as well as daily meetings with a baron from the capital city for more than a month. However, Keltin had never been a guest of one of these people before. Not only that, but the fact that Mr. Whitt was his sister's employer added another layer of potential awkwardness, as Keltin refuse to allow himself to do anything that could possibly jeopardize Mary's position in the household.

Mr. Whitt continued.

"We'd expected you some days ago."

"I stopped off in Bracetown for a short hunting job that went poorly. I'm sorry that it made me late."

Mr. Whitt waved his hand dismissively. "Don't trouble yourself. I imagine your occupation has more than its fair share of risks associated with it."

Keltin shrugged. "All occupations carry some degree of risk with them."

"That's true enough, though I doubt the sort of risks that I run would daunt someone like you. After all, how intimidating can a meeting discussing annual revenues with your investors be when you've faced down a charging beast?"

"I doubt that I could do anything like that, sir. I'm not much for getting up in front of people. I'd rather be hunting."

"So would I, though I hunt purely for sport. Do you get a chance to do much sport hunting, Mr. Moore?"

"Not much."

"Perhaps I could convince you to come with me and some of my friends in the near future. I'm planning a grouse hunt at the end of the season, and I'm sure that we would all be fascinated to watch a professional hunter like you in action."

Keltin smiled politely, unsure whether Mr. Whitt was being sincere or merely polite.

"Thank you sir," he said. "Though I'm not sure that I'd be very entertaining for your friends. As I said, I'm not the best at speaking with groups."

"You wouldn't be speaking so much as shooting, which I'm sure you're far more comfortable with. Besides, you'd likely already be friends with at least one of the other participants."

"I would?"

"I believe so. In fact here he comes right now."

Keltin turned in the direction that Mr. Whitt was pointing. He saw a man walking towards them from the house. He bore a shock of white hair that seemed to have come to him early in life as his face showed a youthful exuberance. His eyes had a stunning intensity to them that seemed to remind Keltin of someone. Mr. Whitt smiled and clapped the man on the shoulder, turning towards Keltin.

"Mr. Moore, allow me to introduce you to Severn Destov."

"Hello Mr. Moore," said Mr. Destov. "I'm very glad to finally meet you. My daughter has told the entire family a great deal about you."

Suddenly Keltin realized where he had seen those intense eyes before. The man before him was Elaine's father! Keltin was too surprised to voice a greeting as he extended his hand to find Mr. Destov's handshake firm, his smile warm.

"I owe you a long overdue expression of gratitude, Mr. Moore," he said.

"I appreciate that," Keltin managed to say. "Though I could just as easily say that I owe my life to your daughter. She led the charge against the tusked giant when it had me trapped in the barn."

Mr. Destov's snowy white eyebrows went up. "Is that so? I never heard that part of the story. You'll have to tell me more about it later. Are you staying for dinner?"

Keltin glanced at Mr. Whitt.

"Mary mentioned it, but I wouldn't want to intrude…"

"Nonsense!" said Mr. Whitt. "We're having a few friends over for dinner, and I'd love for you to be there as well. I know I for one would be fascinated to hear some stories of your hunts, and while I've never tracked something that might have tracked me back, it would be grand to have a new, sympathetic ear for some of my tired old hunting stories."

"In that case, I'd be honored to come to dinner."

"Splendid. I'll see that another place is set. Now if you'll excuse me."

Mr. Whitt left them to make his way back to the house. Keltin turned to Destov, feeling more than a little uncertain. How much had Elaine told her father about Keltin? Had she told him of her feelings for him? Keltin looked at Destov and saw his eyes full of genial friendliness. Keltin cleared his throat.

"I must admit, I'm still a little surprised to see you, sir. I'm afraid that I don't understand why you're here."

"I can answer that easily enough," said Mr. Destov as he gestured for Keltin to walk with him through the grounds. Keltin fell in step with him as Elaine's father began speaking. "Have you been keeping up with current events in Malpin?"

"I read what I can in the papers, though most of what I know is from your daughter's letters. It sounds like the Heterack Empowerment has finally transitioned into a somewhat stable new government."

Destov made a slight grimace. "'Somewhat stable' is a most appropriate description. The Vaughs have taken control of nearly every branch of government, and their Supreme Minster Halev is introducing new laws and policies every week. Beyond that, the loss of the Loopi craftsmen and laborers has proved a severe handicap in our ongoing attempt to restore our nation to what it was before the tragedy of the Three Forest War."

"I would have thought that the gold coming in from the rush in Drutchland would have stimulated the Malpinion economy."

Destov chuckled softly. "I'm afraid that most of the wealth from the banks of the Wylow has been divvied up between the mining company owners and their investors. You can believe that Mr. Whitt is among those secretly kicking themselves for not acting quickly enough to get a piece of that action. But for the common man, it will be some time before any positive effect trickles down to the lower classes."

"Are you worried that there may be a revolution, like in Krendaria?"

"No. Not with the Vaughs in power. Their grip is too tight on the populace. At first it was simply dirty politics, but recently the most outspoken opponents of Halev have begun to run afoul of the League of Protection, the state's police force. The LOP has been finding all sorts of legal violations among political dissidents, especially with the laws changing so quickly. As a solicitor, I've tried to represent a few of those who were brought to trial, but the cases were farcical at best. In all honesty, this is why I have been searching for some time now for the possibility of employment outside of my home country."

Keltin shook his head. "I had no idea things were that bad."

Destov nodded. "I'm afraid so. Luckily, your sister Mary chanced to mention to Elaine that Mr. Whitt was looking for someone with experience in both business law and government agencies outside of Riltvin. Once I had sent a list of my credentials and a letter of introduction, Mr. Whitt was good enough to invite me to come to discuss the possibility of employment."

"Are you going to work for him, then?"

"I believe so. Working as an agent for Mr. Whitt's interests should prove both stable and lucrative. Don't let his genial demeanor fool you. He's a shrewd businessman with a cunning, quick mind."

"So that means that your family will be coming here?"

"Would you expect them to stay in Malpin?"

"No, I... I'm sorry. I just..."

Keltin hesitated. Destov seemed pleasant enough, but they'd only just met. How could he explain how he felt about the man's daughter? Should he even try? He was still debating with himself when Destov spoke again.

"No need to apologize. This is all quite new to you, I'm sure. I would like to continue to talk with you, but I really should finish some pressing business of Mr. Whitt's before the day's out. I'm sure our host would encourage you to explore the grounds as you like. Dinner is typically served at seven."

"Thank you. I'll see you then."

Elaine's father shook Keltin's hand again and turned away. Keltin watched him go and for a long time, his thoughts remained a thousand miles away from the lovely green landscape around him.

* * *

Keltin emerged from the room that had been provided for him, scratching at the unfamiliar, fine suit that had been loaned to him for dinner. He endured it stoically as he made his way along the halls until he finally found the dining room. The space was enormous with a ceiling so high that its ornate details were lost in the twinkling candlelight. The room was dominated by a massive table with comfortable seating for more than a dozen diners. Most of the other dinner guests had already arrived, and Mr. Whitt smiled broadly from the head of the table as Keltin entered the room.

"Ah! Mr. Moore. Come in. I don't believe I've had the pleasure of introducing my wife to you yet."

"No sir, thank you." Keltin gave his best gentlemanly smile to the finely dressed woman at the opposite end of the table from her husband. "Good evening, Ma'am. Thank you for inviting me to be here."

"Oh the pleasure is ours, Mr. Moore!" she gushed in a surprisingly high-pitched voice. "Please take a seat there, across from Mr. Garsun. Let me make introductions for you. Of course you already know my husband and Mr. Destov. This is Mr. and Mrs. Pennock and Ms. Olshield, old friends of our family. Mr. Garsun serves as my husband's personal secretary, and of course we have Father Rafferty, always a welcome guest at our table. Everyone, this is Mr. Keltin Moore, the brother of our governess, Mary. He's a great beast hunter, recently returned from one of his grand adventures."

Keltin felt his cheeks go warm as he nodded to each in turn, taking his seat in-between Mr. Destov and an empty chair, with Isaac Garsun sitting directly across from him. Mr. Pennock leaned over the table from his place at Mr. Whitt's side to speak to Keltin.

"A beast hunter, eh? Now there's an engaging profession. I do hope you'll rouse us with a few tales of your recent exploits. I never tire of hearing a good hunting story. Tell me Whitt, did I ever tell you of the time I went hunting at Dabnishire?"

Pennock and Whitt were soon deeply conversing about pleasure hunting while the women at the table spoke of people and events that Keltin had no knowledge of or interest in. He would have liked to engage Destov in conversation, but the solicitor was making a show of giving his full attention to his employer's conversation. Instead, Keltin studied Isaac Garsun out of the corner of his eye. Mary had mentioned the young man several times in her letters over the last few months. It seemed like each time he was brought up, Mr. Garsun had become kinder, funnier, and more intelligent to her. Keltin looked at Garsun for anything that might make him immediately dismiss the young man, but found nothing. Despite his employment as a secretary, he had a healthy pallor, with a build that was slender but not spindly. His face was friendly and he had intelligent eyes. Only once did Garsun look in Keltin's direction, realized he was being watched, and quickly looked away.

Mary arrived just as the soup and cheese were being served. Keltin was startled to see his unassuming sister wearing a dress that seemed far above her station, though Mrs. Whitt smiled at her warmly. Perhaps it had been a gift from the lady of the house. It certainly seemed to have an effect on Isaac Garsun as the two of them shared a quick smile as Mary took her seat at Keltin's side.

"How are the children, Mary?" asked Mrs. Whitt.

"Very well, Ma'am. They've had their supper, and are enjoying their reading now."

"You're a wonder with those two, my dear. Mr. Moore, we're all so glad that your sister has become a part of our household."

Keltin smiled politely even as he noticed Mary and Garsun continuing to look at each other with half-hidden smiles. He glanced in their direction. Mary gave him a small smile, but Garsun immediately blushed and looked away to feign interest in some tale Mr. Pennock was sharing about chasing down a grousehound on foot when he was a youth. For his part, Keltin could immediately tell that Pennock was lying through his teeth about the encounter, but decided it was better to keep such thoughts to himself. Luckily, the dark brown soup was most distracting, filled with tangy spices and generous slices of turnips, carrots, onions, and scallions. Keltin hadn't realized how hungry he had been until he looked up from his empty bowl to realize that everyone else was only half-done. He blushed, worrying that he was looking all the parts of a country bumpkin when he noticed that Father Rafferty was watching him with a kindly smile.

"Well, Mr. Moore," he said. "I've never met a beast hunter before. It seems like it would be terribly dangerous work. Why did you take up the trade?"

Keltin relaxed slightly, feeling more at ease with the reverend than some of the other, more distinguished guests.

"I learned it from my father. The Moores have been beast hunters for four generations. I'm proud to carry on the tradition."

"Does your father still hunt?"

Keltin fell silent. Mary reached over and placed a hand on his arm.

"Our father passed away some time ago," she said.

Father Rafferty smiled gently. "I'm sorry for your loss. You must miss him."

"He was clearly a good man, if his children are any indication," said Mrs. Whitt.

Keltin glanced at Mrs. Whitt and received a kind smile in return. Perhaps she was merely being a good hostess, but Keltin was suddenly very grateful that Mary had found such excellent people as her employers. The conversation moved on, and it wasn't until they were midway through the next course of stuffed pheasant and spiced potatoes that Keltin was roused from his thoughts by Mr. Whitt. The conversation at the head of the table had shifted from hunting to investing in mining operations, and the subject of the discovery of gold in Drutchland had been brought up.

"You were recently in Drutchland, weren't you, Mr. Moore? Were you able to observe much of the goings-on among the mining companies there?"

Keltin swallowed his mouthful of potatoes and nodded. "I worked for several of them while I was in Lost Trap, though I couldn't say much of the way they conducted their business. I was... occupied."

Keltin's host gave him a broad smile and a wink. "I'm sure you were. Well, why don't you tell us a little of your adventures while there? I think we've all been patient enough, but I must insist on you telling us something before the meal is over. I'm sure we'd all be fascinated."

Feeling eyes on him from all sides, Keltin wished he could politely refuse, or better yet, he wished that his apprentice Jaylocke was with him. As a Weycliff wayfarer, Jaylocke had lived his entire life on the road, entertaining all sorts of audiences across the continent. It was Jaylocke that typically took up the telling of the tale of any of their adventures together, which often resulted in better business for the both of them. Still, Keltin had heard Jaylocke's version of their adventures in the boomtown of Lost Trap enough times that he was able to frame the events in a fairly interesting sequence. It also helped that both Mr. Whitt and Father Rafferty proved to be very attentive audience members, each asking questions and giving every indication that they were on the edge of their seats listening to his tale. Keltin slowly found himself relaxing a little in the uncomfortable role of a storyteller, and while he never dared to embellish any details of the tale, he found himself taking some genuine pleasure in describing the hair-raising final hunt for the deadly Ghost of Lost Trap.

"Marvelous!" said Mr. Whitt as Keltin finished his account. "I'm sure no-one else could have accomplished such feats as you did. And it sounds like you were properly rewarded for your efforts. I wonder, have you given any thought as to how you will spend your newfound wealth? You don't strike me as the sort to throw it away on drink and frivolity."

"No sir. Actually, I haven't spent very much of the money yet, aside from giving my regular donation to the church."

"I'm sure you'll be blessed for your generosity," said Father Rafferty.

Keltin gave the churchman a small smile. "In my business, there's no point in taking needless risks."

"Still," said Mr. Whitt, "I'm sure you were left with a pretty pile of pence after your oblations. Have you considered investing your money? I have any number of ventures right now that would welcome a junior investor."

Keltin was caught completely off guard. He glanced quickly in Mary's direction, but her stunned expression seemed to match his own surprise. Keltin tried to think over all the possible ramifications of becoming a business partner of Mary's employer. After a moment, he took a breath and turned back to Mr. Whitt.

"I appreciate the offer, sir, but I've already made plans with several of my fellow hunters. We intend to use our combined money to start a beast hunting company."

Keltin was relieved to see that Mr. Whitt didn't seem offended by the refusal, though he did arch an eyebrow in curiosity.

"That's interesting. I don't think I've ever heard of a venture quite like that. How do you plan to conduct your business?"

"I haven't had a chance yet to decide on a lot of the particulars, as I've been on the road for some time. But my friends are coming to Maplewood to exchange the bulk of our gold for Riltvin jeva. Once that's done, we'll set up shop somewhere."

"Where do you think you'll base your business?"

"I honestly hadn't really considered that yet."

"May I make a suggestion?" said Mr. Destov. "You may want to choose a large city. There's a larger customer base that way, and you can make your business more easily accessible."

"But there aren't any beasts in the cities."

"I appreciate your concern," said Mr. Whitt. "But I think in this instance it would be better to make yourself easy to find for your potential clients. Let them come to you. Or, at least have a place that they can leave word that they want you to contact them."

"I suppose you're right," said Keltin. "Maybe I'll look into a larger city then."

"May I suggest Collinsworth?" said Mr. Destov. "Many of my duties take me there, and it seems to me to be a growing city of commerce. It's also fairly well connected to the surrounding territory by their fine railroad system. It's also closer to the hill country and the northern territories, not to mention the nations beyond Riltvin."

"Yes. I'll look into it. Thank you both for your insight. I fear that I'm a terrible novice when it comes to this sort of thing."

Mr Whitt grinned. "Don't bother yourself about it. This is our trade, just as hunting beasts is yours. There's no shame in seeking out the expertise of someone with experience."

The rest of the dinner conversation moved away from Keltin's plans, and he gratefully lost himself in the final courses and dessert, trying not to show that he noticed all of the little looks that Garsun and Mary kept giving each other. At last the meal ended and the dinner group began to break up. Mary had to leave early to put the children to bed, and Reverend Rafferty excused himself to head home. Keltin was invited to join the others for cards and drinks in the parlor, but he turned them down, still feeling out of place despite the polite company. Returning to his room, he found that his pack and gear had been unpacked for him and his few clothes had been laundered. Only his tattered coat had been left untouched.

Looking at the bed, Keltin realized that despite being tired, he couldn't bring himself to sleep just yet. He took up a fine lantern from his bedside, and went in search of the gardens again. The evening air had cooled the summer heat, and a bright moon shone on the distant lake. Keltin sat in one of the rattan chairs and took a deep breath of a passing evening breeze. This felt infinitely more comfortable than the Whitt's mansion. He couldn't imagine living in such wealth. Although, he reminded himself, he had more money now than he ever had before in his life.

It occurred to Keltin that the entirety of his adult life had been spent in a constant scrabble to make ends meet. Whether it was sending money to support his mother and sister or trying to make his monthly payments to Mrs. Galloway, so much of his time had been caught up in worrying about where he would get his money and where it needed to go. But that wasn't an issue anymore. His mother was staying with her brother's family, and Mary's every need was seen to by the Whitts. Keltin felt a sudden, unexpected pang within him. He was finally in a position to easily take care of those that he cared for most, and they didn't need him.

He breathed a long sigh, and started to rise from his chair when he heard the slight creak of hinges behind him. Turning towards the house, he was surprised to see Isaac Garsun walking towards him. Keltin stood up as Mr. Whitt's secretary approached him.

"'Evening, Mr. Garsun. Something you need?"

"Oh! No, Mr. Moore. Please, call me Isaac. I was hoping to talk with you, if you don't mind."

"Of course. And you can call me Keltin."

"Ah… thank you."

Keltin sat back in his chair as Isaac took a seat next to him. The young man stared at the table for a moment, clearly struggling to put voice to the words in his mind. Keltin waited, forcing himself not to guess what might be coming.

"Mr— Ah, Keltin, I wonder if Mary has mentioned me very much in her letters to you?"

"Some."

Isaac cleared his throat and plunged ahead.

"You should know that I care deeply for her. She's a very special girl. Of course, you'd know that, but I… well, Mary means a great deal to me."

He glanced up, but Keltin didn't reply as he watched the young man and waited for him to continue.

"Keltin, you should know that your sister and I have been courting, somewhat, of a fashion. It's hard to do very much in our current positions, but there it is. I wanted you to know, as her brother. I didn't want you to think we were keeping it a secret from you."

Keltin nodded slowly.

"I appreciate that. And you are right, Mary is very special."

"Yes." Isaac showed no signs of relaxing as he continued. "The thing is, I know that your father is gone, but I would like to do everything as properly as I can. Though it's still a little early, I'm not sure when I may again have the opportunity to speak with you face to face." Isaac took a shaky breath. "Keltin, I'd like to ask your permission to ask for your sister's hand."

Keltin was silent. He thought of his little sister in pigtails, running through the woods behind their home and playing with her overly-serious big brother. He thought of his father, wise and friendly, always certain of what to say and do. It should have been him sitting here, having this conversation. Suddenly Keltin missed his father with an intensity that he hadn't felt in years. Steeling himself, he looked into Isaac's uncertain eyes.

"You need to understand something, Isaac. Mary is my only sister. She means more to me than you'll ever know. I've protected her and taken care of her as best I could ever since our father died. I don't know you, but I trust my sister's judgement. If she thinks that you are worthy of her time, it's not my place to say otherwise."

Isaac seemed to wilt with relief. "Thank you, I—"

Keltin held up his hand and Isaac froze.

"There's one more thing I want to say," said Keltin. "You don't know me except for what my sister might have told you. So let me tell you this about me. I don't like bullies, and I've tried hard to keep from being one myself. I'm a beast hunter for a number of reasons, not the least of which is a deep belief that it's my duty to protect those that need protecting. My father, my uncles, my grandfather… my family taught me that. I'm not going to threaten you like a boastful, blustering older brother trying to make himself feel big and important. I'm only going to tell you the truth. If any man ever hurt my sister, I would come for him. No matter where I was, no matter how he might hide or try to make himself ready for me, I would come for him. Do you understand?"

Isaac looked away a moment, took a deep breath, then met Keltin's gaze. Looking into the young man's eyes by the flickering light of the lantern, Keltin was surprised to see a spark of strength and determination that hadn't been there before.

"I understand, but what you've told me doesn't change how I feel about her. All I can do is swear to you that I will never hurt her, and I will do my best to take care of her for the rest of my life."

Keltin looked into Isaac's eyes for a long moment before nodding.

"I believe you. All right, you have my permission, for what it's worth."

Isaac reached out a hand to Keltin. "Thank you. Thank you so much."

Keltin shook his hand and arched an eyebrow. "Keep in mind though, you may have my permission, but it's really up to Mary."

Isaac nodded and risked a smile.

"I know. I think I may be even more scared to talk to her than to you."

Keltin smiled back. "That's good. I'll wish you luck then."

"Thank you, Keltin. And I wish you luck in Collinsworth."

"Thank you. Good night, Isaac."

"Good night, Keltin."

The young man rose and left. Watching Isaac go, Keltin had a sudden, painful realization. Nervous as he may have been, the young man was far braver than Keltin was. Keltin might have stared down a charging beast dozens of times, but Isaac had faced a total stranger, possibly a dangerous stranger, and bared his soul to him. An image of Elaine forced itself into his thoughts, and Keltin nodded grimly. Yes, timid Isaac Garsun was much braver than Keltin Moore had ever been.

CHAPTER 2 – PUTTING DOWN ROOTS

Keltin stared into the rat's beady black eyes. The black-furred rodent was more than a hand's length long without its ropey tail. It returned Keltin's gaze boldly for a moment before turning and slipping back through a hole in the wall. Keltin shook his head. Now he understood why they had gotten the office space so cheaply. The bakery next door seemed to draw rats from all over Collinsworth, if not all of Riltvin. Keltin was sure there was at least one nest, maybe more, stashed away in the walls. His sharpened hunter's ears seemed to twitch every time he heard their scuttling feet or scratching teeth. Perhaps it had been a mistake to decide to use the upstairs portion as a living area.

Still, the space was otherwise well-suited for their needs. The downstairs had previously been used by a bookkeeper's firm, with a spacious receiving area and several frosted windows to allow some natural light in. Beyond the receiving area there were two offices and a third room that had been used for storing ledgers. Keltin had claimed one office for his own use, and planned to use the storage room for the storing and maintaining of their weapons and gear. He still didn't know what he would use the second office for.

Bor've'tai appeared in the doorway to Keltin's office, a

broom in his large, ape-like hands.

"I've finished sweeping the reception area," said the dignified Loopi in a rich bass voice. "Do you need any sweeping in here?"

"I already did it."

Bor've'tai nodded, setting the broom aside and entering the room to sit in the chair opposite the barren desk. Keltin looked over the long expanse of empty wood between them and shook his head.

"I almost wish that they hadn't included these desks in the deal," he said. "I feel silly with nothing on it."

"What would you put on it?"

"I don't know. Jaylocke suggested a rifle, or perhaps the mounted head of a coiling creeper."

"That sounds like something he would suggest."

"I just saw another rat."

Bor've'tai frowned.

"We'll have to get rid of them before we can open for business. Shall I board up their holes?"

"At some point. But unless we kill them off they'll only chew new ones."

The bell at the front door jingled. Keltin and Bor've'tai got up and entered the reception area to find Jaylocke with three steaming lamb pies balanced in his hands and a wide grin on his face.

"There's a definite advantage to setting up shop so close to a bakery," he said. "Lunch is served."

"I don't know how I feel about eating goods from a business that has a rat problem," said Bor've'tai.

Jaylocke shrugged. "We've had worse on the road."

"Not by choice."

"I'm sure it's fine," said Keltin, taking one of the pies. "Besides, I was thinking of going by the Claxons' shop and seeing if they sells any traps."

"Oh?" said Jaylocke. "Are we converting to trap hunting rather than stalking?"

"You use the right method for the right quarry. Besides, if

we shot a rat with any of our guns, we'd blow a hole through the little monster and a few walls behind it. No need antagonizing our landlord with more property damage."

"Fair enough, but we have bigger concerns than rats that we should discuss."

"I know… I know…"

"We can't have a business without a name for it."

Keltin heaved a sigh and set his pie down. "I'm no good at this sort of thing. If we have to have a name, why don't we just have something sensible? I still think 'The North Riltvin Beast Hunting Company' sounded find."

"It did, it sounded fine. And that's the problem. We need something that will stop people in their tracks. Something that shows just how amazing our company is. Something like 'The Guild of Nightmare Slayers'."

Keltin made a face in between bites of his lunch.

"I don't like the idea of calling ourselves a guild. Not after Drutchland. Besides, nightmare slayers sounds too ostentatious, and doesn't really describe what we do."

"Well we have to name the company something, Keltin."

"What about 'The Beast Hunter'?" said Bor've'tai.

Keltin turned to him.

"'The Beast Hunter'? But there are three of us."

"True, but you're the one with the reputation. Think about it. People have always come to you, seen you as the leader, the expert, the authority figure. To them, you are *the* Beast Hunter."

"I think you're on to something there," said Jaylocke with a growing grin. "It's got a nice, stoic sound to it. Like Keltin's a lone, dangerous man that only lives to kill monsters."

"But it isn't true," said Keltin. "Well, not precisely. Anyway, we're partners. I'm not interested in taking any recognition from either of you."

"We know that," said Bor've'tai. "But for better or worse, we will be best served letting you be the face of our company. You are the most experienced of the three of us, after all. We should also consider that there are some people, even in

Riltvin, that won't react well to a company that advertises itself as having a Loopi and a Weycliff Wayfarer among its hunters. It's better to let people think of you first, then have us follow along as needed."

"Besides," said Jaylocke, "think of the thematic power of a name like 'The Beast Hunter'. Picture a family up in the hill country. The father —tired from a hard day's labor— sits carving a toy for the baby while mother helps older sister with her letters and numbers. Suddenly, there's a scream in the night. There's something outside. It claws at the door, filling them with fear before it leaves again, sure to be back the next night. The daughter looks to her mother with terror, and she looks back, her face nervous, but reassuring. 'Don't worry, darling,' she says. 'Tomorrow, your father will go to… The Beast Hunter!'"

Keltin held up his hands. "All right, all right. If both of you are so insistent, then we'll keep the name. It doesn't matter much to me either way."

He set aside his empty plate and took up his hat from the stand by the door.

"I'm off to the shop. Try to keep the place in one piece while I'm gone."

Keltin left his friends and stepped out onto the streets of Collinsworth. It was good to see the town returning to a semblance of its normal self now that the mad rush north was over. Months ago, the town had been a riotous mash of hopeful prospectors all trying to buy supplies for the trip to Drutchland. While there were still those who no doubt felt the allure of distant gold, Keltin was glad to see that the town had settled into a more natural rhythm.

He soon left the merchant district and was just on the outskirts of the residential area when he found the shop he was looking for. It was built next to the family's home, along with a nearby covered forge and workshop. Keltin heard the distinctive ping of metal on metal from the workshop and went to investigate. He found a great barrel-chested man in a heavy leather apron making precise strikes on a wheel rim held firmly in place by a wiry apprentice.

"Be right with you," said the smith without pausing in his work, pounding the metal until he was satisfied with its shape. He straightened and turned to Keltin as the apprentice shoved the worked iron into a bed of hot coals.

"What can I do for you, sir?" asked the smith.

"I was heading for your shop and thought I'd introduce myself. I'm Keltin Moore. I think I've met your daughter a few times."

The man's scarred eyebrows shot up. "Oh yes, Mr. Moore! It's good to finally meet you in person." The smith pulled off his glove and gave him a strong working-man's handshake. "My name's Abel Claxon. Jessica's told us an awful lot about you."

"I'm not sure what she could say. I've only been by a couple of times in the last year."

"That's more than enough to keep Jessica going." Abel turned to his apprentice as the young man joined them. "Jonah, this is the nephew of Byron Moore."

The young man nodded respectfully and gave Keltin a handshake that was almost as firm as his masters.

"Jessica is in the shop," said Abel. "I'm sure she'll be happy to see you. Will you be in Collinsworth long?"

"Actually, I've rented a space in town. I'm starting a beast hunting company."

The man's eyes lit up.

"Is that a fact? That's wonderful! Just what the countryside needs. I hope you know how much we working folk respect the work of the Moore family. Your Uncle Byron is a local legend among gunsmiths. Do you still carry any of his pieces?"

Keltin nodded. "My hunting rifle is one of his. And I have one of the few close weapons he ever made."

"I would dearly love to see them, if you ever care to bring them by. I'm sure my wife would fix you a splendid supper, if you'd honor us. I'd love to hear tales of your adventures. And if you ever have need of new gear or guns, please come to me first. I'll sell you the very best I can make."

Keltin smiled, recognizing where Abel's daughter had inherited some of her bright, friendly personality.

"Father! I've brought your lunch."

Keltin turned at the sound of a familiar voice. Jessica was a pretty young blonde woman with a talent for smithing that her father had genuinely encouraged. She looked up from the footpath and lit up with a dazzling smile as she saw Keltin.

"Mr. Moore! It's so good to see you!"

"Thank you. How are you, Jessica?"

"Very well. It looks like you've finally met my father?"

"Yes, I was just telling him that I've started a beast hunting business here in town."

"That's wonderful! I'm so glad. Oh! Father, here's your lunch. I nearly forgot."

Jessica turned to her father's apprentice.

"Here you are, Jonah. Shaved beef on glazed toast."

"Thank you. That's my favorite."

"I know."

The blacksmith's daughter gave Jonah a smile as she handed over the package. Keltin took notice of that smile and made a mental note to mention it to Jaylocke. The previous spring, they'd paid a visit to the shop and the wayfarer had suggested that Jessica had been sweet on Keltin. Whether that had been true at the time or not, it was clear that the girl's affections were firmly placed elsewhere. Keltin turned back to the girl's father.

"Actually, I was hoping you could help me with something. We're having issues with rats in our offices. Do you carry traps?"

Abel frowned. "Not that I remember. Jessica's in charge of our outside merchandise."

"I can look in the storage room, father, but I'm fairly sure we don't have any in stock."

"Well, that's no matter. We should be able to make you some fairly easily. It'd primarily be a matter of shaping the proper sort of springs for them. Jonah, do you think you could manage something?"

"Yes sir. I'll start on it tonight."

"I appreciate it," said Keltin. "I suppose we'll just have to make due until then."

"Wait," said Jessica. "What about this?"

She moved to a corner of the workshop and picked up a small object from the cluttered worktable. Turning, she produced a tiny pistol in the palm of her hand. Keltin took it and examined the workmanship.

"This looks like a Haurizer pocket pistol, but not quite."

"It's one of my own," said Jessica.

"I wanted her to see how a small piece differed from a larger one," said Abel, pride clear in his voice.

"What kind of shot does it take?"

"Haurizer Poppers."

"What's the effective range?"

"Several yards," said Jessica. "It'll go farther, but after twenty feet or so it loses most of its kick. Would you like to try it?"

"All right."

Keltin followed Jessica along with Abel and Jonah to the makeshift range in the back of their property. Abel handed him a small box of Poppers and Keltin fed one into the breech of the tiny pistol. He took a little time to familiarize himself with handling the almost comically small gun. Several shots and a few adjustments later, Keltin was able to score three bullseyes in a row. He turned to see Jessica and her father both grinning at him.

"I'd love to see you do that with a real gun," said Abel.

"Targets are easy," said Keltin. "They don't move, and they aren't trying to kill you."

"Do you like the gun?" asked Jessica.

"It's not my usual sort of gun, but it's well made. How much are you asking for it?"

"Oh, it was just for practice. I wouldn't feel right charging for it."

Keltin noticed Abel's face cloud over.

"Well then, how much would you charge for a Haurizer

pocket pistol?" asked Keltin.

Jessica thought for a moment.

"Twelve jeva."

"All right. I'll give you fifteen for the pistol and a box of Poppers."

"But Mr. Moore—"

Keltin raised his hand. "You do good work Jessica, but if you want anyone to take you seriously, you need to start selling some of it. Besides, I had some success up north last winter. Take the money."

Jessica bit her lip thoughtfully. Keltin caught Abel smiling and nodding slightly at him over the girl's shoulder. Keltin gave a subtle nod in return as Jessica spoke up.

"All right. Thank you, Mr. Moore!"

"My pleasure."

The transaction was made, and Keltin bid them all a fond farewell before leaving and making his way back to the office. Keltin opened the front door and was surprised to see a stranger sitting in their waiting area. He was tall and long, with short, sandy hair and a trim, matching mustache. When he stood, Keltin had to look up at him.

"Hello," said Keltin. "Can I help you?"

"Yes, I think so. Are you Keltin Moore?"

"That's right."

The man smiled politely and extended a long-fingered hand to him.

"Marius Harper, Collinsworth Gazette. I spoke with your business partner and agreed to come down to talk with you and see if there might be a story in your new business here."

"Oh, ah… all right. I hadn't expected that. Could you excuse me for a moment?"

"That's fine."

"Thank you."

Keltin went to the backroom where he found Jaylocke and Bor've'tai sorting their gear.

"Why did you bring that reporter here?" Keltin hissed.

Jaylocke shrugged, seemingly indifferent to Keltin's tone.

"Well, I was out running an errand when I walked past the Gazette's office and thought that now that we have a name for the business, it's time to start spreading the word."

"You could have asked me first."

"I didn't think you'd mind. I've already told Mr. Harper all about you and your adventures. He's mainly here just to get a quote or two from you."

"Jaylocke…"

Bor've'tai placed a gentle hand on Keltin's shoulder. "Impulsive as our partner may have been, a story in the paper could indeed drum up good business for us. Just be yourself. You'll do fine."

Keltin looked into the Loopi's deep brown eyes a moment before letting out a heavy sigh.

"All right. I'll try."

He squared his shoulders and returned to the reception area. The newspaperman stood again and smiled. Keltin cleared his throat.

"I'm sorry about that. What was your name again?"

""Please, just call me Harper. Marius was my mother's idea, and I was never consulted. So, is this a good time?" he asked. "Or should I return later?"

"No, it's fine, though I apologize for the state of things around here. We're still getting this place cleaned up."

"Please don't concern yourself about it."

Keltin led the reporter to his office, taking a seat behind his empty desk and inviting Harper to sit across from him. The reporter took out a pad and pencil.

"Mr. Jaylocke certainly piqued my interest with his tales of your adventures. I was hoping I could get some of the details from you that he was uncertain about."

"All right."

"Let's start with where you come from. You're a native Riltvinian, aren't you? Mr. Jaylocke told me that you come from a family of beast hunters in the northern hill country. Is that true?"

"Yes, it started with my great-grandfather."

"Do the members of your family still hunt?"

"I think I still have an uncle in the south that hunts occasionally."

"But you're the only one hunting in Riltvin."

"Yes."

"So in a way, you're carrying the family tradition all on your own?"

"I suppose you could say that."

Harper nodded as he scribbled notes in his notebook.

"Mr. Jaylocke also mentioned the influx of beasts in Krendaria last year. What can you tell me about that?"

Keltin proceeded to describe the events of the Krendarian campaign as best he could, though he often was unsure what details Harper would find interesting. It turned out that Marius Harper seemed interested in anything Keltin had to tell him. He asked about everything Keltin could remember of the desperate battle to save the crops of Dhalma Province and the terrible days spent trapped in the farmhouse of Elaine's uncle.

They had just begun to talk about the final encounter with the tusked giant when Keltin suddenly tensed. With a sudden surge, he reached into his pocket and withdrew his newly purchased pocket pistol. Mr. Harper jumped half a foot as Keltin took quick aim and fired into the shadows of the room.

"Plaguing hex!" exclaimed the reporter as Keltin went to inspect his shot.

With a grunt of satisfaction he bent down and lifted a very dead rat up by its tail. Harper looked at the bullet hole in the rodent's head with a gaping stare. Keltin cleared his throat.

"Sorry about that," he said. "We're getting traps made for us. Until then we're making do." Keltin gave a rueful smile. "I suppose it wouldn't reflect very well on The Beast Hunter if our customers found that we had rats in our offices."

Harper swallowed and shook his head, his eyes wide as two-jeva coins.

"I don't think you have to worry about anyone doubting that you're The Beast Hunter, Mr. Moore."

* * *

"I never said that!"

"Which part?" asked Bor've'tai.

Keltin got up off his bed and crossed the room that the three of them shared above their offices. He handed the paper to the Loopi.

"Hardly any of it, truth be told," he said, then pointed to a particular section. "The worst is this part. He makes me sound like the hero of a smear novel."

"Which part is that?" asked Jaylocke.

Bor've'tai read aloud.

"'Just as his family has done for generations, Keltin Moore has dedicated his life to the protection of the innocent from creatures dredged up from the stuff of nightmares. While lesser men would bolt the doors and quake in their insecurity, The Beast Hunter routinely plunges into the darkness to put down the monsters of the night. This is his duty, his very essence, and you can tell it from the first moment that you look into eyes that have seen more than any normal man will ever see.'"

Jaylocke grinned. "It sounds fairly accurate to me, though I wouldn't have been so subtle."

Keltin gave the wayfarer a withering look. "I didn't ask for him to write me up like that. No one will take us seriously after this."

"Don't worry so much," said Jaylocke. "It's just one newspaper story, and a glowing one at that. Just take it for what it's worth and don't worry about it."

"I'd offer the same advice," said Bor've'tai.

Keltin started to reply when there was a sudden sound from downstairs.

"What was that?" asked Keltin.

"It sounded like someone knocking on the front door," said Bor've'tai.

The sound came again. Keltin went downstairs with Jaylocke and Bor've'tai trailing behind him. Keltin opened the front door to find a stranger waiting on the steps. The man was in his middling years, with a potato nose and a look of concern on his plain features.

"Can we help you?" asked Keltin.

The man looked at the three of them with uncertainty. "Are you... which one of you is The Beast Hunter?"

Keltin suppressed a grimace. He still wasn't sure this name was such a good idea.

"I'm Keltin Moore. What can I do for you?"

The man focused on Keltin with some obvious relief, extending a large, weathered hand to him.

"My name is Clemmons, sir. There's... well... there's something on my property that... ain't natural. I didn't know whether to talk with the constable or the priest, but when I read about you in the Gazette, I thought that maybe I should come talk with you."

"Well that was fast," said Jaylocke. "That story only came out today. Your land must be in the residential district."

The wayfarer's quip was lost on the poor man, who shook his head in reply.

"No sir, I was in town already for supplies and just happened to buy a paper and saw the article about your adventures in Krendaria and Drutchland."

"See, Keltin? We're already getting business from that article."

"Let's not get ahead of ourselves," said Keltin. "Why don't you have a seat, Mr. Clemmons, and tell us about your problem."

"Thank you kindly." Clemmons sat and began his story. "I have a farm about ten miles north of Jackson. I was pulling weeds in one of the fields near-to-two weeks ago when I saw it. I stood up to stretch and saw what looked like a puff of smoke wafting through the trees. I thought it was a little odd, as I was pretty far from my nearest neighbor. I wondered if perhaps someone was making camp on my land, and went to investigate. But when I got closer I saw that there was no fire, just a bluish cloud of smoke. As I watched, it curled up a tree trunk to a squirrel that had been chittering away at me.

Suddenly the squirrel went silent as the smoke covered it. It struggled a moment, then dropped dead out of the tree. The smoke went back down, and I swear, it's like it started to… eat the squirrel." The man shuddered. "I've never seen anything like it. I ran all the way home."

Keltin nodded. "We saw similar beasts in Krendaria last year. Have you spotted the smoke beast again, since that first time?"

"Just one other time. I ran for my life as soon as I saw it. Now I'm afraid to go out in my fields, and I'm especially afraid for my family while I'm away. Please, can you do something?"

Keltin glanced at Bor've'ta, who gave him a slight nod.

"I think we can help you, but we'll need some time to discuss how to handle it. Are you staying in town?

"I'm planning on leaving on the Jackson stagecoach tomorrow morning. Until then, I'm at the Pembroke Hotel."

"Fine," said Keltin. "We'll have someone come by later this evening to give you the particulars."

Clemmons rose, a look of relief evident in his features.

"Thank you so much! I'm glad I saw that article. By the way, do you have any idea how much this will cost?"

"That's one of the things we'll need to discuss."

"That's fair. In truth, I'm just so glad that you're willing to help me, I'll pay whatever it takes to get that thing off my land."

"Don't worry, Mr. Clemmons, we'll do all we can to get rid of that beast for you."

The farmer left and Keltin turned to his two partners.

"Well, we have our first customer."

"And he's got a beauty of a first bounty for us," said Jaylocke grimly. He turned to Bor've'tai. "I suppose you'll be going. We'll need a Sky Talker to bring down a smoke beast."

"Will you be able to handle it?" asked Keltin. "I remember the one we faced in Krendaria being a real challenge for you."

"I've grown stronger since then," said Bor've'tai. "A single smoke beast shouldn't be a problem, provided I can find it."

"That won't be a problem for our expert tracker," said

Jaylocke, throwing an arm around Keltin's shoulders, "though I'm not sure how you'd track a cloud of smoke. No matter. I'm sure you two will figure it out."

"You're not coming with us?" asked Bor've'tai.

"Someone has to mind the store, don't they? Besides, I don't think this sounds like a three man job. Do you, Keltin?"

"No, two sounds right. But I think you should be the one to go with Bor've'tai, Jaylocke."

The wayfarer's eyes widened. "Me? Why? You're The Beast Hunter, after all."

Keltin shook his head. "That doesn't mean I need to go on every hunt. Besides, you took charge of that hunt in Brakersville last month, remember?"

Jaylocke frowned. "I do remember, and I didn't enjoy it. I'd feel much better if you lead the way as always, Keltin."

"That's why you need to do this. Jaylocke, you can't be an apprentice forever. If you're ever going to prove to your people that you've learned a new trade and are ready to become a man, you need to start taking charge of hunts. Besides, Bor've'tai will likely end up doing the lion's share of the actual hunting. You just need to be there to deal with the people, make decisions of where to make camp, decide how to hunt the beast, make sure you and Bor've'tai stay safe, all of that. Things that you can't really do if I'm there."

Jaylocke squirmed. "I'd still rather be with you."

Keltin returned his look silently. Jaylocke finally sighed and nodded.

"I know you're right. I suppose I have no excuse. Besides, I won't be alone. My ancestors are with me again. And I've got a great shaggy mountain to keep me safe."

Bor've'tai ignored the wayfarer and turned to Keltin.

"Have you given any thought as to what we should charge Clemmons for this?"

"We'll know better once we've had a chance to go over what gear you'll be taking and what funds you'll need for expenses."

"That sounds fair to me."

"Fine. In that case, Jaylocke, you should probably go start sorting your gear. Once you're done, we can figure out what to charge him, and you can go tell Mr. Clemmons the details."

"What if Clemmons isn't happy that you won't be coming with us?" asked Jaylocke.

"Then you'll just have to convince him that you can do just as good a job as I can. You were an actor for years, Jaylocke. I'm sure you can manage it."

Jaylocke grumbled as he left the office in the direction of the gear room. Bor've'tai watched him go, then gently closed the door and turned to Keltin.

"You're becoming much better at that," he said.

"At what?"

"Being a leader."

Keltin shrugged. "I never really asked to lead anyone. I just fell into it."

"There's a lot of people I could name that are grateful you did." Bor've'tai tilted his head slightly. "So why are you sending Jaylocke and I on this hunt?"

"I told you. You need to go because it sounds like we're dealing with a smoke beast, and you're the only one who can handle it."

"So why send Jaylocke along?"

"He needs the experience."

"Is that all?"

"Are you expecting that there's something more behind it?"

Bor've'tai's expression was impassive as a statue.

"Is there something more?" he asked.

"Not that I know of."

"All right."

Keltin heaved a sigh and turned towards the window. "It isn't that I don't want either of you around, if that's what you're thinking. It's for Jaylocke's sake. His girl Ameldi is still waiting for him, along with the rest of his people. He can't go home until he's fully learned the trade of being a beast hunter."

"Do you think he's done that?"

"He's getting close. His aim has gotten better, and he was

always good at moving carefully through the woods. His tracking still needs some work."

"Is that all?"

"No. He needs to learn responsibility. Jaylocke is too comfortable following my lead. He can't afford to get lazy. That's what got him into this fix in the first place. Do me a favor? While you're on this hunt, don't let him charm or wheedle you into making decisions for him."

"Don't worry. I should be able to resist him." Bor've'tai gave the ghost of a smile before going serious again. "How about you? Will you be all right here by yourself?"

"I should be. I was on my own for years before meeting you two in Krendaria. If anything, I'll probably struggle most with the tediousness of waiting for you."

"Mmm, perhaps. But I worry that you may have to deal with something terrible, and we won't be there to support you."

Keltin turned away from the window towards his Loopi friend. "Why would you worry about that?"

Bor've'tai shook his head.

"I'm not sure. It's just… a feeling I have." He took a deep breath and opened the office door again. "Be careful, Keltin."

Bor've'tai stepped out of the room, leaving Keltin to sit alone and ponder his friend's words. Was there a greater significance to his concern than friendly worry? Bor've'tai was a Sky Talker, after all. Keltin still understood very little of the Sky Talkers' power, despite seeing them in action during his time in Krendaria and Drutchland. He knew they had some sort of influence on the natural world, and he'd seen Grel'zi'tael, Bor've'tai's teacher, show insight verging on precognition more than once. But beyond that, the power of these gifted Loopi remained a mystery to him.

Keltin kept himself busy by helping his friends make their preparations for the upcoming hunt. Despite his obvious reluctance, Jaylocke had faithfully gone to Clemmons with their proposal, returning soon after to report that the farmer had accepted both their plan and their proposed fee. The rest of the day was spent planning the logistics of the trip. Evening had fallen by the time they had finished, and Bor've'tai volunteered to fetch them something for supper. Keltin was surprised when he heard the door open again only moments after the Loopi had left. He turned to see Bor've'tai come back upstairs, a pensive look on his face.

"That was quick," quipped Jaylocke. "I suppose you're planning on a light supper?"

Bor've'tai ignored the wayfarer and turned to Keltin.

"I found someone standing outside our door. I think she was trying to decide whether to knock or not. She says that she knows you."

"Really? I wonder who it is."

"She didn't give a name, and I didn't ask. She seems... troubled."

Keltin gave the Loopi a questioning look. Bor've'tai could only shrug slightly. Keltin got up from his chair.

"Well, I'll go see what it's about."

Keltin went downstairs to find the young woman standing in the front room near the door. She was thin, too thin, with sunken cheeks and an overabundance of rouge. When she looked up at him, he felt her sunken eyes pierce deep into his heart to find memories that had long been hidden safely away.

"Hello Keltin," she said.

It took a moment for him to find him voice.

"Hello, Angela." His mouth worked for a moment before he managed the next few words. "I... didn't expect you. How are you?"

"Fine. Thank you. And you?"

"Fine."

Silence. Keltin turned to see if perhaps Bor've'tai and Jaylocke had come downstairs to give him an excuse to introduce them, but they had respectfully remained out of sight. Keltin turned back to see Angela watching him, her eyes full of uncertainty.

"Would you like to sit down?" he said.

"Yes, thank you."

Keltin led Angela to his office and opened the door for her. She stepped past, leaving a wake of sickly sweet scent in the air behind her. She sat in one of the chairs facing his desk. He hesitated for a moment, deciding whether he should sit on the other side of the great expanse of empty oak. He decided it best to sit on the same side of the room as her, though he made sure to keep his distance.

"You're looking well," she said.

Keltin tried to return the compliment, but knew he couldn't make it sound believable. The truth was that she looked worse than the last time he had seen her nearly a year ago. It had been a brief, painful visit as he had been passing through town on his way to Krendaria. He had reluctantly stopped by the home of ill-repute where she lived and worked, delivering a small bundle of letters from Mrs. Galloway, his landlady and Angela's mother.

Angela shifted uncomfortably and Keltin realized that he'd been lost in thought without responding to her. She spoke again.

"I wrote to you. Did you ever get any of my letters?"

"Yes." Keltin considered making an excuse, then decided against it. "I'm sorry I didn't write back."

Angela nodded, her narrow shoulders sagging slightly. Keltin felt a pang of guilt at the thought that he had hurt her, then wondered how similar Elaine's reaction may have been when he had stopped writing to her. He quickly pushed thoughts of Elaine aside however, surprised at himself for somehow feeling unfaithful just by sitting next to Angela.

"So, what brings you here?" he asked.

Angela sighed, as if she had been expecting something, and was disappointed.

"I saw the article in the Gazette saying that you were in town. I thought I'd come visit you." Her eyes rose to meet him, her gaze unfriendly. "I knew you wouldn't come visit me."

Her voice carried a touch of bitterness, but Keltin felt no guilt this time. He felt affronted, and a little angry. Why should he come visit her? She was firmly in his past, something she should have accepted when he didn't respond to any of her letters. He'd moved on. Besides, he'd never step foot into the Blue Rose again, if he could help it. If that made her feel indignant, then so be it. Nobody was forcing her to stay there.

"Have you heard from your mother?" he asked.

"Not recently. We stopped writing."

Keltin nodded without speaking. She was still as stubborn as she ever had been.

"I'm sure she'd still like to hear from you."

"I don't think so."

There was another long silence. Angela let out a long breath and stood up.

"I suppose I shouldn't have come. Sorry."

Keltin stood just as her hand was on the door.

"Angela," he said. "I'm sorry."

He said it reflexively, but he meant it. She paused.

"I'm sorry too," she said, though he couldn't tell if it was an apology or an observation. "Goodbye, Keltin."

She left the room. Keltin could hear the front door open and close. He sat back down in his chair. He heard Jaylocke and Bor've'tai moving around above him, but he didn't go up to them. He sat and watched the candle on his desk until it burned out, then sat in the darkness, continuing to think of what might have been.

CHAPTER 3 – A CALL TO ACTION

Keltin was in the act of emptying one of the rattraps into the rubbish bin behind The Beast Hunter when he heard the bell ring at the front door. Eager for something to break the monotony of sitting around the office, he rushed back inside and into the front room. He was surprised to see Severn Destov waiting for him. Elaine's father gave him a polite, if not pleasant smile.

"Mr. Moore. Good afternoon. I hope I'm not interrupting anything."

"Not at all. I'm actually grateful for the visit. It's painfully boring just sitting around here. I didn't realize that you were in town."

"Mr. Whitt has given me charge of overseeing his business interests in eastern Riltvin and neighboring counties. Collinsworth is a good center of operations for that purpose. In fact, I'm here on his behalf. You see, he has some investments that are under risk, and was hoping that you could help him."

"I'm not sure what I could do. I'm only a beast hunter."

"That's why he needs you. How do you feel about going back to Krendaria?"

Keltin felt a sudden pit in his stomach. He didn't have

many pleasant memories of his time in Krendaria. It had been his first time away from his home country and the first time that he had hunted with companions. Of course, he'd met some fine people, and made some lasting friendships including Bor've'tai and Jaylocke. And, of course, it was in Krendaria that he had first met Elaine. But there had been a great deal of loss as well. Good men had died, some of them under Keltin's reluctant leadership. Krendaria had pushed Keltin, tested him, and while he had grown a great deal while there, there were things that had happened that were better left in the past.

Mr. Destov waited patiently. Keltin took a deep breath.

"Krendaria isn't a place someone goes to lightly," he said.

Mr. Destov nodded, his face somber. "That's a fair answer. But Mr. Whitt needs you there. And… I may need you there."

"Maybe we should go into my office so you can tell me everything."

"That would be best."

Destov started to explain the moment they sat down.

"The collapse of the Krendarian government was a terrible tragedy, but it also created opportunities for some shrewd businessmen and their investors. Mr. Whitt and a few partners have managed to buy a great deal of the farmland that was abandoned during the incursion of beasts last year. They've sent skilled laborers into Dhalma Province to organize and hire the local population to cultivate its rich farmland."

"I hope they aren't planning on planting now. It's far too late in the season."

Mr. Destov shook his head. "This endeavor was initiated while most eyes were turned north towards Drutchland and the gold strike. There was hardly any competition when purchasing the farmlands, and Mr. Whitt and his partners snatched up a good chunk of Dhalma Province for a song. It was a shrewd, long-thinking move that will pay dividends down the road, as long as things go according to plan."

"In my experience, most things rarely go according to plan."

"True. There's a great deal still to overcome before the first harvest is safely in. Carvalen's hold on the populace is tenuous at best. Minister Erickson likely won't hold his throne through the season, and Parliament has even less power than he does. And even if the government does hold together, there's the seasonal influx of beasts to consider."

Keltin shook his head. "After last year's campaign, I would expect the beast population in the area to be drastically depleted for at least another year or two. Trust me, we killed an entire hell's worth of the boils."

"I don't doubt you, but without an organized Krendarian military, any number of beasts is a potentially disastrous problem."

"Aren't there any local freelancers that the new owners can hire?"

"Very few. Those that survived the campaign either fled Krendaria during the chaos or left to find gold in Drutchland. So far, we've only been able to find one experienced hunter that's local to the region, but he's overtaxed with the amount of land he's responsible for and recently sent an urgent message requesting support. As soon as the message reached Mr. Whitt he remembered our conversation at dinner several months ago and thought to hire the services of your new beast hunting company. I'm just glad I found you in business, although I was under the impression that you had some additional partners in this venture. Mr. Whitt was interested in hiring the full services of your company."

"I'm sorry, but my other two partners are currently on a hunt."

"Do you know when they might return?"

Keltin shrugged. "That's hard to say. They won't arrive in Jackson until tomorrow at the earliest, and then they have the hunt to do and the trip back. It may be two or more weeks before they return."

"That's... unfortunate. Mr. Ross, our current beast hunter, sounded most desperate in his request for aid. I'm not sure we can afford to wait for your partners to return."

Keltin shook his head. "I'm sorry, but Dhalma Province is

not an easy place to work in, even with partners. On my own, I'm not sure it'd be worth the risk."

Mr. Destov let out a long sigh and looked up, his eyes showing a sudden emotion and vulnerability that surprised Keltin.

"Mr. Moore, I understand your position, and I wouldn't ask you to take any unnecessary risk for a purely financial venture, but… well… I have a personal reason to ask you to make this trip. It concerns my family."

Keltin's heart clenched inside him. He leaned forward.

"Is something wrong?"

Destov looked Keltin squarely in the eye. "Yes. Mr. Moore, I need you to be in Krendaria right now, because I may need to ask you to get my family out of Malpin."

"Why? Has something happened there?"

"Not yet, but it may, and soon. Conditions in my home country are swiftly deteriorating. Ever since the Heterack Empowerment, there's been growing unrest under the increasingly totalitarian regime of the Vaughs. The leaders of Malpin have seen the chaos of revolution on their southern border and do not want to see another Krendaria in their own nation. Political dissenters are being silenced, and state control is creeping into every industry and business practice."

"I don't understand. I thought all of the Loopi were driven out over a year ago. Who is the government worried about?"

"Not all of the Loopi were able to leave the country, and there are still plenty of humans and even a few Heteracks who opposed the Empowerment in some fashion."

Keltin suddenly understood. "People like you."

Destov nodded grimly. "Elaine told you?"

"A little. She's mentioned how you tried to fight for the rights of your Loopi clients in court, and then tried to get them fair value for their goods when they had to flee the country."

"It felt like such a hollow gesture in light of all that they were going through, but even my insignificant acts have drawn the attention of the MLP."

"What's that?"

"It stands for the Malpin League of Protection, the Vaugh's personal police force. My wife said in her last letter that they had come by our home in Kerrtow, asking to see me."

"Then why are you here? Why didn't you stay with your family to help them get out of the country?"

"I needed employment outside of the country to provide them some amount of security. Besides, at the time I left it seemed like it would smooth over the emigration paperwork if I already had employment elsewhere, though that seems to make little difference now."

"Why?"

"There are rumors of the borders being closed. My wife is doing her best to settle our accounts and make preparations for the journey, all while under the scrutiny of the MLP. But if the borders are closed, then she will be trapped, along with Elaine and my two sons."

Destov paused to rub his face with his hands. When he met Keltin's eyes again his gaze was sincere. Desperate.

"Mr. Moore, I don't pretend to know you very well or understand your relationship with my daughter, but I trust her judgement, and she believes you to be an honorable man. Please. If she's right, I ask you to help my family. I have little to pay you with right now, but I would consider it a personal favor, and would never forget it."

Keltin spoke without hesitation.

"I'll help you. What do you need me to do?"

Mr. Destov's shoulders sagged with relief . "Thank you. For now, go to Dhalma Province, as we were discussing before. Meet with Mr. Ross, and help him as much as you can. I'll send word to my wife to finish her preparations quickly and take the family to the southern border. With luck, the borders will remain open, and you will be able to meet them and escort them to the nearest train station with connections to the Western Line."

"And if we're not lucky?"

"If the borders close, I will tell them to go as far south as they are able. Then you will need to get away from Mr. Whitt's holdings, go to the border, sneak across, find my family, and escort them south to Krendaria."

"Where will I meet them?"

"I'm not sure. I have some contacts who may be willing to keep them hidden until you come for them."

"But if they're hidden, how will I find them?"

Destov spread his hands helplessly. "I honestly don't know. Hopefully it won't come to that. I just needed to know that I could count on you to help if things go badly."

Keltin nodded. "You can count on me. I'll leave on the next train going east."

Mr. Destov breathed a heavy sigh of relief and reached out to take Keltin's hand. "Thank you, Mr. Moore. I can't tell you how much it means to hear you say that. I wish there was some way that you didn't have to make the trip alone. Even if you don't have to help my family across the border, it will be terribly dangerous for you in Krendaria."

"Don't worry for me. I'm used to this sort of thing. Besides, I know a place where I can get the best gear money can buy."

* * *

"That's quite a list," said Jessica, looking over Keltin's hastily scribbled notes.

Keltin nodded. "My partners took most of our gear on their own hunt, and I need to leave in a hurry. Whatever you don't have I can buy in town, but I wanted to come here first."

Jessica nodded. "All right, I'll see how much I can pull together. It will take me a moment, though."

"That's fine. Maybe I'll go say hello to your father while you do that."

Keltin stepped outside and made his way to the forge. He found Abel running a long steel tube through a special turn-gear to add the necessary rifling to the interior that would help the bullets fire straight through the gun. His apprentice Jonah was busy preparing coke for the furnace when he looked up and saw Keltin.

"Hello, Mr. Moore. Did those traps I made help you at all with the rats?"

"Yes, thank you Jonah. We hardly see any of them anymore."

Abel looked up from his work.

"Hello, Mr. Moore. Can I help you with something?"

"No thank you, I just thought I'd come out to visit while Jessica pulls together some things for me."

"Have you got a hunt, then?"

"Of a sort. I'm going back to Krendaria."

Abel's face darkened. He walked around his bench to stand next to Keltin.

"That's still a mighty dangerous country to journey through right now. What's taking you there?"

"Business. I've been hired to deal with the seasonal increase in beast sightings in Dhlama Province."

"Are your partners going with you?"

"They're already on a hunt. I'll be going alone this time."

Abel seemed to consider that for a moment, his eyes wandering over his worktable as he thought.

"Hold on a moment," he said.

He turned and went to a nearby rack of shelves covered with a variety of projects in steel and iron, all in various stages of completion. He returned with the largest revolver Keltin had ever seen.

"If you're going to go beast hunting alone, you should carry a gun like this."

Keltin held up a hand in protest.

"Thank you, but I already have a sidearm. My grandfather left me his Grantville service pistol from the Three Forest War."

Abel nodded. "Grantvilles are reliable, I won't deny that. But there's no pistol made by them that could handle the same specialized ammunition that your rifle takes. But this," he hefted the revolver in his hands, "this will take Reltac Spinners, Haurizer Smashers, Capshire Shatter-Rounds… whatever you like."

Abel held out the gun and Keltin took it, feeling the sturdy weight of a serious firearm. The revolving chamber had space for five shots, just like his hunting rifle. He turned it over in his hands to examine the bindings.

"Is it an original?" he asked.

"Modified. I wanted to experiment with high caliber side-arms. I started with a Brunson carbine, shortened the barrel and put a pistol grip on it. I added a small shield for powder blowback, and shaved off as much steel as I could to reduce the weight while keeping it fully functional."

"It's still heavy," said Keltin. "I doubt that an average buyer would be interested in it."

"It isn't intended for an average buyer." Abel gave Keltin a sideways look. "It's intended for a beast hunter."

Keltin's eyebrows went up.

"Is that a fact?"

Abel nodded. "Mr. Moore, I was serious when I told you that I want to be able to provide you with all of your hunting needs. Your Uncle Byron was a local legend among private gunsmiths, and I'd be honored to carry on his tradition. I've been training Jonah to build with a hunter in mind, and Jessica is picking it up as well. As long as The Beast Hunter is in business, I want people to know that the Claxon family are the ones providing his weapons and gear."

Keltin thought for a moment.

"I'd have to try it out first."

Abel turned to Jonah. "Go in the shop and get Mr. Moore some specialty shot. Shatter Rounds, Spinners, whatever we have."

"We have an order of Alpenion rounds filled with Belferin acid," said the apprentice. "Should I bring those as well?"

"Those are mine," said Keltin. "I ordered them last spring before I left for Drutchland. They'll fly the same as the other specialty shot, so let's not waste them. They aren't cheap." He turned back to Abel, hefting the weighty firearm again. "Well, let's go try out this... what would you call it? It's not a carbine anymore, but it's almost too big to be a revolver either."

The gunsmith shrugged and gave a little grin. "Maybe a hand cannon. Do you think that would attract beast hunters?"

Keltin gave him the ghost of a smile. "If this thing has the kind of power that I expect it does, you could call it whatever you want and it would attract beast hunters."

* * *

Keltin stood on the train platform waiting for the call to board. He shifted the unfamiliar weight at his hip where the hand cannon sat in its large holster. He thought of the note he'd left at the front desk for Jaylocke and Bor've'tai and almost wished that there was more that he had to do before leaving, just to give them a chance to come back in time to come with him. While he'd hunted alone for years before going to Krendaria the first time, in the last year he'd come to rely on Bor've'tai's stoic, reassuring presence and Jaylocke's sunny disposition. Going to Krendaria without them almost felt like a betrayal.

Pushing the thought aside, he focused on watching the steaming, sighing engine as it sat like a great steel beast lying in anxious anticipation. He was just about to check his pocket watch for the time when he heard someone calling his name.

"Good evening, Mr. Moore! Are you taking the evening train as well?"

Keltin turned and was surprised to find Marius Harper, the gangly, tall reporter who had interviewed him for the Collinsworth Gazette.

"Good evening, Mr. Harper," said Keltin. "Yes, I'm going east. And you?"

Harper nodded. "All the way to Carvalen. Our man in the Krendarian capital had to come home, and I'm going out to replace him."

"Isn't that a dangerous assignment?"

"Could be. But I've dealt with dangerous assignments before. What about you? Are you getting off before the border?"

Keltin shook his head. "I'm headed for Carvalen as well."

"Really?" Harper perked up like a hound that had found a scent. "What's taking you out there? Business?"

"That's right. I've been hired to help with some beast problems in Dhalma Province."

Harper nodded, his mind clearly moving swiftly as he processed this news. "That's very interesting. Returning to the place where you almost died, ready to face creatures of nightmare again to defend the innocent."

Keltin gave a tight smile that he hoped hid his embarrassment. "Well, someone has to protect the workers," he said lamely.

Looking past the reporter, Keltin spied Mr. Destov a short distance down the platform making his way towards him. Harper continued, not noticing the man approaching them.

"Absolutely. Well, this train ride has become much more interesting. I hope you don't mind a traveling companion? Perhaps I could write a little something about your return trip to Krendaria."

Keltin felt an immediate unease. While he was certain Harper had no malicious intent, the idea of someone questioning him about his trip made him nervous, particularly when he considered what he may have to do if the border with Malpin closed. Destov had come to a stop at a polite distance from them, and Keltin forced himself to be pleasant and relaxed.

"I'm open to talking, though I'm not sure if there's a story in anything I'd have to say."

"You let me be the judge of that. If nothing else, we can while away the hours by swapping stories. I may not be a beast hunter, but I have been in some tight spots as a war correspondent down south. I'll see you on the train."

Harper turned and climbed up into the car. Destov approached Keltin once the newspaperman was gone.

"Is that a friend of yours?" he asked.

"More of an acquaintance. He writes for the Collinsworth

Gazette and did a piece on me earlier this month."

If Destov was concerned about Harper's presence on the train he didn't show it. Instead, he leaned forward and placed a hand on Keltin's arm, holding out an envelope with the other.

"I just wanted to come here to wish you luck, and to give you this letter of introduction. Once you get to Carvalen, take this to the address on the envelope and someone there should see to your transportation to one of Mr. Whitt's farms."

Keltin took the letter and placed it in a coat pocket. Destov watched him with a piercing, somber expression.

"Thank you again for what you are willing to do. God willing, you won't have to do anything dangerous." He caught himself and smiled. "Well, no more dangerous than what you would do normally."

Keltin gave him a crooked smile.

"Don't worry, Mr. Destov. If the worst comes, I'll see your family safely to you."

"I believe you. God be with you, Keltin."

"God be with all of us," said Keltin before turning and climbing aboard the train.

CHAPTER 4 – FAMILIAR TERRITORY

The first time Keltin had entered the capital city of Krendaria, it had been on foot, forced to walk the last dozen miles because of pre-revolutionaries bombing the tracks. Now, Keltin watched Carvalen through the train window as they slowly made their way to the station. Framed by the Sky Top Mountains covered in their permanent blanket of snow, Carvalen seemed like a city out of time. The capital of Krendaria was old, older even than the nation itself, filled with the history and architecture of centuries. As the first buildings began to slide by his window, Keltin frowned. The scars of the great fires of the year previous were everywhere. Entire blocks stood empty, and even now there were still blackened piles of rubble on street corners and piled up in alleys. Nearly every stone surface bore the plaque-like mark of smoke damage. Keltin mused darkly about how the violent acts of a few days could destroy centuries of art and culture.

"It seems that repairing the city is a low priority of the current administration," Keltin observed.

Harper nodded as he sat across from him staring out the window.

"Were you here for the fires after Parliament fell?" he asked.

"No. I was in the northern country when the revolution hit. I haven't seen the capital since last fall."

Harper craned his long neck to study the damage as they passed the burned out shells of warehouses bordering the train yards.

"When I got this assignment, I reread the piece the Gazette did about the fires. It said that the flames climbed over a hundred feet into the air. Nobleman and revolutionary alike were killed in mid-step on the streets by the heat and smoke."

"I saw a great fire in Lost Trap while I was there. Most of the buildings were wooden though, and it wasn't nearly as large as Carvalen."

"Was the entire town lost?"

"No. We were blessed to have Loopi Skytalkers with us. They called down a heavy snow that kept the flames from spreading."

"And was your business partner, Mr. Bor've'tai, one of them?"

"He was."

Harper's eyes were distant as he continued to watch the city out their window. "I've never seen a Sky Talker use his powers before. It must have been incredible to be there when it happened. It's no wonder that some people are so afraid of the Loopi and the power they can control."

Keltin didn't reply.

Soon the train came to a stop and Keltin was stepping out into Krendaria's capital city. The air was stale, filled with the choke of coalsmoke and the grease of the train yards. There were few other people on the platform, and Keltin turned slowly to examine his surrounding as he considered his next move.

"Do you have someone meeting you at the station?" asked Harper as if reading Keltin's thoughts.

"No, I'd only gotten the job offer the day I left, so I doubt word of my coming has gotten here any faster than I have. But I was given a letter of introduction from a representative of my employer. I just need to find the address on the envelope."

"May I see it?" Harper frowned at Destov's neat handwriting and shook his head. "It isn't familiar to me, but I don't know Carvalen very well yet. If you'd like, you can come along with me to my local contact. It shouldn't be hard to get help finding your address there."

Keltin was about to politely decline out of a habit of self-confident independence, but hesitated. What would it hurt to get a little help with directions? Besides, he was eager to get out of the fire-scarred city as soon as possible. He gave Harper a grateful smile.

"I appreciate that. Thank you."

Harper grinned. "Well, it's not all altruism on my part. This is a dangerous city, and I wouldn't mind traveling with someone equipped as you are for a little longer."

"Fair enough, though that reminds me of something."

Keltin reached into one of his pockets and withdrew a small paper box. Sliding it open, he removed ten rounds and proceeded to load them into his rifle and the hand cannon. Harper watched him with interest.

"May I ask what you're doing?"

Keltin held up the box for the newspaperman to see.

"Candleshot. Minimum powder charge and a wax payload. I use them for target practice, but they should also work as a nonlethal ammunition in case we run into trouble."

Harper's smile was thoughtful.

"I don't know too many men that would have concerned themselves with something like that," he said.

Keltin didn't respond, as he had chosen not to mention to the newspaperman the other contingency he had if things went truly awry. In one of his vest pockets he carried the pocket pistol he'd purchased from Jessica to kill rats. He'd brought it on a whim, rather than any planned purpose. Still, if he had to cross the border, it might be good to have a small, easily concealable firearm. He tried not to think about the fact that the pistol's Haurizer Poppers, while lacking in power, were nonetheless a potentially lethal ammunition. If he had to shoot someone with the pocket pistol and wasn't careful…

He snapped closed the chamber to the hand cannon.

"I kill beasts, not men," he said aloud.

Harper nodded and turned to lead them away from the station. Keltin studied the town as they made their way down its scarred, tired looking streets. A year ago it had been a hotbed of contentions, a city on the brink of revolution with tension in every expression. Now, the city looked haggard and beaten, like the bloody loser of a street fight. People walked with their heads bowed, barely sparing a warry glance at strangers. It occurred to Keltin that the people who had warned him of the danger in Carvalen may have misjudged the state of affairs in the city. This wasn't a place of bubbling violence anymore. If there was danger, it lurked in the dark shadows, not out in the open.

Keltin looked at a woman in rags carrying what looked like someone else's washing in a heavy basket, trying to skirt the worst of the garbage in the streets. He wondered if the common people like her were any better or worse off than they had been before the revolution. After the fighting and the fires were over, what had really changed? As fragile as the current government's hold on power was, Keltin was sure that a new upper class would eventually establish itself, leaving the rest of the people just where they were before. At least, those that had survived.

Eventually they arrived at a small, unobtrusive building that showed the stains of smoke but was otherwise still intact. Inside they met Harper's contact, a man with cracked spectacles and haunted eyes. He easily gave the necessary directions to the address on Destov's letter, and Keltin turned to bid Harper farewell.

"I enjoyed visiting with you on the trip," said the newspaperman. "Good luck in Dhalma. Perhaps we'll see each other again in Collinsworth when this is all over."

Keltin agreed and departed, wondering just how much still stood between him and that distant reunion.

* * *

The sun was riding low in the sky by the time Keltin reached the Lona farm. He sat up on the buckboard next to the driver that had been tasked with delivering him there. Looking at the farm, Keltin half-expected to see the same sort of hastily thrown-together fortifications he had seen the last time he had been in the province. But the workers seemed far less concerned about beasts than they had been the year before. The only fortification he saw was a rough earth wall that had been started but never finished, now eroded by a year's worth of rain and snow. The driver noticed him looking at the embankment.

"Luckily, we haven't needed to build that thing back up, though I can't imagine there being enough beasts around here that you'd need to."

Keltin made no comment as the driver pulled the wagon to a halt by the barn. He jumped off the buckboard and pulled down his pack and gear. Turning, he spied a man walking towards him across the farmyard. He was short and stocky, his face and arms burned brown by many days spent in the sun. The man stopped a few feet in front of Keltin, seemingly taking in his rifle, gear, the hand cannon at his hip, and the three-foot long Ripper hanging from his shoulder.

"You must be the new beast hunter we asked for," he said.

"I am. My name's Keltin Moore. Are you Mr. Ross?"

"No, my name's Largos Yull. I'm the foreman of this farm. Ross is around here somewhere though."

Keltin handed him his letter of introduction from Destov. Yull scanned it for a moment.

"Well, Mr. Moore, it says here that you were a part of the campaign that was up this way last year."

"That's right."

Yull seemed to consider that for a moment before continuing.

"I was working on a farm out east, but we heard what you folks did. Hexing brave of the lot of you. You likely saved a lot of lives."

"You're Krendarian? I thought all of Mr. Whitt's foremen were from Riltvin?"

"Most of them are, but there are a few natives in the lot, and most of the workers are still Krendarian."

Keltin nodded, looking out at a nearby field, where workers crouched among the green leafy potato plants pulling out offending weeds.

"I'm glad to hear that. Dhalma was all but abandoned when I was last here."

Yull frowned. "Well, it isn't like it was before last year. None of the old families are here anymore. Nearly everyone left. It's all foreign investors now that own these fields." Yull shrugged and cleared his throat. "Well, I'm glad you're here, either way. My boys and I will focus on getting the crops in. You can have all the beasts to yourself." He turned and pointed at a long, low building next to the barn. "The workers are all staying in the bunkhouse, but there's a spare room in the farmhouse that you can stay in when you're here. You go on in. Ross is probably in there somewhere."

Keltin thanked the foreman and turned towards the farmhouse. Walking up the beaten earth path to the door, he allowed himself in. There was little light inside, and he squinted in the gloom to make out a narrow hallway with several doors leading into the rest of the house and a stairway up to the second floor. Closing the front door, he turned just as a young woman came into the hallway. Her eyes flashed wide and she gave a startled yelp. Too late, Keltin realized just how he and all his armaments must look to her.

"I'm sorry," he said quickly.

He started to set his rifle down on the boot board when he heard a low, snuffling growl from somewhere in the house. There was a clacking of claws on hardwood floor, and suddenly the doorway to one of the rooms was filled with the dark silhouette of a massive, four-legged creature. Instinctively, Keltin yanked his rifle into his shoulder, lining his sights even as he tried to make out any features of the beast in the dim light. His fingertip had just touched the trigger when the girl shouted out desperately.

"No Wait! It's just Kuff!"

She thrust herself in front of Keltin and stood facing the massive creature, showing the palm of one hand and speaking in a gentle, firm tone.

"Al-Hah!" she said. "It's all right. It's all right."

The great creature visibly relaxed, its bunched shoulders slackening as it leaned forward to nuzzle the girl's hand. As Keltin's eyes adjusted to the light he realized what he was looking at. It was a tamarrin hound, a fierce species of beast that had long ago been domesticated by the Krendarians and selectively bred for the hunting of other beasts. Fully-grown, a hound stood four-feet at the shoulder with long, muscular bodies and curiously feathered tails. Keltin had seen such hounds while in Krendaria the year before, and knew them to be both fiercely loyal and incredibly deadly once fully trained. It was clear that the girl was unafraid of the creature as she offered it her hand. The hound sniffed it once -perhaps looking for a treat- before turning and leaving them alone again.

The girl turned back to Keltin.

"I'm sorry," she said. "Kuff is still learning how to act around strangers."

"It's my fault. I should have knocked first."

The girl looked away nervously, giving Keltin a chance to study her features. Her hair was long and pale blonde, framing a face that looked about the same age as Jessica Claxon's. She wore a rough cotton dress and an apron that was clean despite a number of old stains on its surface. Keltin coughed and tried to imitate one of Jaylocke's friendly smiles.

"I'm sorry for startling you. My name is Keltin Moore. I'm a beast hunter. I've been hired to help protect the workers on the farm."

She gave him a tight, uncertain smile. "My name is Wendi. I work in the kitchen here. You'll want to meet Mr. Ross. Kuff belongs to him. I'll go find him for you."

She turned and hurried upstairs. Keltin stepped further into the house. He peered around a doorway to find a living room and a comfortable blaze in the fireplace. The tamarrin hound's massive form lay curled up before the crackling fire, warming his sandy brown back against the glowing embers. His eyes were closed and he seemed content, but Keltin knew enough of the creatures to remain at a respectful distance until they were better acquainted.

"Well I'll be plagued," said a voice from up above. "It is you!"

Keltin looked up to see a man descending the stairs. He had the hardened, weathered features of a man on the cusp of hardy old age. He stepped into the living room and smiled, clasping his weathered hands on Keltin's shoulders.

"Captain Moore! It's been some time."

Keltin gave him a curious look. His craggy features were somehow familiar, but Keltin couldn't place him.

"I'm sorry, have we met?"

The man shrugged. "In a way, though I saw more of you than you did of me. We hound trainers kept mostly to ourselves under Baron Rumsfeld, but we all knew about Captain Keltin Moore and his team of stalker hunters."

Realizations dawned on Keltin.

"You were part of the campaign," he said.

"That's right, and I'm plaguing glad that it's you that's come to help me. I couldn't have asked for a better man. Well, barring another trainer, of course."

Ross took a seat by the fire and waved Keltin towards an overstuffed chair across from him. Keltin sat down, grateful for the soft cushion underneath him after the long hours spent bouncing on a buckboard. Kuff immediately lifted his head at the sight of Ross, but a dismissive wave of the hand and a mumbled command saw the hound lower his head back to the floor.

"Wendi told me that you already met Kuff," he said, nodding at the hound. "I'm sorry he acted like that. He's only half a year into his training, and still learning when to be a hound and when not to."

"He wasn't there for the campaign then?"

Ross shook his head, his features hardening. "No. I lost my hound on that hexed campaign. Got tangled with a barbed thresher. She…"

Ross went silent.

"I'm sorry," said Keltin. "We all lost friends on that campaign."

Ross nodded. He spat savagely into the fire, leaving it to hiss for a moment in the glowing flames before he took a deep breath and turned his attention back to Kuff.

"This one is out of one of her litters. Kept him for myself. I would have liked to give him more time to train before taking him on hunts, but I didn't have that luxury, being the only hunter in a hundred leagues. Well, until you showed up, that is."

"I don't understand. Where are the other Krendarian hunters? Where are your fellow trainers?"

"It wasn't just hounds we lost in the campaign. A lot of trainers are gone now, including Captain Tallow."

"I didn't know he died. I'm sorry."

"It's all right. It happened after you and your company went into the northern country." Ross sighed and shook his head. "Things were bad all around by that time. We did our best to hold the line that Baron Rumsfeld set, but when the fires in the capital started, the campaign fell apart. Those that weren't native to Krendaria fled the country. Those that had family here went to their homes, trying to protect their loved ones and goods from the chaos spreading out from Carvalen."

"But what about now? Why aren't there more native hunters here in Dhalma Province?"

Ross shrugged. "Most of them left. Many fled the country during the revolution. The rest went to look for their fortune in the Wylow Gold Rush."

"But you didn't."

"No. I'm a hound trainer, not a prospector. My hounds are my family, so I stayed here to see to Kuff's training. Besides, I had to stay to see after Wendi."

"Is she your daughter?"

"She could be, couldn't she? No, her family and I were neighbors. I found her after I came home from the campaign. Her family hadn't survived the beasts. She didn't have anywhere to go, and I couldn't leave her alone, so she came to live with me. Makes herself useful with cooking and cleaning. She's a good girl. She couldn't stand the thought of being left alone again when I was hired to come out here, so I brought her along."

Keltin heard a soft creak of the floorboards beyond their room. Kuff's ears twitched as well, and the two of them looked up to see Wendi appear in the doorway.

"Supper's done," she said softly. "I've put out an extra plate for you, Mr. Moore."

"Thank you," said Keltin, trying another smile on her, but she didn't look his way and left without another word.

Dinner proved to be a potato soup with chunks of spicy Krendarian sausage and good crispy bread with butter and marmalade for spreading. Keltin did his best to eat slowly, but he couldn't help getting multiple helpings of everything before him.

"This is delicious," he said to Wendi.

The girl finally gave him a shy smile and placed another ladleful of soup in Keltin's bowl without waiting to be asked. Ross finished chewing a mouthful of bread and leaned towards Keltin.

"Well, let me tell you something of what we're facing here. I know you're already familiar with the terrain and the beasts that we usually see, and God be praised, we won't have nearly as many to face this time, though our numbers are certainly not as impressive as they were last season."

"Can we expect any help at all from the Krendarian military?"

"Not very likely. There were plenty of desertions when the war was lost with Larigoss in the south. I think Parliament is trying to keep the best troops it has left close to the capital, just to keep order. "

"Even still, they can't afford to ignore this area. The crops are just as needed now as they were last year."

"It's not that they don't see the need. The problem is coordination. Minister Erickson was deposed nearly two weeks ago with no replacement, and a seat in Parliament these days is as permanent as a stool in a roadside pub house. There just isn't anyone who's managed to pull the government together to get something done. Until then, it'll be up to the people to see to their own needs."

Ross went on to explain the logistics of the region and just what sort of task they had set out for them. Mr. Whitt and his partners had purchased a total of nine different farms of varying sizes across the province. Four of them were adjacent to the Lona Farm, while the other four were more scattered, two in the west, one to the south, and a final one to the north and east. Ross had established a routine of patrolling through the farms and their fields with Kuff, spending one day to the west, south, and north-east farms for every four he spent at the base of operations here at the Lona farm. He and Kuff had already brought down three beasts consisting of a serpent stag, a spiked thresher, and a winged strangler.

"Any sign of a tusked giant or warp beast?" asked Keltin.

"No, and let's hope it stays that way," said Ross, pinching his left ear for good luck.

"What about the other farms in the province, the ones that Mr. Whitt doesn't own? Are they being worked? Do they have hunters?"

"I've seen men working the fields, but I haven't spoken with any of them. Do you think we should?"

"I do. Even if we're not working together directly, it doesn't hurt to know who your neighbors are when beasts are about. At the very least, you should introduce Kuff to them so they know not to shoot at him if he turns up unexpectedly on their property."

"All right. We can do a patrol of Mr. Whitt's properties starting tomorrow. There are several farms he doesn't own along the way that we can visit."

"Good." Keltin set aside his empty bowl and yawned. "In that case, I'd like to get some rest. Do you stand watch over the workers?"

"No. The bunkhouse has a sturdy lock, as does the barn and the stable. Don't worry. Kuff sleeps outside. He'll let us know if something comes calling." Ross turned to Wendi. "Could you show Mr. Moore to his room? I'll do the washing up."

Keltin followed Wendi out of the dining room and up the stairs to the second floor. She led him to a bedroom down the hall, stopping just outside the doorway to allow him in. Keltin lit a candle on the nightstand and laid his gear down at the foot of the bed.

"Is there anything else that you need, sir?" asked Wendi.

"No, thank you. You've been very kind."

Wendi smiled without looking at him. "Well, goodnight."

"Goodnight."

She closed the door and Keltin sat down on the bed. It was too soft for his liking, but the linens were clean and tidy. He pulled off his boots and readied himself for bed. He considered writing a letter to either Jaylocke or Mary, but decided against it. With any luck, he wouldn't be in Krendaria all that long. Just a few weeks until the harvest was done and then he'd be home again. That is, if he didn't have to make a trip to the Malpinion border. Keltin quickly said an evening prayer, blew out his candle, and climbed into bed, but he didn't sleep. His thoughts were miles away, hoping desperately that Elaine and her family were safe.

CHAPTER 5 – THE HOUND

The morning was cool and crisp, with a slight bite of chill that signaled the gradual changing of the season. Already, some of the leaves were beginning to turn. Keltin leaned against the fence outside the farmhouse and looked out at the trees beyond the cleared fields, searching for telltale signs of movement. Workers passed by him, giving his weapons a curious look but otherwise not approaching him. After a few minutes of waiting, he was confronted by Yull on his way to the fields.

"All settled in?" he asked.

"Yes. We're going to make an inspection of all the farms that we're responsible for."

Yull blew out his cheeks and nodded.

"Well, I suppose that's your duty, and I'm not your foreman. Still, I don't like having you both gone at the same time. I'd hoped that having two of you here would mean that one of you would always be nearby. After all, we've got the majority of Mr. Whitt's property right here."

"We may do that once we've had a chance to inspect all of the farms, but for now, I'd like to see what sort of job we have ahead of us."

"I suppose I'll just have to hope that nothing happens to

one of my men while you're off wandering the countryside."

Yull walked off in the direction of the fields without a word of farewell. Keltin watched him go without taking any offense at the foreman's words. He didn't envy the man having to worry about the constant threat of beasts while trying to do a job that was hard enough on its own. Soon, Ross and Kuff emerged from the front door of the farmhouse. In his hands, Ross held an impressive scattergun, while on his hip he had what looked like a service revolver, possibly from the Krendarian military. Kuff was wearing a studded collar to protect his vulnerable throat and seemed eager to get going.

"Sorry to have kept you waiting," said the hound's owner.

"It's all right. Are you ready to go?"

"Yes. Let's."

They left the farm and made their way westward, following the roads when possible and crossing fields and stands of trees when it wasn't. Keltin took a deep breath of the cool air. After weeks cooped up in the company office and traveling through Riltvin and Krendaria, it felt good to finally be out on a hunt again. Here, he knew what was expected of him and felt confident that he would deliver when needed. While he never could forget about the needs of the Destovs or his family and friends, for the moment all those worries were set aside for more immediate concerns. Even the threat of danger was welcome in a way. It forced him to concentrate on the moment, and leave worrying about the future for some other time.

They'd traveled in silence for half an hour when Ross struck up a conversation.

"Prefer a rifle for hunting, eh?" he said, careful to keep his voice soft and low.

Keltin nodded. "My uncle was a gunsmith as well as a beast hunter. He made this rifle for me."

"I suppose it would be useful in the open, but with these close trees, I would have thought you'd prefer something more like this." Ross lifted his scattergun for emphasis.

Keltin shrugged. "I prefer precision shooting to blasting

great gaping holes in my quarry. It's the way my family has always hunted."

"And is precision shooting the reason you carry that?"

Ross pointed to the hand cannon on Keltin's hip.

"That's an experiment. I'm friends with a gunsmith and his family. He wanted me to try it out."

"Looks like it would kick like a mule."

Keltin shrugged. "It does."

They continued on, always moving cautiously and careful not to make too much noise or draw attention to themselves. Each stir of leaves caused all three of them to pause, listening and watching. Sometimes they spied the bird or rabbit that had caused the sound. Other times, they waited and watched for several minutes before moving cautiously in the direction of the sound, usually only to find that there was nothing there.

Keltin remembered when he had first started training Jaylocke and how surprised the wayfarer had been to learn that most of what passed for beast hunting was silently investigating rustles of wind and the scampering of small woodland creatures. Keltin likened it to fishing, full of long periods of monotony occasionally punctuated by heart-pounding excitement. Except that hunting beasts was more than just a matter of trying to hunt down his prey. Often, it also included avoiding becoming prey yourself.

After one particularly long wait after a soft crash in the brush, Ross breathed a whispered command to Kuff.

"*Poe-See*," he said. "Come Kuff."

The hound didn't budge, continuing to stare at the space where a small bird had long since flown away. Ross had looked at the bush once more, as if debating whether the hound saw something he didn't. After a pause, he turned back to Kuff and gave the command again, more firmly this time. The hound continued to hesitate, until a third, sharp command was given, and he finally turned to follow his master. Keltin had kept most of his attention on the bush throughout the episode, trying to see if there was anything he himself had missed. Eventually, he decided that he had been right, soon finding that his assumption was correct when he circled the bush and found that there had been nothing at all inside it.

It concerned Keltin that the hound had forced him to second-guess himself. Of course, it was dangerous to become too comfortable on a hunt. Careless beast hunters were soon dead hunters. But jumping at shadows had its own risks. Over time the senses became dull and overtaxed. Fatigue came more quickly as well, and foolish errors became easier and more frequent. It seemed as if Ross had read these thoughts in Keltin's expression as they continued on.

"I'm sorry," he said. "Kuff is still in training. If I'd had the choice, I would have waited another season before bringing him on a hunt. But he's the only hound I have."

"I understand," said Keltin. They continued on for a few minutes as a thought occurred to him. "What's it like, hunting with a fully trained hound? Captain Tallow and the rest of you trainers always kept to yourselves, so I never really saw your hounds in action."

Ross sighed and looked at Kuff. "A fully trained hound is like a tool in its master's hand. It goes, comes, attacks, turns, leads, tracks... It's like having a trusted old gun that hears the way you breathe, reads the way you smell. A great hound can almost read your thoughts and will do anything you tell it to... or die trying."

Ross cleared his throat, rubbing at his eyes with the back of his fist and cursing quietly under his breath. Keltin attempted to steer the conversation elsewhere.

"If we spot a beast, how should we proceed? I don't want to get in the way of you two, or to teach Kuff any bad habits."

"I appreciate that," said Ross, shaking himself from his reverie. "But Kuff needs to learn how to be around other hunters, whether they're people or hounds. Right now, he knows two commands for hunting: attack and turn. If I tell him to attack, he'll fight until he can't fight anymore. If I tell him to turn a beast, he'll chase and harry it, doing his best to drive it back towards me and my scattergun. As far as what you can do, if I give him the signal to turn, be ready to shoot the boil as it comes towards us. If I give him the signal to attack, hold your fire, even if you think you have a clear shot. Don't be offended. I remember the stories about your marksmanship from the campaign, but you'll forgive me, he is my hound."

"I understand, but what if the fight is going poorly for him?"

Ross took a deep breath. "There's a command for him to back down, but Kuff is still learning it. If we encounter a beast that's a little easier to manage, I may use the encounter as a chance to help him practice it."

"What are the commands for attack and turn, just so I know what you're telling him to do?"

"Attack is *Daag*. Turn is *Walloo*. Stand down is *Al-hah*."

"I heard you use another one earlier. What was it?"

"*Poe-see*? That's come. We're still working on that too." Ross hesitated before continuing. "There's one other thing. If I feel that Kuff isn't ready for a particular beast, or if it's too dangerous for him…"

"I'll take care of it. Just keep him back."

Ross visibly relaxed. "Thank you. I will."

The rest of the day passed with little conversation as Keltin and Kuff continued to pause and check each stray sound or flash of movement before continuing on. They also stopped and introduced themselves to the men working the fields of several farms that were not owned by Mr. Whitt and his partners. Keltin was glad to find that the men they encountered all seemed grateful to see them, realizing that any beast hunter in the neighborhood was a good thing. By mid-afternoon, Ross pointed to a distant field of tall maize.

"That's one of Mr. Whitt's fields. We're getting close to the Parson Farm."

They passed by the maize and continued on to a field of pumpkins nearly fully orange and ready for harvest. Keltin looked out over the field and noticed something stir on the far end. He stopped, pulling the brim of his hat low to shield his eyes from the gray sky above. He saw it again. Something was lurking just along the tree line. Keltin moved carefully to the fence surrounding the field of gourds, setting his pack and the Ripper down and bracing his rifle on top of the fence. Ross drew close to him to whisper in his ear.

"What do you see?" he asked.

"Not sure. It's still in the trees on the far side. Keep Kuff close, all right? I don't want him to scare it off."

Ross nodded, whispering a command to the hound. Kuff dutifully laid down and placed his head between his paws, looking up at his master with inquisitive eyes. Keltin kept his focus across the field, watching the telltale signs of movement among the densely growing trees and bushes. Suddenly he spied a creature that he was all-too familiar with from the year before. A stork-legged beast emerged from the foliage. The creature stalked forward carefully, its bald, vulture-like head twisting from side to side, its beady eyes searching for potential prey.

Keltin advanced the revolver chamber of his rifle to a Capshire Shatter Round. While he preferred taking down this particular monster by firing the explosive round into the beast's spindly neck, making the shot from the other side of a field was unlikely at best. Instead, he aimed for its slender body, one third of the way down the trunk, dead center of the boil's lungs. He breathed out, breathed in, and fired.

The gunshot shattered the stillness around them. The beast was knocked completely off its feet, thrashing in the dirt for a moment before it managed to struggle back to its spindly legs and stumble off into the trees. Keltin turned to see Ross nodding in admiration of the shot. Keltin allowed himself the ghost of a smile.

"Can't do that with a scattergun," he said.

Ross gave a good-natured chuckle. "Maybe not, but I've got another weapon I can use." He turned to Kuff, who had leapt to his feet at the sound of the gunshot. The hound stared in the direction the beast had fled, his body tensed like a spring just waiting to be sprung.

"*Daag* Kuff! *Daag!*"

The hound leapt into the air, flying over the five-foot

wooden fence in a single bound and bolting over the pumpkins at a blistering sprint, barking all the way. Keltin and Ross took off after him, following the sound of the barking as the hound disappeared among the trees. They had just reached the far side of the field when the timbre of the barks changed to a higher, more excited yelp. Then they went silent.

"He's got it now," said Ross, hurrying forward. "This way!"

They hurried through the dense brush, following the direction of the last barks they had heard. Soon Keltin heard another sound. Violent rustling, savage growls, and panicked hissing. Chasing down the sound, they finally emerged into a small clearing and found where the hound had run down the stork-legged beast. Kuff had leapt up onto the fleeing creature, clamping his massive jaws around its long neck. His powerful muscles quivered as he shook the beast, whipping its head and body around savagely. The beast's legs kicked and twitched even as its dead black eyes stared at the hunters. Ross watched Kuff for a moment before shouting at him in a firm voice.

"*Al-hah!*"

It took Kuff a moment to register the command, but eventually he released the beast and stepped back, leaving the corpse to twitch and spasm for another half-minute before coming to its final rest. Kuff looked up at Ross with a canine grin, his long fangs glistening red. Ross immediately went to his hound, praising him loudly and scratching behind his long, pointed ears. Keltin meanwhile went to the still form of the beast. He looked down at it as images nearly a year old came rushing back to him.

"Bring back some memories?" asked Ross.

Keltin nodded. "I lost a man to one of these boils on my first patrol. It was one of the reasons I spoke out against Baron Rumsfeld's use of military tactics to hunt beasts."

"I remember hearing about that from Captain Tallow. You likely saved a lot of hunters' lives by doing that."

Keltin shook his head. "Maybe. It was too late for Ru, and his friend Weedon never recovered. In the end, I couldn't help either one of them."

Ross didn't answer. Keltin looked up to see the hound trainer looking at him with a thoughtful expression.

"Come on," he said after a moment. "The foreman of this farm likely won't be thrilled to know that we found a beast in one of his fields, but at least we can tell him he won't have to worry about it anymore."

CHAPTER 6 – A NEW COMPANION

"I must be getting old," said Ross as they slowly made their way down the road winding its way between the fields. "I find myself looking forward more and more to a warm meal and bed every day."

"There's nothing wrong with enjoying some creature comforts. You'd be a fool to prefer sleeping out in the open when beasts are about."

Ross gave him a predatory grin. "Well, there are fewer about now, aren't there?"

Keltin nodded absently. They'd made a complete patrol of Mr. Whitt's farms and managed to find and kill a serpent stag along with the stork-legged beast they'd brought down on the first day. Not a bad start to the job. And certainly much easier than it had been a year ago.

Autumn had come like the breaking of dawn. At first, the change had come in subtle hints. A slight nip in the air. An occasional golden leaf among a sea of green. Then suddenly it seemed like they had woken up to find the sounds, sights, and smells of fall all around them. The heady scent of ripened crops was everywhere, and already the foremen had their workers beginning the final labors of harvesting, storing, and processing for shipping. Nearby, Keltin could see a team of men armed with spades, busily digging up plump potatoes to be shaken off, cut, and deposited in a waiting wagon. He thought he saw Yull among them, but couldn't be sure at the distance. He allowed himself a small smile. For the moment, things seemed to be going well all around.

Soon the farmhouse was in sight, and Keltin spied the rustle of curtains at a top-floor window.

"That'll be Wendi," said Ross with a smile. "No doubt she's been watching for us since this morning."

But it wasn't Wendi who met them at the door. Kuff gave a low growl as Marius Harper stepped outside and approached them with a pleasant smile.

"Hello again, Mr. Moore! Surprised to see me?"

Keltin blinked, then smiled and shook the newspaperman's hand.

"I certainly am. I didn't think we'd meet again until we were both back in Collinsworth. Weren't you going to stay in Carvalen to write a story about conditions in the capital?"

"Oh, I've already written two pieces about the capital. One documenting the state of the government, and another representing the plight of the common man on the street. Now I'm following up with a new piece focusing on what's being done to try to avoid the same catastrophe that befell this poor nation just one year ago. I had the idea that our readers would likely be interested to hear the current state of affairs in Dhlama Province. Luckily, I already knew where Mr. Whitt's offices in town were thanks to you, and I was able to gain permission to come up here to record my observations."

"I'm surprised that Mr. Whitt's partners were willing to agree to that."

"It did take a little coaxing, but I managed to convince them that a favorable article in a prominent paper would likely garner some good publicity. Show them in a light that makes them look like saviors helping out the poor populace, rather than shrewd businessmen taking advantage of other people's misfortunes."

"But is that true?"

Harper shrugged. "I won't know until I see where the crops end up being sold… and at what price."

"They may not be happy with you if you don't write the favorable piece you promised."

"I never promised anything. I only suggested the benefits of a positive article, if that's what I end up writing."

Keltin nodded, unsure how he felt about the easy duplicity of the Collinsworth Gazette reporter.

Wendi appeared in the doorway behind Harper. Her subdued features belied her relief upon seeing Ross and Kuff safely returned. She focused on the large hound, giving him a scratch between his long, pointed ears.

"Hello Kuff! Did you bring down a beast while you were away?"

"He gave a good accounting for himself," said Ross. "We'll tell you about it over dinner, if it's ready."

"It is. Come on inside and wash up, and I'll get it on the table. Oh, and Mr. Moore, a letter came for you while you were away. I left it on your bed."

Keltin took the stairs two-at-a-time and hurried into his room. He didn't recognized the handwriting on the envelope and turned it over to find the sending address. The letter had come from the office of The Beast Hunter with Jaylocke's name prominently displayed. He tore open the envelope and began to read.

Dear Keltin,

Well, this is a fine "Welcome home!" No sooner do we return, brave slayers of the mythical smoke beast, when what are we met with? No piping hot dinner or turned-down sheets. Just a note on the desk saying you're off on an adventure and forgot to take along your good-humor and level-thinking. I'll let you sort out which of us is which.

That aside, I do wish it would have been possible to come with you on this one. I realize that you had to leave posthaste, and I'm not worried about you managing all those beasts by yourself. It's the other reason that you're there that concerns me. If you do have to go north to fetch Elaine and her family, be extra cautious. There are more dangers than beasts in Malpin. Word is that the Heterack Empowerment is turning the place into something of a military-state. My advice? If you must go there, get in, get out without being seen if you can, and if someone in a uniform tries to stop you, smile and wave, then shoot them dead if they twitch. I'm sure I don't have to tell you, but when defending those you care about (and perhaps love) there are some scruples that are worth setting aside temporarily.

Write back if you can, though we may not be able to respond right away. The Beast Hunter already has another work order for a lumber camp up north. Bor've'tai is very excited to be among his former peers in the fine craft of hacking down trees. At least, I assume he's excited. Hard to tell with him.

May your ancestors walk with you.
Jaylocke

Under this, in a surprisingly delicate hand, was a second, smaller note.

Keltin,
Heed the advice that Jaylocke has given you. Malpin is no safe place, though you may find allies if you stay off the beaten path. It pains me deeply that I'm not able to be of service to you, especially now that you are going to a place that I would be most familiar with, and in the service of someone we both care deeply for.

The best advice I can give you is to seek out the Brothers of Kerrtow once you are in Malpin. While I dealt with them little myself, I know that they were a great help to Grel'zi'tael and Shar'le'vah when they were fleeing south. I think that you can trust them. Also, if you meet anyone that you think you can trust while in Krendaria, consider asking for their aid as well. Remember your own counsel. There is no shame in asking for help when it is needed.

May the God of Light keep you safe.
Bor've'tai

Keltin set the letters down and felt a sharp pang of loss

without his two friends. They were both right, of course. If Keltin did have to go to Malpin, both of them would have been incredibly helpful to have had with him. On the other hand, it might have been especially dangerous for Bor've'tai as a Loopi, and perhaps Jaylocke as well as a Weycliff wayfarer. Keltin wouldn't have wanted to put either of them at risk. Perhaps it was just his wish to not be alone on a mission that was so far removed from what he was accustomed to that made him long for his two truest friends.

Keltin's thoughts were interrupted by a gentle rap on the door.

"Come in."

The door opened, but Wendi remained outside in the hall.

"Mr. Moore, supper is ready, if you'd like."

Keltin quickly stood up and followed her downstairs. He found Ross and Harper already sitting at a table spread with sausage pie and maize pudding, with a golden brown loaf of bread waiting nearby. Harper smiled as Keltin took a seat beside him.

"It seems I may have to write another piece about your past exploits, Mr. Moore. Mr. Ross has just been telling me some of your adventures during the campaign that I hadn't heard before."

"Really? I can't imagine he'd know much more than what I've told you. We didn't work very closely together at the time."

"I tried to tell him that most of my stories were just the scuttlebutt and rumors passed around the rest of the hunters," said Ross.

"Those are often the best stories," said Harper. He sighed. "I do wish I could have been there to document it in person."

"I'm not sure you would have wanted that. It wasn't a very easy campaign."

"You're forgetting that I've been a war correspondent. I've seen plenty of action. I even had to participate in a suppressing maneuver in the trenches of the Larigoss war. Come to think of it, I'll bet they would have appreciated a man like you down there. Have you ever considered changing careers, Mr. Moore? I'm sure you could have found great success as a crack military scout, or better yet, a skilled marksman."

"I'm not a soldier."

Harper shrugged as he served a generous slice of sausage pie to Ross. "Some men don't have the luxury of choosing. War comes regardless of the common man's hopes and desires. It sweeps up people like dust before a tornado, scattering them wherever it will." He chuckled. "Pardon my flowery prose. But look at the state of Krendaria, still reeling from the bloody blow dealt to it last year, and smarting from a land-grab by Larigoss in the south on top of that. Then look at Malpin in the north. Strong, hungry, and drunk on its own power. A tight-fisted regime requires far fewer signatures on a declaration of war."

"What is the latest news from Malpin?" asked Keltin, his thoughts on Elaine and her family.

"More dangerous all the time. There's an election coming up in a few weeks for the seat of Supreme Minister, and the front contender is a Heterack named Grik Pallow. If Pallow is elected, he'll be the first of his people ever to take that office."

"I thought Polace Harlev was Supreme Minister. Doesn't he have the backing of the Vaughs?"

"Both Harlev and Pallow are tight in the pocket of the Vaughs, but Pallow has the ear of the people. He blames Harlev for the economic downturn they've had since the Heterack Empowerment. He said that it would have been better to keep the Loopi craftsmen and laborers on a tight leash, rather than drive them from the country. It's a clever tactic with an easy scapegoat, and it looks like he's headed for a landslide victory."

"What would that mean?"

Harper's expression was grim. "It could mean a more militant regime than our continent has seen in more than a generation. Closed borders, trade embargoes… it all gets very messy if the neighboring nations can't find some common ground. It could even mean war."

Keltin shook his head. "I don't believe there will be a war. Malpin is surrounded on three sides. It would be a slaughter if they instigated anything. Besides, there'd be nothing to gain."

"There's land. Krendaria is severely weakened, and has a lot of prime farmland in the north country, including this province. Malpin could march a few thousand soldiers across the border with little opposition and lay a firm claim before any of Krendaria's allies had time to react."

"Don't count out Krendarian heart too easily," said Ross. "We've gone through hard times for certain, but my people have seen bad times before and rose above it. If Malpin comes south, we'll be ready for them."

Harper smiled at the hound trainer.

"I'm sure that you're right. I certainly saw my share of Krendarian courage to the south against Larigoss." The newspaperman then shifted topics with a social grace that made Keltin envious. "So, you've both made your recognizance of the surrounding farmlands. Now that there are two of you," he glanced at Kuff on the floor beside the table, "pardon me, three of you, what will be your next move?"

"I think we'll split up," said Keltin. "With this many farms under our protection, we need to be able to cover as much territory as possible."

"Isn't that too dangerous? Going out into beast-infested woods, alone?"

"Well, Ross will have Kuff with him, and until this last year, I did almost all of my hunting on my own. Besides, there's little need to sleep out-of-doors, which is the biggest danger on a hunt. We should all be fine."

"Still, I'd feel better if you had someone to watch your back. How about I tag along with you? I'm a fair shot, and I'd dearly love to see a beast hunter at his trade."

Keltin hesitated. "Well... perhaps. We can head out in the morning. You and I can make a circuit of the surrounding farms while Ross and Kuff stay here to watch Lona farm and the other local fields. Though you'd have to be very careful. I can't afford to spend my time watching out for you while I'm working."

"I promise I'll do my best not to be a burden. Just think of me as a passive observer, unless, of course, there is any way that I can be of help."

"Just keep yourself safe. Leave the beasts to me."

* * *

The autumn morning air was cold and crisp. Keltin felt a slight chill through one of the poorly-sewn patches in his hunting jacket and again wished he had invested in a new one. He could have afforded it, after all. But it had sentimental value. Its tough outer layer had saved him from many stray claws, teeth, and spikes over the years, and the removable inner lining had kept him warm even on the banks of the frozen Wylow river. Besides, his father had worn it, his mother had mended it, and then his sister had. And Elaine had.

A twig snapped. Keltin spun and had half-raised his rifle to his shoulder before realizing that it had only been Harper missing a step. The newspaperman gave an apologetic, rueful smile. Keltin gave a tight-lipped acknowledgement of the gesture as he examined the reporter's outfit and kit. True, he didn't look entirely out of place alongside a beast hunter. His clothes were sturdy and sensible, showing many miles of hard wear, and he held his Clefferton bolt action rifle with confidence. But there was something in the man's bearing that was unmistakable. It was a sort of stiff awkwardness, like a man trying to move around early in the morning or when he was too cold to be comfortable.

Keltin spoke softly to him.

"I suppose there wasn't much call for moving stealthily in the trenches."

Harper looked around uncomfortably. "I wasn't sure if I should try speaking with you. Are you sure it's safe to talk?"

Keltin shrugged. "As long as we keep our voices low, we shouldn't draw the attention of the more skittish beasts. As far as the more dangerous ones go, if they're nearby, they're already hunting us."

Harper nodded though he didn't look very reassured. They continued on in silence throughout the morning until they had reached one of Mr. Whitt's farms. Called the Flaherty Farm, its fields consisted mainly of potatoes, squash, and turnips. Keltin spied a number of workers using specialized, pronged shovels to dig up the turnips from their neat rows. Among the workers stood a man scanning the outer edges of the field with an old Matlock rifle in his hands. Keltin approached him.

"Hello, Bryce. How are things around here?"

The foreman of the Flaherty farm turned and fixed him with a somber look.

"Fair enough here, but I expect you'll want to press on to the Graggery farm. They've been having a hard time of it. A man was taken down by a beast."

Keltin sucked in a breath. "Dead?"

"Not since I last heard, but he wasn't in a good way from what I was told."

"Any word on what sort of beast did it to him?"

"Only that the boil got away. Hope you bring down the hexed thing. My men can't work very fast while looking over their shoulder."

"I'll get on it. Stay sharp until you get word that I've brought it down."

Keltin turned and began to stride quickly away, leaving Harper to catch up or be left behind. This was the first casualty of the season, and it set Keltin's nerves on edge. Though it wasn't the first time he had heard of someone hurt or killed by a beast, it stirred the familiar driving fire that had fueled him ever since he was a young boy looking up to his father, uncles, and grandfather as they left on their own hunts. He remembered imagining them like modern-day knights, questing to save innocent folk from monsters of nightmare and legend.

Of course, the real thing was less glamorous than the legends he'd read in his mother's home library. Reality was full of things like tediously long stretches of wandering through the woods, eating cold potted meat from a tin because you had to make a cold camp, and praying that you wouldn't be attacked while stepping out in the darkness to relieve yourself. Still, he'd go through all that and more to protect good people from the sort of tragedy he'd seen so often. The sort of tragedy he'd faced himself more than once.

"Try to keep up, Mr. Harper," Keltin said over his shoulder. "You're finally going to see what's it's like to hunt a beast."

CHAPTER 7 – SPECTERS FROM THE PAST

They reached the Graggery farm just as the sun was setting behind the trees, the sky stained with lacy pink clouds against a blue and orange background slowly giving way to the blackness of night. There were no workers in the fields or the farmyard, leaving an eerie silence in the emptiness. Keltin led Harper directly to the worker barracks. He rapped on the door to the bunkhouse and was greeted by the sound of several crossbars and braces being removed from the other side. The door opened, revealing the golden warmth of lantern light within. The man at the door peered out at Keltin and turned back to call inside.

"It's that new beast hunter!"

"Get him in here and close the door, you slack-jawed git!"

Keltin and Harper were rushed inside, the door secured firmly behind them. Usually a place of banter, gambling and good nature, the bunkhouse was nearly as silent as the farmyard outside. Keltin was confronted by more than a dozen silent field workers all sitting on their bunks, watching him. Thom Parse, the farm foreman, emerged from the back of the bunkhouse where several blankets had been suspended from the rafters to provide some privacy.

"It's a hexed good thing to see you again," he said, his

quiet, strained voice filling the silent common room. He cut a glance in Harper's direction. "Who's that?"

"Marius Harper, he's traveling with me."

Parse grunted a greeting and turned back to Keltin. "We thought we'd have to wait for another full patrol of the other farms before we saw that loafer and his mutt again."

"I came as soon as I heard that one of your men was attacked. How is he?"

"He's back this way."

Keltin followed Parse back to the curtained-off portion of the bunkhouse. Pulling the blankets aside, the foreman gestured Keltin and Harper within the close-quarters before carefully pulling the blankets back into place behind them. The injured worker was striped to his underclothes, his bare chest heaving with each strained breath. A jar of spirits sat on a nearby table along with a small pile of bloodied bandages. Keltin could see little of the man's wounds, only that the greatest injuries had been around his neck and upper torso. As he stepped closer to investigate the man, he noticed Harper watching from a respectful distance, his expression somber but not pale. It seemed the newspaperman was made of stern stuff after all.

Keltin spoke softly to Parse.

"Did anyone see the beast?"

"Not clearly. It was like a blur that came out of the woods and threw itself at him. I had a rifle, but Monse and the beast were both rolling around in the dirt and I didn't dare fire for fear of hitting him. I fired into the air, and the rest of us rushed at the thing with shovels, shouting and cussing at the top of our lungs until it took off, fast as a dart."

"That was very brave of you," Harper said softly. "There are many that would call you and your men heroes."

Parse grimaced and spat on the floor. "We're not hunters, but we couldn't stand by to let one of our own get torn apart by that boil." He turned to Keltin. "Do you know what sort of beast it could have been?"

Keltin knelt down to examine the soiled dressings on the

man's body.

"I have an idea, but I don't know enough yet to be sure. Does he have a fever?"

Parse nodded. "I think the wounds got infected. We're trying to draw it out with hot compresses, but it keeps leaking blood and pus."

"Is he talking much?"

"Nothing but screaming in pain and crying for more whiskey. We poured half a still in him just to get him to sleep."

Keltin nodded and rose to his feet.

"When are you planning on changing his dressings next?"

"In a little while. It'll wake him, and I wanted to let him sleep while he could, if only for the sake of the rest of us."

"All right. Let me know when you're ready to do it. I need to see his wounds."

"Fair enough. Have you eaten yet?"

"No."

Parse waved a hand towards the other end of the bunkhouse. "We've got a pot of beans down there and some travel bread. It's cold, but it'll fill you. None of us are eating very much right now."

"Thank you."

Keltin held the blanket open for Harper and the two of them made their way to the pot of vittles. He scooped himself a healthy portion from the pot and grabbed one of the hard little loaves stacked nearby. He sat at one of the long tables that ran the length of the room, flanked by bunk beds on either side. He bent over his bowl and began to eat, acutely aware of the eyes of the workers upon him. He could imagine what they were thinking, looking at this heavily armed stranger sitting in their midst. Perhaps they fancied him a great hero, or a dark, dangerous figure. Perhaps they even imagined him to be something of a monster himself.

As the silence grew thicker, he found himself wishing for Jaylocke's lively wit and banter to brighten the setting a little. It seemed as if Harper was equally aware of the deep silence. He leaned across the table and spoke to Keltin in a voice that imitated softness, but was clearly meant to be audible throughout the silent bunkhouse.

"So, Mr. Moore. I don't think you've ever told me about your first beast hunt. Do you remember it?"

"Not really. I went on a lot of hunts with my father and uncles when I was young. I can't really remember which one was my very first."

"What about your first hunt on your own, then? Surely that one stands out in your memory."

Keltin finished chewing a healthy portion of bread before answering.

"Yes, I can remember that one. I was sent to hunt down a sleevak that had escaped from a traveling sideshow."

"Those are the beasts that some hunters use to hunt other beasts, correct? Something like Ross and his tamarrin hound?"

Keltin shook his head firmly. "Sleevaks are nothing like tamarrin hounds. Hounds are well-trained and intelligent. Sleevaks are stupid and savage. The hunters who use them are mostly Heteracks from Olpin, and they don't train them, they handle them. Hunting with a pack of sleevaks is a delicate balance of starving them, releasing them into the general area of whatever you want killed, then drawing them back home with live traps and drugged meat. It leaves most of the work of hunting to the sleevaks. I suppose the sort who do it prefer dealing with the devil they know rather than facing the unknown. There were sleevak wranglers in last year's campaign here in Dhalma. We didn't get along."

Keltin scowled, recalling bitter memories. Harper gently cleared his throat.

"But the sleevak you hunted that first time, that one wasn't used for hunting?"

"No, it was part of a menagerie of creatures in a traveling show making the rounds through the bigger towns in Riltvin. The carnival was stopped outside of Jackson when the man caring for the animals made a mistake while trying to feed the sleevak and got himself killed. The boil got loose and started terrorizing the countryside. My father was contacted almost immediately, but he thought that this might be a good opportunity for my first solo hunt. It took me four days to track the thing down. By then, it had killed more than half a dozen livestock and seriously hurt two people, including a child."

Keltin stared at a point in space somewhere beyond the table in front of him as his mind went back in time.

"I finally tracked the thing down to a farmer's henhouse. It had torn away the flimsy wire on one side and gorged itself on everything inside. It was dark, and I couldn't see very well, but I fired at its still form as it lay sleeping against the back wall. It came awake like a demon with a knot in its tail. It threw itself at me, and was only stopped by the undamaged fencing on the side I was standing on. It savaged and tore at the wire, trying to get at me. I emptied all five chambers of my rifle into the beast, and still it kept coming. The wire was snapping under the strain, so I rushed forward with the Ripper and started stabbing at it with the point. The boil was little more than a bloody mass of mangled flesh by the time it died, pierced by the spike of the Ripper and torn in more than a dozen places by its own mindless rage against the thin wire of the henhouse."

Keltin looked up to see Harper watching him silently. He gave the newspaperman the ghost of a smile and a dry, humorless chuckle. "Not much of a heroic start to a new beast hunter's career, was it?"

He was answered by a screaming wail from the curtained-off section of the bunkhouse. Keltin and Harper jumped to their feet and made their way back to the wounded field worker. The injured man's face was red as a beet as he gasped and cried, cursing the pain and begging for whiskey. He was given a long draught until he started to choke on it, then proceeded to groan and gnaw at the spent shell casing that Parse had slipped between his teeth as he changed his dressings.

Keltin stood at a short distance and studied the wounds. Some were clearly the result of bites, with a semi-circle of puncture marks with two deeper than the rest where the canines had penetrated the flesh. Several smaller wounds showed where the beast had unsuccessfully tried to gain another grip with its powerful jaws. Focusing his attention on the most clearly defined bite marks, he studied their radius and estimated the size of the beast's mouth. He continued to examined the marks until they were covered by fresh dressings, then turned away. Harper stood before him, his eyes serious and searching.

"Do you know what sort of beast it was now?" he asked.

Keltin nodded. "I'm almost certain. At the very least, I know what to look for to track it. We'll start in the morning as soon as there's light."

Harper leaned in close to whisper in Keltin's ear. "Are you planning on camping outside?"

Keltin had to wait until the worker stopped screaming before answering. "We'll see if Parse can let us stay in the barn. It'll be safer than outside, and… quieter than in here."

* * *

The air was full of the coldness of dew as heavy gray clouds loomed overhead. The seasonal rains would arrive any day now. Keltin hoped that the workers could bring in the majority of their crops before then. Of course, some small amount of rain wouldn't spoil the crops immediately, but it would mean that their remaining time was quickly running out.

Still, Keltin was no Sky Talker, and had no control over the weather. He would have to focus on what he was hired to do, and let the foremen worry about their harvests. He crouched down to examine the ground where Parse had said that the attack had taken place two days before. He had no expectation of finding a definite trail away from the scene of violence, but hoped that the wet earth might reveal at least one identifying mark or clue for him. Sure enough, a few minutes' searching revealed a cat-like paw-print with clear claw marks at the front of six padded toes. Half-an-hour later and several yards away,

Keltin found another set of prints. He nodded in satisfaction.

"I know for certain what we're tracking now," he said.

Harper looked at the distance between the sets of prints. "Either this beast has an abnormally long stride, or it's got to be quite the giant."

"It's the stride. What we're looking for is called a 'whip leg'. Its legs have three joints and roll like cables or ropes as it runs. It's incredibly fast, has a head like a rock, and isn't afraid of large groups of men."

Harper's expression was grim with a twinge of discontent. "I suppose we'll need to travel especially carefully to find it."

"Not necessarily. In fact, you can walk comfortably today. While we don't necessarily need to traipse around banging pots and pans, making a show of not being cautious will likely draw it to us, looking for a meal. We just need to be ready when it attacks."

The newspaperman swallowed. "All right. I'll follow your lead."

"Actually, it would be safer if you walk in front. It may come from behind."

The day passed in the slow, anxious tedium of a beast hunt. Every falling leaf forced them to stop, listening and looking for any sign of their quarry. Harper was clearly on edge, and Keltin found himself equally bothered, though for an entirely different reason. He couldn't stop thinking of Elaine and her family. He knew it was distracting him, but despite his frustration, he just couldn't help it. Harper's candid appraisal of conditions in Malpin was more worrying than any of the beasts in Dhalma Province. The more Keltin thought about it, the more some secret part of him wished that he could abandon this job and go north right now. He wouldn't, of course. He had a duty to perform, and people were counting on him. But it still rankled him. Perhaps he would try writing a letter to Mr. Destov to ask for any updates he might have received from his family.

He was trying to compose a letter in his head when the beast struck. All was silent and still, then suddenly there was a rush from the left. There was no time for aiming or even clearly registering what was coming at them. Keltin saw a blur out of the corner of his eye, turned, and shot wildly from the hip. The blur stumbled, more from the force of the shot than any sort of accuracy in the placement of the bullet. Keltin used the spit-second of hesitation to pull his rifle up into his shoulder and fire again. He was almost certain the second shot connected, but the whip leg continued to come without hesitation, making a direct path for Harper.

Fortunately, by either design or dumb luck, Harper didn't try to fire at the beast or even attempt to run. He merely fell over. He landed backwards on his rump and the beast sailed over him, scrambling and skittering through the underbrush as it tried to turn with its long, coiling legs. Keltin aimed a killing shot for its chest but the beast gave up trying to turn around and launched itself onward through the woods and away from them.

Keltin stood rooted to the spot for a long moment, waiting to see if the whip leg would double-back and attack again. Eventually, he realized it wasn't coming back, and relaxed slightly. Harper had remained on the ground, though he had managed to pull a pistol from his belt, swinging it around to aim at every falling leaf around them. Keltin spoke to him softly.

"I think it's gone. Are you all right?"

The newspaperman relaxed slightly, running a trembling hand over his eyes.

"Yes, yes I think so. Hex, but that was close."

"Do you think you can stand?"

"I think so."

Harper accepted a hand as Keltin pulled him to his feet.

"It came so fast," said Harper. "I wanted to dodge away from it, but all I had time for was falling backwards." He gave a shaken, rueful smile. "Not very graceful, I suppose."

"It probably saved your life. I know I hit that whip leg at least once, so there should be a blood trail. It'll likely be a long one, considering how fast that thing can move."

Harper clenched his jaw and nodded.

"All right. Let's go get the boil."

* * *

Keltin slipped off his glove and rubbed stiff fingers into his weary eyes. It was getting colder, a rare sign of the end of day when the sun and sky were largely hidden by the surrounding trees. He stopped and judged his bearings. The blood trail had carried them some distance beyond the farms owned by Mr. Whitt, but he hesitated to turn around and go back. Parse and his workers would not be consoled by tales of a wounded beast fleeing into the forest. Besides, It would look bad to his employer if Keltin allowed a worker to be seriously injured without bringing down the beast that had done it.

"It's getting late," said Harper.

Keltin glanced up at the small patch of sky visible through the tree tops.

"It should start getting dark soon," he agreed.

"Should we make camp?"

"I'm thinking about it. It's never ideal to make camp in the open with a known beast on the loose, but if we go much farther we won't be able to see this blood trail anyway."

"Should we go back to the nearest farm owned by Mr. Whitt?"

Keltin was considering his answer when the stillness of the forest was broken by a distant yowl and an answering roar. He froze, trying to register a direction for the sound. There was another primal scream, and Keltin rushed in its direction, moving with careful haste, his rifle held in front of him. As he drew nearer to the sounds, he became convinced that he was hearing two different beasts in the same location. He wasn't familiar enough with the whip leg's vocalizations to be certain that it was one of the beasts, but he was sure that he had heard at least one of the beasts before. The shrieking wail gnawed at his memory, and he struggled to recall what creature made the sound even as he continued to rush towards it.

Suddenly he broke into the opening of a small clearing and was met with a spectacle of extreme savagery. Two beasts rolled together, lashing and slashing at each other with reckless abandon. One of the beasts was clearly the whip leg, its elongated limbs flying around the twisting bodies like braids on a dancing schoolgirl. The other beast...

Keltin sucked in a breath as he recognized the mottled green, scaly body, the bony crest around its head and the four gleaming eyes glaring out over a mouth full of knife-like fangs. A sleevak. Harper crashed into the open beside him. Keltin spun on him, almost lifting him off the ground in his haste to push the man back into cover. As soon as they were behind a fallen log Keltin dropped down and pulled his rifle into position, ready to kill either of the two monsters before them.

The beasts were too involved in their savage combat to pay the two men any notice. They'd ceased their violent rolling and now stood a short distance apart, squaring off and posturing as they slowly circled each other. It was immediately clear to Keltin that the whip leg was losing the fight. While its rock-hard head showed only superficial bleeding wounds, its front left shoulder had suffered a savage bite and was bleeding heavily. It moved with a marked limp, and it was clear that speed was no longer the advantage of the lighter, more agile beast. Meanwhile, the sleevak showed little damage.

Keltin was in the process of examining its superficial wounds when it launched itself forward at the whip leg. The lighter beast tried to dodge to the side but was too slow. The sleevak took hold of the whip leg in the same place where it had bitten before and clamped down. Unlike a tamarrin hound that would have gone for the throat and done a death shake, the sleevak instead used its hooked teeth to keep its prey from escaping as the long claws of its forelimbs raked over the whip leg's exposed body. The trapped beast cried out in desperation, but it didn't have the strength to break away a second time. Flesh, muscle, and tendon were torn away, and soon the dying beast's exposed viscera was steaming in the chill air, its long legs collapsing to the earth to twitch like bits of string tugged by a housecat.

Victorious, the sleevak immediately began to feast on its fallen opponent, tearing dripping chunks from its flanks and swallowing them whole. Keltin took the chance to examine the sleevak as it fed. Looking closer, he realized that the bony frill around its head had been distinctively cropped, and a blue-tinged brand had been burned into its flank.

Harper inched closer to him, his voice barely more than a breath in his ear.

"Are you going to shoot it?" he asked.

Keltin hesitated, then shook his head. "No. Someone owns that monster."

He pointed at the brand and the cropped frill. Harper shook his head.

"But you and Ross are the only hunters working for Mr. Whitt. Where did it come from?"

"Obviously, someone at one of the neighboring farms around here has hired their own beast hunters. Ones that wrangle sleevaks."

"What are you going to do?"

"Right now, we're going to hurry back to the nearest farm. I'm not going to sleep out in the open with sleevaks loose if I can possibly help it."

"What about tomorrow then?"

Keltin felt his jaw clench as he spoke through his teeth. "Tomorrow, we're going to find out who's fool crazy enough to use sleevaks to hunt here."

CHAPTER 8 – PREJUDICE

Keltin was angry. He knew it. He could almost see himself from the outside as he practically stomped through the woods in search of the next farm. In a distant, detached part of his mind he knew that he was being irrational, but the blurred line between justifiable outrage and blind anger was too vague to distinguish.

Sleevaks were dangerous. They killed indiscriminately, were notoriously hard to handle, and were all-but impossible to control. Keltin had only ever known one group of sleevak wranglers personally. A group of Heteracks from Olsivo, they had been a part of the Krendaria Campaign. Under the direction of their leader Captain Rok, each of the wranglers had been arrogant, clumsy, and spiteful, nearly killing Keltin and his friends with their stupid pets, then playing the part of the victim when their precious monsters were killed in self-defense. Worse, they had demanded compensation, not in money, but in vengeance, demanding that Bor've'tai and his fellow Loopi be cast out of the camp to survive on their own in the beast-infested woods. Keltin thought of the blind prejudice of the Heteracks and felt the glowing coals of anger flare yellow-hot inside of him. He'd never been so close to hunting something other than a beast as those plaguing wranglers.

Of course, the sleevak he had seen the day before couldn't be owned by the same wranglers. They had all died in a brutal attack by a tusked giant. But the fact that yesterday's sleevak was owned by someone else hardly changed Keltin's mood. Whoever it was, they were risking the lives of every field worker in the region, not to mention Keltin, Ross, and any other legitimate beast hunters working the same area.

Harper cleared his throat. Had he been trying to speak with him? Keltin had been so caught up in his dark thoughts that he hadn't noticed. The calmer portion of his mind told him that he was being reckless and forced him to slow down and travel more carefully. There were still dangerous beasts around after all, including the sleevaks.

He forced himself to bury his anger enough to speak with the newspaperman.

"Did you say something?"

"I was going to ask whether you think we'll find the owner of the sleevaks at the next farm?"

"We'll know when we get there."

"Have you considered what you will say once you meet them?"

"I need to find out how many boils they've got out here, and where they're deploying them. I need to know what –if anything— they're doing to control their monsters. And I want them to know that I don't appreciate them using sleevaks without letting any of their neighbors know about it."

"They may not be very eager to hear what you have to say."

Keltin spat. "That's too plaguing bad, because they're going to hear it. And they'd better listen, or they may just start finding all of their precious pets dead in the woods with bullet holes in their ugly heads."

They pushed on until they broke through the trees to find a field of workers harvesting gourds. Keltin was looking beyond the field at the farmhouse on the other side when he heard a distant, familiar shriek in that direction. Sleevaks. Turning, he made his way around the fence surrounding the field, well-aware of the cautious looks coming his way from the field workers. One of them called out to him.

"Ho there!" he said, making his way across the field to intercept him. Keltin noticed the man's hand hovering an inch away from the handle of a pistol in his belt.

"Just where do you think you're going?" demanded the man.

"Are you the foreman of this farm?"

"That's right. Who are you?"

"I'm a beast hunter hired to protect some of the farms around here."

"We've already got our own beast hunters."

"That's why I'm here. I think you have some sleevak wranglers working for you. Is that right?"

"Suppose we do? I don't see where it's any of your business."

Keltin's eyes narrowed. "It's my business because I'm traipsing around these woods risking my hide to protect men like you, and I don't appreciate having to watch my back from both beasts and sleevaks at the same time. Now, I'm going to go have a word with those wranglers. Are you going to stop me?"

The foreman seemed to take Keltin's measure for a moment before looking away and waving him towards the farmhouse.

"Makes no difference to me," he muttered. "I'm not overly fond of those slimy boils myself. Just don't cause any trouble for my men."

Without a farewell, Keltin turned and made his way to the farmyard grounds. A bestial cry from the barn turned him in that direction as Harper continued to trail along silently in his wake. Lifting the simple latch, Keltin pulled open the door with a creak of the rusty hinges and peered inside. His nose was immediately flooded with the natural smells of a barn. Hay dust, old manure and rust along with something else... something sharp and unpleasant. Opening the door wider, he saw the source of the stench. Eight steel cages dominated the barn's open, central space. Inside each one a sleevak thrashed and growled, creating a reverberating din in the echoing space. Half a dozen Heteracks were busying themselves with the creatures, using long blacksmith's tongs to drop great hunks of meat between the bars of each cage, allowing the beasts to snatch and gobble up their bloody dinner. At the sound of the creaking barn door, one of the Heteracks looked up sharply from where he stood cutting meat from a side of beef.

"No visitors during feeding time!" he snapped. "Wait outside!"

Keltin hesitated. His righteous indignation urged him to insist on talking with them now, but even in the midst of his high emotion he realized how potentially dangerous the wranglers' task must be even without distractions. Embarrassed and unable to think of anything to say, he swung the barn door closed with a bang and latched it shut. Finding a nearby workbench he threw himself on top of it and sat staring moodily at the dirt before him. Harper hesitated at his side for a moment before finding his own place to sit and wait a short distance from him.

A drop of water appeared in the hard-packed dust, followed by another. Soon, the ground was spotted with the splattering of a light, cold rain. Keltin removed his broad-brimmed hat and let the cold wetness seep through his hair. He felt a large drop hit the back of his neck and he shuddered. Slowly, he felt his anger cool as the rain continued to fall on him like a damp rag placed over his childhood head by his mother when his temper would get the better of him.

The barn door opened and the Heterack that had spoken to him before stepped out. He was a typical specimen of his race, incredibly broad in the shoulders, with a large, flattened face and a massive tawny mane that framed his head and neck like the fur lining of a lady's coat. His features were serious, but not harsh as he approached them.

"Sorry for the rough words," he said, his voice deep and clear. "But it's never safe to be distracted around the sleevaks when they're eating." He paused to take in Keltin's appearance before continuing. "You're not one of the field workers. You look like either a military scout or a beast hunter. Which is it?"

"Beast Hunter. I'm Keltin Moore, from Riltvin."

The Heterack nodded, then surprised Keltin by extended a thick, muscular hand.

"I'm Bol, from Olsivo in the north of Malpin," he said. "I'm in charge of this crew." The Heterack shook Keltin's hand then gave Harper an inquisitive look.

"Marius Harper, Collinsworth Gazette," said the newspaperman by way of introduction. "I'm following Mr. Moore in an effort to report on conditions here in Dhalma Province."

The Heterack shook Harper's hand before turning back to Keltin.

"It's good to see another beast hunter out here. I was beginning to think we were the only ones in the whole province."

Keltin was caught off guard again. His only impression of Heteracks up to that point had been as bullies and bigots. Of course, most of the Heteracks' animosity during the campaign had been directed towards the Loopi and Weycliff wayfarers. Keltin had only drawn their displeasure by openly associating with Bor've'tai, Jaylocke, and their peoples. Still, this Heterack didn't act at all like Keltin had expected. He was too well spoken, too amicable, if not openly friendly. Keltin struggled for a moment to think of what he wanted to say.

"Well, I'm not surprised you haven't seen more hunters around if you prefer to use those things."

Keltin pointed towards the barn. Bol gave a humorless chuckle, as if he were hearing an old argument that he had given up trying to win.

"All methods of hunting beasts are dangerous, just in different ways. Sleevaks are just a tool to us. We know how to use them because we understand them."

"I understand something of them myself. They were used in the campaign in this province last year."

"You were in the campaign?"

"I was."

Bol nodded slowly and seemed to examine Keltin a second time. "I see. My crew was away when we got word of the call for hunters. By the time we learned of it, it was too late to join. I heard it was a twisted fete, though."

"You could say that. We were up against more beasts than I'd ever seen in one place before. It also didn't help that I had to worry as much about the wranglers' sleevaks as the beasts themselves."

"Sounds like they didn't know what they were doing. You never release sleevaks when there are people within a certain radius of the release point."

"Really? Then why did I see one of your sleevaks just yesterday?"

"Where?"

"Half a day's walk to the west, near Gronson farm."

Bol shrugged. "We didn't know anyone would be in the area. My employers own that region. What were you doing out there?"

"I was on the trail of a whip leg."

"Well, if we'd known you were there, we wouldn't have released the sleevaks. We make sure all of our workers know when we're going to release them. The foremen have become very good at shuffling their crews around to work where the sleevaks aren't."

Keltin didn't answer. Harper cleared his throat.

"It sounds like you have a very organized operation going here, Mr. Bol."

"We have to. Sleevaks are predictable and effective, but incredibly dangerous if you aren't careful." Bol turned back to Keltin. "I don't fault you for trailing the whip leg into our territory. You didn't know we were here. But in the future, if something wanders onto our side of the province, consider it taken care of. We'll do the same if something crosses into your territory. If you survived last year's campaign, you must be quite the hunter."

Keltin could only make a tight-lipped smile to acknowledge

the compliment. He felt his ears burning hot despite the cold rain. Again, Harper spoke.

"It sounds like this was all a simple misunderstanding. I'm glad to know that there are such capable men protecting these fields and workers."

"Thank you. Well, if there's nothing else, I need to get back to my creatures. Good hunting."

"You too," Keltin managed to say before the Heterack turned and went back inside the barn.

Keltin stared at the closed barn door for a long moment before turning and walking away, leaving Harper to follow him through the steadily falling rain.

CHAPTER 9 – HIDDEN FIRE

The autumn rains had come in earnest, and all the workers were rushing to bring in the rest of the crops. As soon as there was light until the last shred of day was done, they labored in the fields cutting, digging, picking, and piling. Already, teamsters and their wagons had begun coming up from Carvalen, delivering the produce back to the capital to either be sold in local markets or shipped via the railway across the continent to wherever the distant landowners would turn the best profit.

Keltin was also keeping busy. It seemed everyone wanted a beast hunter watching over them, and no-one was ever happy when he had to rush to the next person waiting for him. He saw little of Ross and Kuff, and even Harper had stopped traveling with him quite as frequently, as the newspaperman was keeping himself busy riding along with the teamsters up and down their route to Carvalen. More than one of the teamsters had asked Keltin if he would ride along with them for protection, but he refused them, reasoning that the workers in the field were at greater risk than the drivers and their mules on the road. Besides, he was busy enough running from one farm to another, sometimes in pursuit of real beasts, though most of the time he ended up chasing shadows to reassure the nerves of men worn thin by long hours of labor in the rain.

It was with real relief that he finally returned to the Lona farm in the middle of a particularly wet day, free of any desperate missives begging for his attention. He looked forward to a well-deserved rest in the upstairs bedroom that had been allotted to him and a hot meal or two prepared by Wendi. He gratefully opened the front door and stepped into the mudroom, shedding his jacket and hat before sitting on a bench to remove his sodden boots. As he began to untie the soaked laces, he heard a sudden thumping from upstairs. Curious, Keltin stepped out into the entryway and called up the stairs.

"Hello? Is everything all right up there?"

There was another violent thumping, and Keltin rushed upstairs, not sure what he would find when he got there. He began throwing open bedroom doors and soon found Ross laid up in bed with a nearby chair that he had clearly been slamming on the wooden floor to get someone's attention. The hunter looked up at him with feeble, watery eyes that spoke of the advanced stages of a nasty cold.

"Moore!" he croaked, obviously causing himself great pain in forcing words through his aching throat. "Thank God in Heaven it's you."

"You don't look very good, Ross. I think you've spent too much time out in the rain. Maybe Wendi could make you some hot soup."

Ross winced, squeezing his eyes shut and shaking his head violently.

"Wendi's gone," he whispered.

"Gone? What do you mean gone?"

Ross' eyes snapped open and he snarled at Keltin like a strangled frog.

"I mean she's gone! The blasted fool girl. I got a message from Charrow farm. A worker was killed by a beast, and the boil's still in the area. They desperately needed someone to deal with it. I was going to, but I'm sick as a slug. I told Wendi we'd have to wait for you to come back, but the girl didn't listen.

She waited until I went to sleep, then slipped out and took Kuff with her."

The fatigue of the road immediately disappeared from Keltin's body. He hurried to Ross' side.

"How long ago did she leave? Did she take anything with her?"

"We got the message yesterday. She was gone when I woke up this morning. Left a note. I think she also took my scattergun."

"All right. I'll be back."

Keltin turned and raced back to the stairs, descending the first third before vaulting over the bannister to land heavily in the entryway and rush back into the mudroom. He was dressed again and outside hurrying to the Charrow farm in less than a minute.

What was Wendi thinking? Keltin knew that Ross had taught her some of the commands for Kuff, but did she really imagine that that made her a beast hunter? No, she was too intelligent for that. So why had she gone? Keltin shook his head, sending raindrops flying from the brim of his hat. Wendi had a good heart. With Ross unable to go and no idea when Keltin would come back, she'd done what she thought was best. Despite her fears, she was doing what she felt she could to potentially save lives. The more Keltin thought about it, the more certain he was of her intentions. More than that, he realized that he wasn't angry with her, only worried. He'd seen too many others pay the ultimate price with equally good intentions. Beasts had no regard for nobility and courage in the face of inexperience.

Charrow farm bordered Lona farm to the north and east. Keltin cut across a recently harvested field without bothering to search the ground for any sign of Wendi and Kuff's passing. The rain had ruined any chance he might have had at tracking them, leaving him no choice but to get to Charrow farm as quickly as possible and pray that he could find them before something tragic happened. As soon as he reached the farm he searched about for anyone that he could question. He found a group of workers, looking wet and miserable as they tried to eat their lunch under the poor cover of a wagon partially loaded with gourds. Keltin rushed up to them and shouted over the shushing of rain.

"Did you see a girl go by with a tamarrin hound?"

He was met by a chorus of blank looks. He tried a different question.

"Was there a beast attack here recently?"

One of the men crouched behind a wagon wheel snorted. "Aye there was, no thanks to you."

"What sort of beast was it? Where did it happen?"

"A little late to show such a fiery interest, ain't it? Tosh is dead already."

Keltin went straight to the man. Crouching down, he caught hold of his shirt, yanked him out from under cover, and propped him up against the side of the wagon. The man stared at him in open-mouth shock as Keltin leaned in close, letting the rain drip from the front brim of his hat onto the man's face.

"I have no time for your smart mouth," Keltin said in a low voice. "There's a brave girl out there with more grit than a little sopmouth like you will ever have. She's trying to hunt down the beast on her own, and I've got to find her before she gets herself killed. Now tell me everything you know about the beast attack or so help me I'll crack your skull open like one of these gourds."

The man's eyes went wide and he swallowed like his tongue had suddenly gotten too big for his mouth. Another worker appeared at Keltin's side.

"The beast attacked just on the eastern edge of the potato field," he said. "I don't know what sort of beast you'd call it, but it looked like something out of a nightmare. No arms, no legs, no head even. Bullets just bounced off it, and we couldn't even get it off of Tosh as it ate him."

Keltin's blood went cold. An armored leech. A formless, heavily-shelled lump the size of a man with a mouth hidden on its underbelly full of fine teeth and a poison that would kill with a single scratch. Keltin dropped the worker he was holding down into the mud, gave the helpful fellow a quick nod, and set off to the east.

The potato field had already been harvested, its good, rich earth broken by the shovels and rakes of the workers and then churned into a thick muck by the rain. Keltin was forced to go the long way around the field lest he run the risk of becoming stuck fast in the deep mud. He watched his step to avoid slipping and falling into the muck even as he tried to remember everything he could about the armored leech and plan just how he would kill it.

The beast's outer shell was far too thick for a conventional round. A Reltac Spinner would penetrate it, but would it have enough power left to do any real damage after breaking through? Explosive shot like the Capshire Shatter rounds might break it open, but again, would it cause any damage? A Haurizer Smasher wouldn't break through the shell, but might be enough to stun the beast. Then again, it might not.

No, the answer wouldn't come from any of his specialty ammunition. The beast simply had no weak points that were accessible while it was flat on the ground. He'd have to get more aggressive. Get in close. The Ripper's blade and spikes would be just as useless as bullets, but the sturdy hook on its side could be used to catch underneath its edge. If he could flip the beast, he could use the hand cannon at his hip to finish it with a point-blank shot to its exposed underbelly. With his best plan in mind, he swung his rifle over his shoulder and pulled the oversized revolver from its holster, filling all five chambers with Capshire Shatter rounds before clicking it back into place. He then pulled the Ripper off of his other shoulder to hold it ready in front of him just as he reached the eastern edge of the field.

Stepping among the trees, he finally forced himself to slow his furious pace. He imagined he could feel the rain turning to steam on his shoulders and back as he stood gasping for breath. Gulping and swallowing air, Keltin forced his thundering heart to slow down to allow him to better hear his surroundings. He strained his ears, but all he could hear was the overwhelming, surrounding noise of falling water splattering on every surface around him. He continued to try to steady himself as he began to stalk slowly forward, listening all the time and offering a silent prayer that he would find Wendi before the beast did.

An hour passed slowly, feeling like an eternity of fruitless searching. Keltin resisted the urge to call out for the girl, focusing instead on listening and searching for any clue of her passing. At last, he heard something. Perhaps a human cry, perhaps the yelp of a hound. Whatever it was, it was distant, but clear. Keltin raced towards it as a second sound came from the same direction, followed by a third. Now he could distinguish between high-pitched barks and a female voice, though he was still too distant to make out what was being said. When he heard the sharp report of a gunshot he gave up all pretense of caution and sprinted through the forest, leaping over low bushes and crashing through larger ones, desperate to reach the chaotic noises ahead of him.

Suddenly he burst through thick, damp foliage and was confronted by a violent scene. Kuff was there, leaping and snarling as he darted forward to savage a large, dark lump that quivered and flexed on the forest floor. The leech flinched each time the hound attacked, his long canines sliding harmlessly over the hard outer carapace. Wendi stood nearby, screaming a single command over and over while clutching Ross' scattergun to her shoulder.

"*Al-hah* Kuff!" she cried. "*Al-hah!*"

But the hound was too infuriated and confused by the strange beast. He continued to feint and retreat, trying to find some weakness while only narrowly avoiding a fatal bite with each failed attack. Keltin turned his attention from the hound and beast to the girl still screaming nearby.

"Wendi!"

She turned, her expression rapidly shifting from shock to relief mixed with desperation.

"Mr. Moore! I can't stop him!"

"Keep trying! I'm going to flip the beast on its back. Keep Kuff away from its mouth. It's deadly poisonous!"

"I'll try!"

Keltin rushed forward, the Ripper held out in front of him. Kuff darted in front of him, racing right over the armored leech, causing it to turn slightly in the hound's direction. Keltin swung the Ripper in a low arc and caught the edge of the beast's shell with the sturdy hook. He heaved on it, but the beast spasmed suddenly, driving the haft of the weapon painfully into Keltin's side. Keltin gasped but held on, struggling with the weapon like a fisherman using a gaff hook to pull a wounded shark into a boat. The beast continued to thrash as Keltin struggled to pull it up and over, unable to get the leverage he needed as he continued to dance away from the beast's deadly underside.

Suddenly, Keltin felt a second pair of hands on the haft of the Ripper. He looked up to see Wendi standing next to him, taking a firm grip on the short wooden handle of the weapon. There was no time for a reprimand or word of caution. They were both in desperate danger and he needed her help. He gave her the briefest nod and turned back to the beast. Planting his feet, he crouched low and pulled up with all his might.

"Heave!" he cried.

He felt a surge of strength from Wendi, and like a boulder in a farmer's field the beast lifted up off the ground and turned over onto its back. The beast squirmed helplessly, its circular, toothy mouth gnashing at the air. Kuff dove forward, seeing an opening, but was brought up short by a command from Wendi, not a desperate scream this time, but a powerful, authoritative order.

"*Al-hah!*"

The hound hesitated, and Keltin pulled his hand cannon from his belt. He fired three times into the beast, twice into the soft underbelly, and once directly down its fearsome gullet. The explosive rounds detonated inside its exposed body, scattering flesh and gore all around them. By the time the last echoes of the final shot had died away, the beast was lying still, its black shell like a misshapen bowl filled with its dead remains and a slowly growing puddle of rainwater.

Keltin took a long breath and crouched down on the sodden earth, offering a silent prayer of gratitude. As he finished and looked up, he saw Wendi staring down at the beast, her hands shaking slightly. Keltin stood slowly, placing a cautious hand on her arm.

"Are you all right?"

She swallowed and nodded, not taking her eyes from the beast.

"Don't be mad with me, Mr. Moore," she said softly. "I didn't know you would be back so soon. I thought if Kuff was with me, I could... I just... I didn't want anyone else to die."

"I understand. It's all right."

Wendi took a deep, shuddering breath without replying.

"Thank you for your help," said Keltin. "It was very brave."

Wendi made the ghost of a smile.

"Thank you," she said softly.

Keltin turned to follow her gaze back down to the sad remains of the beast. Kuff had taken a few cautious steps forward, and was sniffing at the still corpse.

"Come away from there, Kuff," said Wendi, her voice gentler than before, but still bearing a trace of iron in it. The hound gave a final sniff and backed away from the beast to trot over to Wendi's side. She reached out and rubbed between his rain-soaked ears. "Come on," she said to the hound. "Let's go home and see how Mr. Ross is doing."

The hound gave a canine grin and bounded away, leaving the two humans to quietly follow behind him.

CHAPTER 10 – LAST WORDS

"I still can't believe you went after that beast on your own," croaked Ross.

"You should be saving your voice," said Wendi gently. "Besides, I wasn't alone, I had Kuff with me. Still, I'm very grateful that Mr. Moore came along when he did."

"I'm just glad that you're safe," said Keltin. "And don't forget, I couldn't have done it without you."

Keltin and Kuff both perked up at the sound of feet on the stairs. After a moment, Yull appeared in the doorway to Ross' bedroom.

"I just came up to see for myself that the young lady had made it back safely," he said. "We all heard what happened. It was very brave of you."

Wendi smiled as her cheeks turned a bit rosy.

"Thank you, but I should really get dinner started." She turned to Ross. "Do you think you can handle some potato soup?"

"That's fine," he rasped. "I'll come help you."

"I'd rather you didn't," said Keltin. "I don't need to catch whatever you've got."

Ross sighed and laid back on the bed. "I suppose you're right. I just feel so useless and old lying here in bed."

Yull snorted. "I wouldn't mind swapping places with you, if you feel the need. Well, I'd best go see to the men. Have a good evening all."

Keltin turned to Wendi as Yull left them. "I could help you with dinner, if you tell me what to do."

"I don't really need any help right now. But you did get a few letters in the last mail call. I left them on your bed."

"Thank you."

Keltin went to his bedroom, lit the lamp, and found the somewhat dog-eared letters where Wendi had left them. The first envelope bore Jaylocke's name, and he looked forward to a pleasant word from his apprentice and friend. As soon as he began reading however, he knew something was wrong.

Dear Keltin,

I'm not sure how to begin this letter. Bor've'tai is assisting me, for which I am most grateful, though I almost wish that he would write it on his own. Something bad has happened, and I feel like I only know part of the story. Only you can fill in the rest. I just wish you weren't alone to do it.

I should first reassure you that, as far as I know, your mother and sister are fine. Bor've'tai and I are well, as are the Claxon family and our other shared friendships. That said, perhaps I should start with how things came to our knowledge.

Two days ago, a girl came to The Beast Hunter office long after closing hours. Upon opening the door and seeing her dress, appearance, and demeanor, I suspected she was one of the city's ladies of the night, and had come seeking business from us. I was about to turn her away when she asked for Keltin Moore. Well, I know your character well enough to be suspicious, and asked what she wanted with Mr. Moore. That was when she said she had come on behalf of a coworker of hers by the name of Angela. It took me a moment to recall the name, but when I realized it was the same girl that had visited you earlier this season I was slightly more forthcoming, saying that you were out of town and asked if there was a message for you.

Keltin, what she told me was far from good. It seems that Angela's health had been poor for some time, and had taken a turn for the worst. At that very moment, she was lying in bed in a terrible way, and had implored her friend to find you. Well, I didn't know what to do. I looked to Bor've'tai, and he asked if perhaps we might come to speak with her. The girl agreed, and so the three of us went together to the Gallant Rose.

We were greeted by the Madam who cooled considerably when she learned we were not customers, but allowed us access to the cramped portion of the establishment set aside for the girls' personal use. I won't trouble you with a description of the conditions of the place, except to say that no-one enjoying the satin sheets and pillows in the upstairs accommodations would likely imagine the course bedclothes and tight quarters the girls endured below.

We found Angela in her bed, and she looked most unwell. Quietly, I called on the assistance of my Great Aunt Landria, who you remember had been a midwife with a fair portion of practical medicinal knowledge. On sight alone, Aunt Landria was not able to help me identify what specifically was wrong with the girl, but it was clear that some sort of wasting sickness had been eating her from the inside for some time. Of course, I need not tell you that a woman in her profession has every opportunity to catch any number of dangerous ailments.

She was pale and gaunt, but awake and alert despite her clear discomfort. The girl that had brought us explained to her that you were out of town, and that we had come as his friends. Angela closed her eyes, clearly disappointed. We remained like that for a long time, and I thought perhaps we should excuse ourselves and leave. I was just turning to go when Bor've'tai knelt by Angela's side and placed his hand on her forehead. She gave a start, but didn't seem unwilling of his touch as he looked down at her. He asked her if there was anything that she wanted you to know. She looked up at him for a long time before replying in a voice that I had to strain to hear.

"Tell Keltin I'm proud of the good that he's done. Tell him I wish things had been different. Tell him my happiest memories are from those days, and that I forgive him."

That was all she said. Bor've'tai and I have both spoken together *to be sure that we gave the message to you just as it was said. Bor've'tai said we would deliver the message, and we turned to go. Before we left, she called out once more, and asked if we could get word to her mother that she was sorry, and that she missed her. Bor've'tai has already written a letter detailing that portion of our visit to Shar'le'vah, who will give the message to Mrs. Galloway.*

We left after that. The next day, yesterday, the girl that had come to fetch us returned. With reddened eyes, she told us that Angela had passed from this world in the early hours of the morning. She had some additional words for her mother, which Bor've'tai also included in his letter, but I won't burden you with those.

I can't imagine how you're feeling, my friend. I am so sorry for your loss, and wish that I could be with you to offer what poor comfort my company could provide. I hope that you can find comfort in knowing that Angela is no longer in pain of any sort.

Write back if it will help you. Or keep your peace until we are reunited. Feel no obligation to Bor've'tai or I. We are ever your friends, and will ever be so.

Jaylocke

Keltin set the letter aside. He sat and stared into space for a long while, not moving, not thinking. Eventually, his mind returned to the last time he had seen Angela. Had she known then how badly she was doing? Why hadn't she told him? It occurred to Keltin that she may have been coming to him with the intention of saying goodbye and telling him all those things that she had been forced to share with strangers who passed the word to him. Then again, maybe her intentions had been completely different. Keltin had never been able to predict what she would do or say. Not as children, and certainly not as adults.

Memories came to him unbidden. He recalled sitting in the old single-room schoolhouse in Gillentown. It had been a long walk from their home in the country, but his mother had insisted that her children receive as much education as possible. It was in that old school house that he had first seen young Angela Galloway. She and Mary became fast friends, and Keltin found himself becoming more interested in his sister's companion as time went on. Angela seemed to get prettier every year, and for a time the three of them were inseparable. But times changed, and as they became young adults Keltin noticed Angela becoming more distant. She didn't talk openly to him like she had before. She teased and smiled, sending him little notes during class or watching him at parties while she danced with other boys and he stood uncertainly against a wall.

Then Keltin's father was killed on a beast hunt. His family was suddenly torn apart, and it only got worse over time. His mother had never liked beast hunting, but her displeasure turned into outright hatred for the whole business and anyone involved in it, including her son. Mary did what she could as a peacekeeper between them, but too often Keltin had felt horribly alone in his own home. Desperate for understanding, he had turned to Angela, but she had remained just as distant as ever. Looking back now, Keltin still wondered whether she had simply been insincere or if she perhaps hadn't felt capable of helping him cope with his crushing grief.

Whatever the reason, her distance had spurred Keltin to uncharacteristic impulsiveness. He asked her to marry him. Her shock had been obvious, and she had given him no answer before promptly going home. It took several days for Keltin to nurse his hurt pride sufficiently to call on her again, but by then she was gone. Mrs. Galloway told him that she and her daughter had had a terrible argument, and while she wouldn't say what it was about, Keltin suspected that it had been about his proposal. Regardless, all Mrs. Galloway ever admitted was that hurtful words were said on both sides, and that Angela had left without any clue as to where she might have gone.

Keltin had tried to find her, but as weeks turned into months without word, he found no success. Eventually his mother and Mary moved away and he started lodging at Mrs. Galloway's boarding house, spending as much time hunting beasts as he could. It was nearly a year later that he finally received a single sheet of paper, half-filled with Angela's handwriting and stuffed in an envelope with the return address of the Gallant Rose, a bordello in Collinsworth.

For a long time after, Keltin had nursed a quiet ache in his heart for the girl he had known. Even as time had dulled the pain, she had remained a shadow over him, never leaving him totally free. It kept him from noticing any of the looks that Mrs. Galloway insisted he received regularly from the young women of Gillentown. In fact, the more Keltin thought of it, the more he came to the unpleasant realization that his hesitancy to express his true feelings for Elaine had less to do with her and more to do with the lingering venom in the wounds Angela had caused him.

And yet, as he sat quietly thinking in the darkness of his room, something else occurred to him. While he was sad to hear about Angela's passing, the strongest emotion he felt was... relief. Finally, he was free. Free from the nagging feelings of responsibility and guilt that had hounded him for so long. It was as if a great weight had been taken from him, and as soon as he realized that, his thoughts turned to Elaine.

How much time had he wasted hemming and hawing over his feelings? How much uncertainty and confusion had he put her through as a result? Now that his mind was clear, he realized that he cared for her. Deeply. Suddenly he felt a driving desire to write to Elaine, even though he knew mailing it to her right now was out of the question. He sat at the desk next to the room's large window and began writing. His pen flew as words came to him that he had never dared say before. He was vaguely aware of Wendi calling up the stairs that supper was ready, but he was too eager to continue writing, pressing on late into the night until the light through the window had completely faded, leaving him to continue to work by the light of a warm, glowing lantern.

CHAPTER 11 – TIME TO MOVE

Keltin lay awake in his bed as the pale light of dawn began to seep through the curtains across his window. He'd finished the letter to Elaine some time ago but had been unable to fall asleep, his mind drifting in a dozy haze over the words he had written. Rolling away from the light, he heard a distinct crinkling underneath him. Sitting up, he felt for the source of the sound and found an envelope lying beside him. With a shock, he realized that he had completely forgotten the second letter he had received. Lighting his lantern, he turned over the envelope to find that the handwriting was unfamiliar and bore no postal print. Keltin tore it open and skipped the body of the letter to find the signed name at the bottom. Severn Destov. The warm drowsiness in his mind evaporated as he eagerly began reading the letter from Elaine's father.

Dear Mr. Moore,

I wish I could write this missive under more pleasant circumstances. I've received the reports from the foremen of the farms, and their accounts of your efforts have been most encouraging. I am glad to see that Mr. Whitt's faith in you was not misplaced, and I'm sure that he and his partners will show their appreciation in a most palpable way once you return to Riltvin. Unfortunately, our private concerns have not gone nearly as well.

As you may have already heard, Grik Pallow has assumed the position of Supreme Minister and the borders of Malpin are now closed. I have not heard from my wife and family for several weeks now. The last letter gave no indication of any significant changes, but this gives me no comfort. It could be that the Malpin League of Protection has begun screening letters and correspondence. My wife and I had decided on a special code for just such a possibility, but this lack of any letters at all has me very concerned. Could it be that something has happened to them?

Regardless of my lack of information, I think you will agree that the time to act is now. End your business as quickly as you can, and make your way north to the border. The northernmost town in Krendaria is Wellos, a community built on the border between the two nations along the Royal Highway. There may be other, smaller villages and settlements in the region, but I do not know them. On the other side of the border is Ruley, though you will not be able to reach it via the border crossing. You will have to find your own way across, but I trust that a man with your experience and resources will be up to the task. I can tell you that most of the border is defined by the Bent Knee River, which may be fordable in some places, but will not be frozen over for another month or more.

However you get across the border, your next task must be to find my family. Before I left home, I left implicit instructions with my family that if the border ever closed, they should go to Carris, just a few leagues north of Ruley. I also advised them to make contact with several persons that I know are associated with the Brothers of Kerrtow, the underground group that has worked in the shadows against the Vaughs since the Heterack Empowerment. They are experienced in smuggling both people and Loopi artifacts out of the nation, and will hopefully be able to lend their resources to our needs. Keep in mind that it may be necessary for my family to remain in hiding, making it necessary for you to find the Brothers yourself and prove your intentions to them. How you can do that I do not know. I curse myself for not having more to offer you. I must rely almost wholly upon your judgment and the mercy of God to see my family safely returned to me. I offer my sincerest prayer on your behalf that you are successful. Please make haste, and God be with you.

    Severn Destov

Keltin read the letter a second time, paying particular attention to the sparse details and instructions he had been given and feeling the stark reality of his task. How was he supposed to smuggle himself into a foreign country, find a family that was hiding from the government, and then smuggle them back out? The more he thought of it, the more a dark possibility grew in his mind. What if something went wrong? What would he do if a border guard found him trying to sneak across the border, or an officer of the MLP started asking too many questions? What would he do if someone drew a gun on him or one of the Destovs? Despite the odd fist-fight or display of force, he'd never actually fired a gun at another person before. He wasn't a soldier or mercenary. He was a beast hunter.

On the other hand, he remembered the advice that Jaylocke had written in his first letter after finding out Keltin might be going to Malpin. "If someone in a uniform tries to stop you, smile and wave, then shoot them dead if they twitch. There are some scruples that are worth setting aside temporarily." Keltin wasn't sure whether he agreed with Jaylocke or not, but he knew that if he waited to make his decision until the moment came, it would likely be too late.

A soft voice called from the bottom of the stairs.

"Breakfast is ready."

Keltin drew a deep breath and forced himself to his feet. Regardless of the conditions at the border, he hadn't had any dinner the night before, and the smells coming from downstairs were enticing. He left his room and descended the stairs to find Ross telling Harper about the adventure with the armored leech as they sat in the parlor eating their breakfast.

"Good morning, Mr. Moore!" said Harper pleasantly. "We

were worried when you didn't come down for dinner last night. You're not coming down with Ross's sickness, are you?"

"No, I'm fine."

"That's good to hear. Just so you know, we're on our own this morning." He gave a playful wink. "In addition to being our newest resident beast hunter, it seems that Wendi has taken over the kitchen and dining room in preparation for tomorrow's Harvest Celebration."

"I thought the workers were still bringing the crops in," said Keltin.

Ross cleared his throat, sounding much improved from the day before but still on the road to recovery.

"Yull came by this morning," he croaked. "He said that he and his men worked by lantern light late into the night, so the last of the harvest is already done and we can have our Harvest Celebration tomorrow. It looks like our job here is officially done."

Harper shook his head. "It all seems a bit anticlimactic, doesn't it? Still, I suppose that's the way with your sort of work. Mine too, for that matter. At least we get to enjoy a Harvest Celebration with the workers before returning home. Speaking of which, how do you feel about traveling back to Riltvin together, Mr. Moore? We could leave the day after tomorrow, just as long as you don't want to leave too early, because I certainly plan to do my fair share of celebrating first."

Harper grinned. Keltin shifted uncomfortably.

"I... may not head directly home. Perhaps you should go on without me."

"Really?" Harper gave him a curious look. "Why? There's no real reason to hang about with the job done, unless you have some other work you're planning to take on."

"Of a sort. Yes."

Now it was Ross' turn to be curious. "Is it the sort of work that could use another beast hunter? I wouldn't want to drive you off of it, but perhaps Kuff and I might accompany you? I've missed working with another hunter, and wouldn't mind doing it for a bit longer."

Keltin hesitated. He was uncomfortable lying to his friends, but he wasn't sure whether it was wise to tell them of his plans. After all, crossing the Krendarian/Malpin border would not only be dangerous, but highly criminal to at least one of the nations involved. Keltin didn't feel right putting either Ross or Harper in a potentially awkward position by telling them too much of what he intended to do.

"This isn't an opportunity for more than one hunter," he said. "Sorry."

Ross shrugged. "I suppose it's just as well. Season's coming to a close anyway. Which way are you bound?"

Keltin hesitated for what felt like far too long.

"North," he finally said truthfully.

Ross' brows furrowed. "North? There's not much left of the Province beyond these farmlands except the Bent Knee River and the border with Malpin."

"Which you should definitely be avoiding right now," put in Harper. "I haven't had a chance to tell you the news yet. Malpin has closed its borders."

"I know."

Harper's eyebrows went up. "You do?"

"I received word in a letter."

"Ah, I see. Well, I suppose all we can do is wait and see what happens. I know I don't look forward to the prospect of being a war correspondent again."

"Well, I'd better get my breakfast. Excuse me."

Keltin escaped the curious looks of his friends and made his way to the kitchen to find Wendi sprinkling sugar on a row of small sweet loaves on the table. She looked up at him with a shy, friendly smile.

"Hello Mr. Moore. Are you feeling all right?"

"Yes, I'm not sick."

"I'm glad. I was worried."

Wendi picked up one of the sweet loaves with a padded kitchen cloth and placed it on a plate for him.

"I'm sorry that there isn't more for breakfast this morning.

But you can have this. Be careful, it's still very hot."

Keltin gave her a small smile of gratitude and sat at the kitchen table. He tore open the loaf and sat watching the steam pour out of the perfectly aerated bread. Wendi continued her work, laying down a fresh layer of flour before beginning to knead another large lump of dough. As Keltin watched her, he was suddenly reminded of the many times he'd sat in the kitchen while his mother was cooking. It had seemed like the only time that the two of them had been able to talk together.

"Is the loaf all right?"

Keltin gave a start and realized that he had been staring into space as he reminisced. He gave Wendi a reassuring smile.

"Yes, it's very good. I'm sorry, I was just remembering sitting in my mother's kitchen growing up."

"Did she teach you to cook?"

"She tried, but I was never very good at it. What about you? Did your mother teach you to bake?"

Wendi paused her kneading.

"Yes," she said quietly. "Momma loved to be in the kitchen. She always said that she was just a country cook, but I think she had studied in the city when she was young. Or maybe she knew someone who had. Either way, all of our neighbors said she was the best cook in the territory. She taught me everything I know."

"It shows."

Wendi looked up, her pale blue eyes tinged with vulnerability.

"Do you think so?"

"I do."

She smiled. "Thank you."

For a few moments, they kept their silence, Keltin quietly eating and Wendi continuing her work. Keltin finished his loaf, noticed that the wood box next to the stove was running low, and went outside to retrieve another armful from the stack against the leeside wall. Returning inside to the welcome warmth of the kitchen, he refilled the box, then fed several sticks into the stove as Wendi stood next to him stirring a pot of thickening, golden syrup.

"Wendi, I'm leaving today."

She looked up in surprise.

"Already? Can't you at least stay for the Harvest Celebration?"

"I'm sorry, but I have to go."

"But why?"

Keltin hesitated. For some reason, it felt all right if he talked with Wendi... at least a little.

"There's someone that I met last year here in Dhalma Province. We were trapped together for weeks in a farmhouse surrounded by beasts and became very close. After that, she went back to her family in Kerrtow."

Wendi's eyes widened in understanding.

"But the border with Malpin has been closed," she said.

Keltin nodded.

"You're going north to your girl, aren't you?"

Keltin didn't answer. Wendi stepped closer to him.

"You're going to try to get her out of Malpin."

Keltin let out a heavy breath.

"Her and her family. Her father sent me a letter, asking me to try. So I need to leave as soon as I can. Would you set aside some of that bread for me?"

"Yes. Yes, of course. I've also got plenty of potatoes and a tin of lard you can take."

"Thank you."

Keltin left the kitchen and went up the stairs to his room. Placing his pack on his bed, he began to pull together his few belongings. He was in the process of rolling and stowing away his change of clothes when he heard his bedroom door open behind him.

"We're butchering a hog tomorrow for the Celebration," said Ross in a conservative whisper to preserve his voice. "If you wait, you'll have fresh meat for the road."

"I really should be leaving as soon as I'm able," Keltin said as he continued to pack.

"Game is scarce along the Bent Knee this time of year, and

you won't find many places to buy more supplies very close to either side of the Malpin border."

Keltin turned.

"Wendi told you."

"She did."

Keltin was silent. Ross stepped into the room and drew closer so that his soft voice could be heard clearly.

"Listen, Keltin. I'll not fault you for not sharing this with Harper and I right away. It's your business after all. But if you're worried about either of us trying to discourage you from going, don't. If you want to try to help someone on the other side of the border, good for you. But you shouldn't let your heart do your thinking. You're a good hunter, better than good, so treat this like a hunt. Take the time to plan it out. Gather all the resources you have available so you have the best chance for success, and that includes talking with people who may know more about a region than you do."

Keltin sighed as he realized that in his haste to go to Elaine's aid he had forgotten the words of Jaylocke, Bor've'tai, and Mr. Destov as each of them had encouraged him to seek help from anyone that he felt he could trust.

"All right," he said. "I see your point. Is Harper still downstairs?"

"He is."

"Good. Let's go join him. I might as well lay my cards out for everyone to see."

They found Harper still sitting by the fire waiting for them with a curious expression. Keltin sat down across from him and proceeded to explain his situation. Ross and Harper listened quietly as Wendi drifted into the room stirring a bowl of batter on her hip. Keltin finished by describing Mr. Destov's most recent letter and reading all of the pertinent details to the group. Harper sat back and stroked his mustache.

"Hmm…" he said. "I won't lie to you, Mr. Moore. This is dangerous, and not the sort of danger that you're used to."

"I've dealt with dangerous people before."

"Perhaps, but think of their caliber. Bullies, belligerent

hunters, perhaps a crooked businessman now and then. But this is an entire nation with a strong militant arm curling around its people and borders. You can't bluff your way past all of them, and even a beast hunter as fierce as yourself can't stand against a whole squad of border guards."

"That depends on the terrain," said Ross. "We saw the worth of soldiers against a good handful of beast hunters in last year's campaign."

"And are you planning on shooting each one of them?" countered Harper. "As you said, you're not soldiers. It takes a certain kind of man to look at another breathing person with hopes, dreams, perhaps a family, and put a bullet in his brain. Could either of you do that?"

Ross looked away uncomfortably. Harper turned to Keltin. "What about you?"

Keltin took a long breath before answering. "I was considering that this morning. It turns my stomach to think about, but if it meant the safety of Elaine and her family... yes. I would live with the guilt and pain that came with it, if I had to. But only if I knew that I had done everything I could to avoid it first."

Harper nodded slowly. "All right. In that case, I'm going with you."

Keltin blinked. "You're what?"

"I'll finish my last piece for this assignment and send it to my editor along with a note explaining that I have a rare opportunity to examine conditions on the Krendaria/Malpin border. I won't be able to wait to hear back from him, but I know him, and he would jump at the chance to get a man across the border to report on conditions inside Malpin right now."

Keltin shook his head. "I don't want to put you in danger."

"You wouldn't be. I would. Besides, we'll both have a better chance of success if we go together. I've seen enough of your skills in the countryside to bet that you will be able to sneak us both across the border without being seen. And I've got experience working undercover and talking fast when things get tight. If I'm with you, there's a better chance that we'll be able to talk our way out of sticky situations, rather than resorting to violence. What do you say?"

Keltin was silent. After weeks of waiting and inactivity, things were suddenly moving very fast. He worried that he might already be losing control of the situation. Still, there was little time to doubt or hesitate. Elaine needed him now. He had to act. He had to trust.

"All right," he said. "I'll follow your lead when it comes to dealing with people."

Harper nodded. "And I'll follow your lead in all else. Just give me until tomorrow to finish my last article, and I'll be ready to leave after the Harvest Celebration."

"Agreed."

"Good. In that case, I'd better go get to work."

Harper rose and went upstairs to his room. Ross turned to Keltin.

"Well, it sounds like you'll be staying for the Celebration after all."

"I suppose so. Thank you for helping me to see reason."

Ross nodded silently as Keltin turned and looked into the guttering fire. The thought of taking Harper with him was new and a little worrisome, but he also felt a stirring of hope. Perhaps with the newspaperman along, he truly would have a better chance for success. While he would have preferred Bor've'tai or Jaylocke at his side, any sort of ally would be most welcome in what could become his most dangerous endeavor yet.

CHAPTER 12 – LOOSE ENDS

Keltin kept himself busy the rest of the day and into the next helping prepare the farmhouse to entertain all of Yull's workers. He focused all of his attention on every menial task, from weaving together decorations of maize stalks to setting out cutlery and finding additional chairs for everyone. Of course, his mind remained firmly on the task ahead of him come the morning, but with nothing more to do to prepare, he did his best to lose himself in the spirit of the special holiday.

Wendi had truly outdone herself. Keltin was amazed as she laid out platters of fried potatoes, buttered maize, spiced sausages, and stewed squash. Loaves, rolls, and biscuits were in abundance, with sugar crumble pies and apple cake waiting in the wings along with pitchers of milk, cold cider, and mulled wine . Yull and a few of his men had butchered an impressive hog, spending the better part of the day slowly roasting the meat until it was nearly sliding off the bone. When the time came to begin the carving, even Keltin had to admit that he was driven to distraction by the intoxicating smell of roasted pork.

Ross was at his side for the majority of the day in their preparations, with Kuff following along behind and eyeing the growing feast with the sad longing of an animal too well-trained to steal food, but not above a little begging. Harper remained cloistered in his room for the majority of the day, only emerging late in the afternoon to sit down with an exhausted sigh. Keltin looked at the man sucking deep breaths of air as if he'd been running a league, and wondered just how hard writing truly was. Harper appeared too humble to talk about it, and only made a single announcement with tired pride.

"Well, I finished the piece. It will go with the courier when he leaves in the morning. Do you want to read it?"

"I'll see it in the paper when we get back."

Harper nodded, and Keltin saw in his eyes the same unspoken statement that he had thought to himself.

If we get back.

"I'll make sure the Gazette saves you a copy."

The workers began arriving as daylight started to fade outside. There were more than twenty men all together, but somehow they all found places to sit either around the dining room table or in various chairs scattered throughout the parlor. The farmhouse was soon filled with the din of talking and raucous laughter, though they refrained from touching the tempting food spread out before them. Once the last man had found a chair and Wendi had brought out the last pitcher of cider, Yull stood up at the head of the table and called for silence, which he almost immediately got. The foreman cleared his throat, showing perhaps more familiarity with barking orders than giving speeches.

"Well, the season's officially done. You've all done a hexed good job out in those fields. The food we brought in will feed a lot of hungry people. I figure that makes us heroes in a way, even if we're the only ones who know it. Well done all." This was met with hearty applause until he signaled for silence again. "I also think we should acknowledge Mr. Moore and Mr. Ross. These men risked their lives every day they were here to keep us and our fellows safe from the boils that stalk the woods in these parts. If not for them, you can be sure that some of us would not be sitting here among friends right now.

So thanks to both of you."

There was more applause, and Keltin felt a warm stirring within him. It was rare to ever receive such adulation for an otherwise lonely life, and he allowed himself to console his worried heart in the warmth of the smiling faces of the men gathered around him. Yull then praised Wendi's impressive efforts laid out before them, which received the loudest acclaim of all. He then offered a simple farmer's grace, and the feast began.

While Keltin had spent much of his life eating lonely meals by campfires, he could remember several times when he had enjoyed a well-cooked meal with good company. He recalled family dinners as a child presided over by his father and attended by most –if not all— of the members of the Moore and Milner families. Later, he'd enjoyed a measure of comradery with his fellow hunters while on campaign a year ago, and there had also been a number of pleasant dinners spent at the Golden Home restaurant and inn in Lost Trap with his close friends the previous winter. Thinking back to those times, he felt a little homesick even as he enjoyed the good food and listened to the cheerful conversations of those around him. He missed his friends and family, and wished that any of them could share this festive time with him.

Feeling eyes upon him, Keltin glanced up to see Wendi watching him from across the table. To his surprise she didn't immediately turn away, but gave him a friendly, encouraging smile. He did his best to return the smile, wondering how Elaine might react to his melancholy. He smiled in earnest at the thought. She would likely tell him that worrying wouldn't help, and that since he was doing all he could, he should take heart and enjoy the moment. With a resolve to do just that, he turned to Ross and asked how the training of Kuff was progressing, soon finding himself in a good-natured comparison of successful beast hunts that continued on throughout the dinner, past dessert, and well into the night.

* * *

The celebration petered out eventually as the men went back to their bunkhouse, no doubt to enjoy private stores of spirits that Yull would not allow them to imbibe while in the farmhouse. Keltin was grateful that Yull had volunteered his men to help with the washing up afterwards, leaving little work left for those who had spent so much time preparing for the event. As the last of the workers placed the final plate in the cabinet, the foreman drew aside Keltin and Ross into the parlor.

"Well, I suppose I won't be seeing either of you again. I'm heading down south with most of the lads, and I understand both of you are headed elsewhere."

Keltin shot Ross a curious look, as he had assumed that the hunter would head south with Yull and the others. He had no chance to ask for clarification though as the foreman continued.

"I just wanted to say one last time how grateful I am to you both. I know most of the men might not say such out loud, but I know that every mother's son of them was grateful to have you around. Thank you."

Ross shook his hand.

"It was good to be protecting the farms of Krendaria again," he said. "Even if it was for foreign owners this time."

Yull nodded and shook Keltin's hand.

"I don't know where you're headed after this, Mr. Moore, but I wish you luck and safe travels wherever you're bound."

"I appreciate that. Take care, Yull."

The foreman left, leaving the farmhouse pleasantly silent after the frenzied din of the celebration. Harper and Wendi entered the parlor and everyone agreed again on the quality of the food. Keltin yawned and turned to Harper.

"Well," he said, "I suppose we'd better turn in. We've got an early start ahead of us."

"Yes…" said Harper, giving Ross a questioning look.

"What is it?" asked Keltin.

Ross blew out his cheeks, looked at Wendi, then turned to

Keltin.

"We'd like to go with you. All of us."

"No," said Keltin. "Absolutely not. This is isn't your problem. I'm willing to let Harper come with me because he has his own reasons for wanting to get into Malpin. But you two have no reason to come along, and it's just too dangerous."

"But Mr. Harper agrees that having a woman along may help if we need to come up with some sort of cover story," said Wendi.

Harper shrugged.

"I did say that. But I also said that it was up to Keltin, and that I wasn't in favor of putting Wendi in any danger."

"I'm not eager to do that either," said Ross.

"But you said that you would like to help Mr. Moore if you could," said Wendi.

"I did say that."

"And I did help Mr. Moore with that beast, even if it scared me."

"It would have scared me too," put in Harper. "Nobody here doubts your courage."

Ross turned to Keltin. "The truth is, I have no other plans for the time being, and neither does Wendi. Beyond that, we both consider you a friend, and we both feel there's a debt that needs repaying for you coming to Wendi's aid against the armored leech. Let us at least travel with you to the border. If it looks too dangerous for all of us to continue on, then we'll stay behind and allow you and Harper to go on without us. We can wait on the Krendaria side for you and help you all travel the rest of the way from here. If nothing else, you can enjoy Wendi's cooking for a little longer."

Keltin looked to Harper, who gave him a slight nod. He took a breath, then turned to Ross and Wendi.

"All right. We'll all go north, at least to the border. From there, we'll see what happens."

Wendi surprised Keltin by grinning and clapping her hands.

"Thank you, Mr. Moore! Don't worry. We'll help you

rescue your friend and her family. You'll see."

Keltin returned the girl's brave smile and hoped that she was right.

* * *

The North Road ran through the fields and cultivated forests of Dhalma province. It was a fairly well-maintained dirt track winding its way through the steadily thicker woods of the north country. Keltin had crossed the road dozens of times over the course of his patrols of the territory, but he had never seen any other travelers on it. He'd always assumed it was because of the seasonal incursion of beasts, but now he wondered if perhaps Krendaria's unfriendly northern neighbor might also have something to do with it. After two days of traveling without encountering another soul, it seemed as if the closing of Malpin's borders had cut off whatever small traffic there might have been at this time of year.

For their part, Keltin's companions had mostly kept their peace during the journey, making the best of two nights of wet camps in the steadily falling rain of a late Krendarian autumn. Keltin was grateful to find that Wendi, while not as experienced on the road as Keltin or the others, was a nonetheless stalwart traveling companion. By the second night, he was gratefully accepting a steaming mug of sweet broth from her as she put the finishing touches on a small pot of potato stew. He had to admit that she reminded him a great deal of Elaine for her determination to make the best of a difficult situation.

"I suppose we'll reach Wellos in the morning," he said once the stew had been dished out. He turned to Harper. "I was thinking we'd learn what we could there before deciding how to attempt our crossing."

"That seems sound," agreed the newspaperman. "I doubt we'd be able to bluff our way past the border station itself, though it's worth looking into, if only to possibly save ourselves a dip in the Bent Knee River."

"I'll let you and Wendi focus on gathering information in town. Meanwhile, I think it'd be best if Ross and I scout out the southern riverbank to either side of Wellos and try to find somewhere we could possibly cross it. We'll scout about a day's journey in each direction, then meet up again in Wellos to discuss our options."

Wendi shuddered. "I hope that we'll be able to get across at the border station. Even if it isn't frosting, it's going to be awfully cold to have to ford the Bent Knee."

"We may not have to get our feet wet," said Keltin. "There's plenty of timber. We could build a raft and ferry ourselves across if we find a calm enough section."

"However we do it, have you considered where we'll go once we're across?" asked Harper. "I'm not sure if it's wise to make straight for civilization once we get across the border. The Malpinion border guard is sure to be at its thickest in the towns closest to Krendaria."

"Destov said that he was going to send his family to Carris. I think we should go directly there, and bypass any other towns along the way. No point in taking too many chances out in public."

"Do you know where in Carris they are supposed to be?"

"No. They'll likely be in hiding. All he said was that I should seek out the Brothers of Kerrtow somewhere in the city."

"Hmm," Harper stroked his moustache thoughtfully. "It's good news for them if they've managed to connect with the Brothers, but with no contact information it will make our job much harder."

"Why is that?" asked Wendi. "Who are the Brothers of Kerrtow?"

"They're an underground organization dedicated to supporting the displaced and disenfranchised Loopi from the capital city and surrounding countryside. From what I've heard, they do everything from expediting Loopi emigration to stealing Loopi holy relics from state-owned museums to smuggle out of the country."

"Can they be trusted?" asked Keltin.

Harper shrugged. "I think so. I know that they have no love for the Vaughs or the MLP. I suspect the hardest part will be getting them to trust us. I'm sure that they're tight with secrecy and fearful of infiltration."

"It's a shame that your paper doesn't maintain a foreign correspondent in Malpin," said Ross. "We might have gotten some help from them."

"Oh we do, but he's up in Kerrtow. Besides, even if he could put us in contact with the Brothers, there's no telling that the cell we meet would have any direct connection with the one helping the Destovs. There's just no way of knowing how organized they really are, since that's one of their most carefully guarded secrets."

"Well, we're going to have to find them somehow," said Keltin.

"You worry about getting us across the border and to Carris," said Harper. "I'm very good at ferreting out information. I'll find them."

Keltin nodded and prayed silently that the newspaperman was as good as he thought he was.

* * *

Wellos was the sort of town that seemed to exist primarily as a place to pass through rather than stop and stay for any reason. There was a modest inn, a pub, and post office, as well as a store or two to keep the local people supplied with their daily needs. Keltin sat with his companions at a corner table in the town pub, watching the other patrons while Ross fetched their food. Keltin had wondered if he might find more Malpinion refugees in Wellos than they had seen on the road. He'd imagined bedraggled, desperate people clutching what few belongings they could carry as they tried to decide where they would go to restart their lives. But the pub was practically empty, and besides himself and his companions everyone there seemed to be a local. He wondered if it was a sign of the efficiency of the border guard and considered how that might affect their chances of bluffing their way northward.

Ross' footsteps echoed in the eerily quiet room. He set down their plates with a clatter before taking a seat and resuming his report of the Bent Knee River stretching off to the east.

"It never got less than twenty feet across," he said in a low tone, "though the current was slow enough. The forest has grown up pretty densely along the banks, but there's a likely-looking bend with some gravely shores that might suit us, if we wanted to try to raft across."

"That's better than I found," said Keltin. "Less than a mile from the border station the banks got rocky and the water got fast. There were a number of small drops, and even some rapids in places. If we want to find a place to cross, it won't be to the west, at least, not within a day's travel." Keltin turned to Harper. "What were you able to learn in town?"

The newspaperman shook his head. "Everything's dried up around here. The town's lifeblood was traffic to and from Malpin, such as it was. It sounds like travelers were becoming scarce before the formal closure of the borders, with new restrictions coming almost every week. That tells me that we can't expect a hastily mustered border guard scrambling to cover themselves. This has been some time coming, and it's likely that the men at the station have already seen dozens of attempts to bluff through customs."

"Sounds like our best option is to go east. We'll need to make a stop at a local general store for some extra supplies."

"What do we need?"

"Extra rope for raft lashings. We'll also want a good-sized saw to cut some sturdy saplings to make it out of. We may also—"

Keltin fell silent at the sound of the tinkling bell above the pub's front door. Turning, he was surprised to see Bol, the Heterack sleevak wrangler along with several of his companions. Harper immediately leaned over and whispered to Keltin.

"We'll need to go over and say hello," he said. "It will seem odd if we don't."

"How do we explain our being north together?" asked Keltin, keeping his eyes on the broad-shouldered hunters as they made their orders at the bar. "They know that we're both from Riltvin."

"I'm reporting on the border closure. I hired you to guard me along the way."

Keltin didn't have time to question the story as the Heteracks turned from the bar and entered the taproom. Bol immediately noticed them, and left his companions as Keltin and Harper both rose to their feet to meet him halfway.

"Mr. Moore," said the Heterack in a polite greeting. "I hadn't expected to see you this far north after the end of the season."

"Harper wanted to write a story on the border closing. I agreed to make a little extra money keeping him safe on the road."

The Heterack nodded. "It's still a dangerous place, to be sure, though I doubt he would have needed more than one abled beast hunter to keep him safe."

He nodded slightly to indicate Ross, Wendi, and Kuff seated behind them. Keltin was just registering the need for another lie when Harper filled the silence without a misstep. "Oh, we were just accompanying our friends back to their home in the north-western corner of the country. We were planning on parting ways here, and were just having our last meal together."

"Ah, I see," said Bol without a hint of incredulity. Keltin was suddenly very grateful that Harper was with him. The Heterack turned back to Keltin.

"How did you fair for the rest of the season? We didn't see anything of you after your single visit."

"I tried to keep my distance from your territory," said Keltin. "I didn't want to have any unfortunate run-ins with your sleevaks." He paused a moment, then decided to try being courteous. "I hope they made it through the season in good health?"

"They did, though one got into a bad roll with a quilled terror. It took a triple dose of drugged meat to knock it out enough to get all the quills out. We were lucky though. One of the quills came dangerously close to an eye. Too deep, and even a single quill could reach the brain and kill the boil deader than stone."

The clink of tankards signaled that the Heteracks' order had arrived, and Bol gave Keltin and Harper brief, firm handshakes in parting.

"I'll wish you both luck on the road then. We're returning home to Olsivo first thing in the morning."

"You don't anticipate any problems crossing the border?" asked Harper.

"Not really. We've got the proper visas and work exceptions. When you're in the business of hauling dangerous cargo around the countryside, you get used to having all the necessary paperwork at all times."

Keltin and Harper bid the Heterack goodbye and returned to their table. Unwilling to continue their earlier conversation with the Heteracks nearby, Keltin and his friends fell to eating silently. As Keltin ate, a nagging thought occurred to him. This was an opportunity to put something behind him. After a moment, he stood, gave a reassuring look to his curious companions, then went to the Heteracks' table. Bol looked up at him as he approached.

"Yes, Mr. Moore? Was there something else that you needed?"

"I was hoping to have a word with you. Alone, if you don't mind."

Bol gave him a curious look, but shrugged.

"All right. I was going to go check on the sleevaks soon anyway. Come along with me."

Keltin followed the Heterack outside and around the back of the pub to find two wagons with the caged sleevaks securely lashed down in the back.

"Are you worried about leaving your wagons unattended?"

asked Keltin.

"Not really. Who would bother a pack of sleevaks, even caged ones?"

"Fair enough."

Keltin hesitated, trying to put voice to his uncertain thoughts. Bol watched him a moment before speaking again.

"So what was it you wanted to say, Mr. Moore?"

"I… I wanted to apologize. I didn't think very well of you when we first met. You see, Last year when I came to Krendaria to participate in the campaign, I met some other Heterack sleevak wranglers from Malpin. They were bullies, and worse, careless with their creatures. One day, they released their sleevaks too close to my team of hunters as well as a gang of field workers. We had to kill three of the beasts to protect ourselves."

Bol grimaced and spat. "I don't have any patience for wranglers like that. These creatures are dangerous, and should be handled carefully. What part of Malpin were they from?"

"Olsivo, like you."

"Do you remember any of their names?"

"Their captain was named Rok."

"I knew him. Not well, but by reputation. A runny carrion feeder from what I heard. Haven't seen him around for… well, since the campaign."

"A tusked giant took him."

"Good."

Keltin nodded, pushing aside the unpleasant image of Captain Rok to focus again on Bol.

"Well, I just wanted to say that it was wrong of me to assume that you were the same sort of hunters, just because of what you are and where you're from. I'm sorry."

Bol extended a large muscular hand to shake Keltin's.

"I'll accept that, as long as you remember that not all of my people are worthy of contempt and fear, especially with conditions as they are."

"You don't agree with what's happening in Malpin?"

"I'm not a politician. I'm a hunter. Speaking of which, I

need to see to these creatures. Good luck to you, Mr. Moore, wherever you go."

"Thank you, Bol, and you as well."

Keltin left the Heterack and went back inside to his friends, wondering how many more of the common people of Malpin felt just the same as Bol, the sleevak wrangler from Olsivo.

CHAPTER 13 – WELCOME TO MALPIN

Keltin sat in a tree looking down at the spot in the Bent Knee River where they had decided that they would make their crossing. The rest of his companions remained a short distance south at the cold camp they'd made, spending the day cutting poles and lashing them tightly together. Keltin meanwhile had been tasked with watching the river for any signs of patrols on either side of the water.

After more than a full day's observation, Keltin was certain that there were no border guards patrolling the Krendarian side of the river, but was convinced that regular patrols were being made on the northern banks. While the guards never got near enough for Keltin to be able to see any sign of them, his trained ears picked them up at regular intervals throughout the day. Checking the time against his pocket watch, he estimated that the guards came by every forty-five minutes or so. A narrow but feasible window to make their crossing.

It wasn't quite dark when he heard a soft call from below. Slipping to the ground, he found Harper, Ross, Wendi, and Kuff all waiting for him in the gloom, holding the results of their day's labors. The raft was crude and small, likely only big enough to carry two of them across at a time. Looking at it in the dim light, Keltin couldn't help imagining what Bor've'tai would do if he saw the poor little craft. Likely, the Loopi wouldn't say anything at all before turning around and immediately setting to work making an infinitely superior raft.

"It's time to decide, Keltin," whispered Harper. "Who do you want to make the crossing with you?"

Keltin took a deep breath, looking out towards the north for a moment before answering.

"I've been thinking about it all day, and it seems like the crossing should be safe enough for all of us to go. I'm not sure what specific help each of you may offer, but it would likely be wise to have us all together in case anything goes awry."

"It's decided then," said Ross. "We'll all go together, and won't come back until we've got your friend and her family in our protection."

"How soon until the next patrol goes by?" asked Harper.

Keltin checked his watch.

"They should be here in about ten minutes. After that, we'll make our move. We'll lose the last of the sunlight soon, so remember to keep your lanterns sheltered or else we'll provide a beacon for the guards to follow us by."

Keltin was sure he wasn't telling them anything that they didn't already know, but it felt good to repeat the instructions. They waited in silence as Keltin alternated between watching the fading light in the sky and checking his pocket watch. Kuff let out a low growl. A moment later Keltin heard the snap of bracken on the other side of the river. He held his breath without realizing it and forced himself to be calm. He tried to tell himself that this was much the same as a beast hunt, except that the goal here was to escape without his quarry ever knowing he had been there.

Unfortunately, doubt still gnawed at him. The whole operation was centered on dealing with people, something that Keltin still felt less than confident about. Beasts were predictable in their patterns and instincts. They could be studied, understood, and anticipated. But a person was irrational and driven by whims that Keltin couldn't even guess at. How was he to know if a border guard stopped to tie a bootlace, or had uncommonly good hearing, or any number of a hundred other unknowable variables?

The sounds of movement to the north faded, and Keltin motioned for the others to follow him. Standing on the bank of the river, Keltin swung a looped rope over his head and tried to hook it onto something secure on the far bank before the daylight was entirely gone. It took him some time to hook the looped rope over something that would hold, and more than once he wished that Jaylocke was along with him, certain that the Weycliff wayfarer must have an ancestor who knew a variety of rope tricks.

Finally he managed to get the loop so tangled in a mess of branches that he couldn't get it unstuck. With the pull-line reasonably secured across the river and Wendi tying the other end to a tree, he quickly made his way to where Ross and Harper had placed the raft in the slow flowing water. Sitting in the center of the small craft, he felt it sink slightly with his weight, and fervently hoped that it would take the weight of the others. With a prayer that he wouldn't sink, he began to pull hand over hand on the rope, dragging himself out onto the water. From the bank, the river had seemed glassy smooth, but the rickety raft seemed to have a mind of its own as it slew and twisted around underneath him. Once, the pull-line suddenly gave about a half-yard of slack, and Keltin had a momentary flash of fear as he pictured himself floating helplessly downstream. He was deeply grateful when his feet touched the bank on the far side of the river. Quickly, he found the end of the pull-line, untangled it, and secured it with a proper knot around a nearby tree trunk before making the slightly less nerve-wracking trek back to the south bank to begin ferrying his companions across.

Harper was the first to climb onto the raft with him. As soon as Harper was onboard and settled, the two of them began to pull themselves hand over hand across the water. The raft rode dangerously low with the weight of the two men, and Keltin felt the chill water begin to soak through his trousers. Luckily, the now properly secured pull-rope kept the raft much more steady, and with Harper's assistance they were able to make the difficult crossing in a fraction of the time. Harper immediately jumped off, leaving Keltin to return back to the south bank to bring Wendi across. She did her best to help pull on the line, but Keltin was beginning to feel his arms and shoulders burning by the time they reached the north side again. Harper helped Wendi to dry ground and leaned down to Keltin.

"I can make the next trip," he said softly.

"I can manage," said Keltin.

"I'm sure you can, but I thought I heard something, and I'd rather you stay here with Wendi."

"All right."

Keltin allowed Harper to take his place and turned his attention to listening for any sign of movement among the shadowy trees. Try as he might, all he could hear were the soft splashes of water against the sides of the raft and the squeak of the rope. The noise was barely more than a whisper, but it seemed to him as if it filled the entire forest. It felt like forever before Harper and Ross returned. The Krendarian hunter helped the newspaperman to shore then immediately began making his way back to get Kuff.

Suddenly a voice cut through the darkness. It was distant, and the words indistinct, but the sound froze Keltin's blood nonetheless. A second voice answered, and Keltin was able to locate them. The speakers were coming from the direction that the border guards had left in. For whatever reason, the two of them were returning. Turning to Harper and Wendi, he saw them staring at him in alarm. Keltin knew that he could slip away without the guards noticing him, but he was less sure that they could manage it. Turning back to the river, Keltin tried to spy Ross and Kuff, but the light was now too poor to see them. The voices were getting nearer now, and Keltin was soon able to make out a conversation already in progress.

"…somewhere. Help me look."

"It's dark as the bottom of a barrel. You'll never find it."

"I didn't drop it that long ago, and if Marie finds I lost it, it's my hide."

The men were getting steadily closer. Keltin sheltered his lantern and pulled his rifle from off his shoulder. Running his hand over the revolver chamber, he thought of the wax shot inside. He'd have to be careful. In the dark, it would be difficult to be accurate, and if his shot went awry and hit either of the men anywhere in the neck or face, it could kill them. He handed his shielded lantern to Harper and whispered in the man's ear.

"When I give the signal, open the shutter and shine the light on them."

Keltin hoped that the light would startle the men and make it easier to make a precise shot. He turned towards the oncoming noise of the men crashing through the brush, the lights of their lanterns bobbing among the trees. He lifted his rifle to his shoulder. Suddenly he heard a violent rustling through the brush. The noise rushed past him and in the direction of the border guards, growling and snarling fiercely. The men cried out in alarm and panic, their lights swinging wildly as they tried to find the source of the monstrous noise. A moment later Ross appeared at his side.

"Come on!" he hissed. "We need to get away from the river!"

Keltin turned and took Harper's elbow to help guild him through the brush. Together, they all made their way further into the forest and away from the sounds of panic behind them. At one point Keltin heard gunshots and he froze inside, fearful of what they might mean. They continued onward until there was no noise but the stillness of the woods and the labored sound of their own breathing. Keltin risked just a little light from his lantern and turned it on his companions. Gratefully, he found them all there, even Kuff. Keltin turned to Ross.

"Why did you sic Kuff on those men?"

"I didn't. I gave him the command to Turn, then gave him the command to Return. He never even touched them. See? Clean muzzle."

Ross turned the light of his lantern on the panting hound, his tongue lolling out of his clean, grinning jaws. Keltin gently rubbed him behind his long, pointed ears.

"Good work, Kuff."

The hound turned his grin to him for a moment before going to sit squarely between Wendi and Ross. Keltin turned to the rest of his companions to find Harper giving him a tight smile.

"Well, we're here," he said. "Welcome to Malpin, Mr. Moore."

Keltin nodded. "The first challenge is over," he said, "and it's gone better than it could have. Nobody is searching for us, and there's no reason for anyone to suspect us if we're seen. Let's try to make a little more distance north and then we can make another cold camp. In the morning, we'll get our bearings, and start making our way to Carris."

The others nodded and Keltin turned, leading his companions onward into the dark Malpinion forest.

* * *

"I think we should have a word before we reach Carris," said Harper as he poured himself a cup of sweet broth from the pot next to the fire. "Keltin has done a masterful job of getting us across the country undetected, but now, we need to come out of hiding, and that's where my part comes in."

"Have you come up with a convincing cover story for us?" asked Wendi.

"I've been thinking of that. I do have an idea, though it won't cover everything. Frankly, I can't come up with a reasonable excuse to have that big fellow along with us," he pointed at Kuff licking the forest floor where the last traces of his breakfast had been. "I think it may be best if he stays out of town along with someone to keep an eye on him. Would you be comfortable with that, Wendi?"

The young woman blinked in surprise.

"Oh, I thought you were going to ask Mr. Ross."

"I was at first, but then I gave it some thought. We don't know what conditions may be like exactly in Carris, but there's a good chance that there may be some danger involved. I think all of us would be more comfortable if you were somewhere relatively safe."

"I agree with Harper," said Ross. "You're the only one I'd trust with Kuff, and I'd likely be better able to handle a sticky spot in town than you could. Besides, it may be a good thing to keep someone on the outside in case everything goes hexed wrong."

Wendi nodded. "All right. I just wish I didn't feel so useless."

"Truth be told, I almost wish I could join you," said Keltin. "I've never been good at lying."

"Sorry, but it's essential that you're there," said Harper. "You're the only one who knows what any of the Destovs look like, and the only one that they would recognize."

"Don't worry, I'll do whatever I have to do."

"Good. Now, with just you, myself, and Ross, I think we can establish cover stories that will hold up reasonably well. Keltin, I know that you're not an actor, so I want to keep things as straightforward as possible for you. You will be a beast hunter from Riltvin that was brought into southern Malpin to help protect the field workers. Got that? It's just like what you've actually done, only you were called to work in Malpin, not Krendaria."

"Can I use my real name?"

"Absolutely. In fact, that's the whole focus of my plan. We need word of you to spread through the town. Hopefully both the Destov family and the Brothers of Kerrtow know that you are coming and are looking for you already. If Mr. Destov wasn't able to get word of his plan to his family, then we'll just have to hope that word will get around to them that you're in town, and that they can put the pieces together themselves. Our job until then is to do our best to spread the word that a beast hunter named Keltin Moore is in town."

"How?"

"I'll play the role of your advocate, shopping around from town to town looking for work for you. It'll give me an opportunity to both spread the word about you while sniffing around for a potential contact within the Brothers of Kerrtow."

Keltin shook his head. "I've never heard of a beast hunter having an advocate."

"Maybe we can play it off as a uniquely Riltvin tradition. These people likely won't know the truth. Besides, it will help add to your mystique. You're such a good hunter, you don't have to search for work. You can afford to have someone do your searching for you."

"Well, I suppose it will make it easier for you to do most of the talking. What about Ross? "

"Ross is less complicated. He doesn't need to draw attention to himself, so he can go in on his own, pretending to be someone caught on the wrong side of the border and trying to find a way back. If the Brothers don't come to you, Keltin, then Ross may be our best chance of finding them."

Ross shrugged. "I'm not much of a play-actor, but I suppose I can blend in with the crowd well enough. How will we keep in contact?"

Keltin found his mind wandering as Harper described complex routines of drop-points and hidden messages. He disliked deceptions, and was still uncomfortable with the idea of trying to be something that he wasn't. Too late, he realized that Harper had stopped speaking. Looking up, he found the newspaperman watching him.

"Are you all right, Keltin?"

"I'm sorry. I suppose I'm still uncertain about all of this."

Harper gave him a sympathetic smile. "I understand. You're an honest man, and this is all far beyond what you're comfortable with. I'll do my best to help you by doing most of the talking for you. Let me worry about building up your legend while Ross focuses on trying to ferret out the Brothers. All you have to do is look intimidating and make yourself available to be contacted by the Brothers when-and-if they see fit to find you. If it helps, think of yourself as the bait."

"How is that supposed to help him?" said Ross.

"Actually, it does," said Keltin. "At least I know where I stand."

"Good," said Harper. "We'll go over the other details as many times as we need to so that nobody forgets or makes a mistake. Remember, as soon as we enter town tomorrow, we'll be on display for both friendly and unfriendly eyes, so we'll need to put on a convincing show."

CHAPTER 14 – THE MIGHTY HUNTER

Keltin paced by the campfire. It had been decided that Harper and Ross would both arrive in town ahead of him so that Harper could start the word around and to avoid Ross looking like he was with them. With that in mind, Ross had left the night before, and Harper had left that morning. Keltin checked his pocket watch for the fifth time in as many minutes. Soon. He could follow them to town soon.

Looking up, he saw Wendi and Kuff both watching him silently. He grimaced.

"I'm sorry," he said. "I'm much more patient on a hunt."

"I'm sure everything will be fine," Wendi said softly.

Keltin nodded absently, not really listening as he resumed pacing.

Eventually the time came, and Keltin quickly took up his pack.

"Keep safe and out of sight," he said to Wendi. "Don't be afraid to use Kuff if things go badly."

"I will. Good luck."

Keltin left the camp and made for the road before turning to the east. Harper had planned it so that Keltin would arrive during the evening crowd for maximum effect. His first order of business was to find the biggest eatery and enter "like a real beast hunter," whatever that meant. He knew that Harper had given him a role to play that was as close to reality as possible, yet he still worried and fretted that somehow he would ruin it all. How would people expect a real beast hunter to act?

The sunlight turned red as it filtered through the trees bordering the road. Keltin's stomach growled, reminding him that he had been too nervous to eat all day. At least it wasn't a part of his mystique that he didn't eat. Perhaps he could get through the evening by simply keeping his head down and focusing on devouring his food. It seemed a fair plan, and gave him some small amount of comfort as the town of Carris came into view.

Studying the town from a distance, he estimated that Carris was somewhere in size between Gillentown and Collinsworth and saw little at first that made it stand out from any of the cities that he had seen in other nations. But as he entered the town's main district, the symptoms of deeper problems began to show. More than half of the shops were closed, despite the oncoming evening. Signs were everywhere declaring "Out of Business," many of them propped in front of boarded-up broken windows. Most troubling was the graffiti, painted in broad red and black strokes with angry brushes. Slurs like "ape," "monkey," and worse were emblazoned across shopfronts along with the rough image of a vile caricature of a primate face. Every business with that face painted on it bore broken windows and an accompanying sign.

There were few people in the streets, and those that Keltin saw moved quickly with their heads down. These were not people beaten down with defeat like those in Carvalen. These were the faces of wary prey. Keltin spied several men in gray uniforms moving like predators through the herd. Everyone seemed to get out of their way without making eye contact. Keltin saw one of the uniformed men from the side and read the initials on his shoulder. MLP. The officer turned and eyed Keltin and his weaponry suspiciously. Keltin turned down a corner and continued on, doing his best to show confidence without confrontation.

Realizing that he should get off the streets, he searched around for a likely soul to ask for directions. Nobody looked promising as everyone hurried along, their gaze firmly fixed on the ground in front of them. After a few fruitless attempts at quietly gaining someone's attention, he selected a man bustling by and stepped in his path.

"Pardon me, sir."

The man gave a start as he nearly ran into Keltin. He looked up in agitation then immediately balked at the sight of Keltin's heavily armed appearance. Keltin spoke quickly in an effort to avoid a scene and draw the attention of the ever-present officers of the MLP.

"Excuse me. I'm new in town and looking for a place to stay. What's the nicest place to eat in town?"

The man blinked and sputtered for a moment.

"Eh? Oh, ah… I suppose that would be Jacoby's."

"And where is that?"

"Just… just down the street, sir. You'll see the sign, on your left."

"Thank you. Goodnight."

The man hurried on without giving a response. As Keltin began to follow the man's directions, he was frustrated to realize that he was already beginning to question his performance. Had he acted too politely? Should he have been more gruff and intimidating? He cursed to himself as he made his way down the street. This business of playing a role, no matter how close to himself, was something he would never get used to and certainly never enjoy.

Jacoby's proved to be an impressive two-story building with golden light spilling onto the street outside. Keltin climbed the steps to the outer porch and took a quick glance through the window at the well-populated round tables and bar within. He breathed a quick sigh of relief at the sight of Harper seated at one of the tables. Taking comfort in having found the right place, he entered through the sturdy front doors to the sound of playful music coming from a player-piano in the corner. He felt a number of eyes upon him but did his best to ignore them as he walked past the tables in the front room and made his way to the bar. On an impulse, he leaned his rifle against the counter and then swung the Ripper from off his shoulder to lay the savage-looking weapon on the bar before him. The man behind the bar gave the weapon a guarded look before addressing Keltin in a somewhat stiff voice.

"Can I help you, sir?"

"My name is Keltin Moore. I need a room, and I'd like something to eat."

Was that too polite again? Keltin suppressed his uncertainty as the bartender replied.

"Well, we can provide you a room, and supper is beef and carrot stew. That'll be seven dunlens."

Keltin froze. With everything else on his mind, he had forgotten to account for the change of currencies in Malpin. What could he do? Should he try paying with either the Krendarian marks or Riltvinian jeva that he carried? He was still trying to decide when Harper appeared at his side.

"I'll handle all of our expenses," he said smoothly before turning to Keltin. "Mr. Moore, I've already gotten you a table. Please take a seat and I'll see to it that your dinner is brought right away."

Keltin nodded, not trusting himself to speak as he picked up the Ripper and his rifle and followed the newspaperman to a table near an impressive fireplace against the side wall. He took a seat and looked up to see that he had drawn more than a few curious looks from the crowd. Despite his uncertainty, he forced himself to avoid looking away. Doing his best to look more confident than he felt, he met each onlooker's gaze until they turned away uncomfortably. When the last of them had looked away he removed a box of Capshire shatter-rounds from his pocket and pretended to slowly count them on the table, feeling for all the world like an actor that had forgotten all of his lines. Harper finished at the bar and sat down next to him.

"You're doing fine," he murmured under his breath.

"I feel like an idiot," Keltin replied softly.

"Just stay strong and silent. I've been talking you up most of the day. In fact, It's probably time to make a little announcement. Just follow my lead."

Harper stood up and addressed the assembled room.

"Excuse me!" he said in a clear, confident voice. "This man is Keltin Moore, the most famous and deadly beast hunter you'll ever see, recently returning from killing beasts in the southern territories. If any of you wish to hire out his services, you can speak with me. If you're plagued by the visitations of some beast or monster of nightmare, this man will kill it, skin it, and bring the hide back to your doorstep in a fortnight."

"You say he's famous?" called a weathered man from one of the tables. "I've never heard of him."

"Have you been to Lost Trap in Drutchland, or Dhalma Province in Krendaria, or the hill country and lumber camps of Riltvin? No sir, I think you haven't, or you'd have heard of the great hero Keltin Moore."

"If he's so great, why doesn't he give some demonstration of it?" called a younger man from another table.

Keltin tried to give Harper a worried glance, but the newspaperman regarded the heckler with perfect coolness.

"If you would care to trot a beast into this restaurant, I'm sure Mr. Moore would be happy to kill it for your pleasure."

Harper was met with a laugh from the crowd, and the young man went red in the face and sat down quickly.

"Well, what sort of things has he done?" asked another fellow. "I'd like to hear some of it, if you can spin a good yarn."

"Ha! I can do that for certain. Turn your chair around, and let me tell you about how Mr. Moore single-handedly tracked down the Ghost of Lost Trap."

Harper then proceeded to regal the crowd with a rousing and highly embellished tale of Keltin's time in Drutchland. The newspaperman clearly had a gift with words, and soon had the entire room's attention as he accepted free drinks from his makeshift stage next to the bar. For his part, Keltin tried not to let his burning red ears show, dipping his hat low and focusing on the stew that had been placed before him.

Suddenly, Harper was interrupted by a young man that had been sitting at the end of the bar. Keltin could see that the fellow had clearly been deep into his cups already as he shouted at Harper in a slightly slurred voice.

"Aw, shut it with your wobble shobbing. If you love the man so much, why don't you take him upstairs with you then?"

Harper gave the man a frosty look. "If you don't care for the story, sir, then you don't have to listen to it."

"How can I help it? You're blabbing it all over here. Well, we don't care what some polished up git with a fancy pickax and his lying trash picker have to say. So why don't you two get a room, or shut your gob."

"Ah sit down, Lough," called someone from the bar. "Let the man tell his story, he ain't hurting you."

"I won't! This man comes here and makes us all out to be fools. What are these two doing here? Maybe they're highwaymen, come to steal women and kill children."

"You're drunk boy, sit down, or go home. Don't bring the Grays in here after us."

But Lough was having none of it. He shoved his stool back and made straight for Keltin, still seated at his table in the corner.

"And what about you, gob? You saying anything?"

Keltin looked up at the young man. He was unarmed, but bore the sturdy build of a hard worker. Keltin had seen plenty of blustering fellows like him, but he'd never had an audience like this before. With Harper's elaborate tales still ringing in his ears, he spoke in an even tone that was just loud enough to be heard throughout the room.

"You should listen to your friend and go home."

The young man's eyes flared. He swung his arm to swipe Keltin's empty bowl to the floor.

"Don't you tell me what to do, or I'll sockmouth your runny face right here!"

Keltin took a deep breath and slowly rose to his feet, carefully setting aside his Ripper and rifle. He stared at the young man coolly as he adjusted his stance, keeping his tone level.

"Go home. You're drunk."

Lough swung a meaty fist at Keltin's head. Keltin easily dodged it by dipping his body low, rising up with a driving fist to the man's stomach. There was an audible rush of air out of Lough's lungs as he stumbled back, face red as a tomato as he clutched at his middle. For a moment it looked as if Lough might throw up, and Keltin watched him carefully as someone came up to the young man to help him.

"Come on Lough, let's go."

But the young man pushed the fellow away and reached into his pocket. Keltin saw a flash of polished steel as Lough flipped open a folding knife. In a single, smooth motion, Keltin pulled his Lawrie hunting knife from its sheath and leapt forward. He clamped his free hand onto the wrist of the hand holding the folding knife and held the blade of the Lawrie against the young man's throat. Lough's eyes went wide with sudden fear. He began to shake, his chin trembling.

"I... I..."

Keltin kept a steely eye on the young man as he spoke to Lough's friend. "Take away his knife before he hurts himself."

Once Lough had been disarmed, Keltin released him to the care of his friend.

"See that he gets home."

Turning away from the pair, Keltin made his way through the silent room to the bartender.

"Is my room ready?"

The bartender nodded and swallowed. "Yes sir. Up the stairs and on your left."

The man fumbled for a minute to detach the room key from a ring under the bar. Keltin took the key and turned to go, giving Harper the barest of nods before making his way up to the room. He unlocked the door, stepped inside, closed the door, and threw himself on the bed to allow all of his pent up tension to finally rise to the surface.

His hands were shaking and his head swarmed with a

pulsing headache, neither of which were the result of the brief fight with Lough. He'd handled far worse exchanges with men before, to say nothing of the scores of beasts he'd tangled with. But the constant pressure of being on display was exhausting. Keltin wasn't sure how he would keep it up.

He stood up and paced around the room until his breathing had returned to a calm, natural pattern. Too late, he realized that he was still hungry, but knew that he couldn't go back downstairs to get something more. He sat in the room's single chair by the shuttered window and tried not to think of the pangs in his stomach until he heard a knock at his door. Keltin tensed, feeling the full rush of tension flowing back into him as he sat up.

"Who is it?" he called, trying to fill his voice with confidence that he didn't feel.

"It's me."

Keltin slumped with relief before rising from his chair and opening the door. Harper hurried inside and closed the door behind him, turning to Keltin was a look of concern.

"Are you all right?"

Keltin heaved a heavy sigh and nodded. "I've dealt with worse bullies. Frankly, it was almost a relief to have a reason to leave, though I wish I'd gotten something more to eat."

Harper gave him a humorless smile.

"Well, it may not have gone perfectly to plan, but at least we've got a story to quickly spread rumors of the legendary beast hunter staying at Jacoby's in town." He lowered his voice. "I'm just worried about the attention it might draw from the MLP."

"Do you think they'll find out about it?"

"There's no question of it. Just from the little that I've seen today I can tell you that the people here don't want any trouble with the authorities. The MLP have likely already received multiple reports of your little scuffle, if only to clear the names of the people doing the reporting. We should expect to answer some questions from the MLP any time now."

"I'm sorry. I shouldn't have let it get violent."

"There wasn't anything else that you could have done. I caught some gossip about that young man after you left. It sounds like Lough had plenty of weight on him before you ever showed up. Apparently, his father owned a carpentry business in town with a Loopi partner. When the Heterack Empowerment came, the Loopi partner wanted to leave, but Lough's father convinced him to stay. Two months later, the shop was burgled and vandalized, forcing them to close it for good. The Loopi partner disappeared, and Lough's father remained an outspoken critic of the Vaughs until he was arrested by the MLP for disturbing the peace. Nobody's heard from him since."

Keltin closed his eyes and bowed his head.

"I wish I'd known," he said softly.

Harper placed a hand on his shoulder. "There's nothing more that you could have done. Don't forget. We're not here to right every wrong that we find. We're here to help the Destovs. Speaking of which, I don't suppose you saw anyone you recognized downstairs?"

"Only you."

"Too bad, though I'm not surprised. We'll just have to wait. With luck, the Brothers of Kerrtow will hear about the new beast hunter in town and get in touch with us."

"I hope they're quick about it," said Keltin. "I'm not looking forward to dealing with the MLP if they become too nosy."

"That's true. We're going to have to walk a fine line between making enough of a noise to draw the attention of the Brothers without getting into the sort of trouble that will make us disappear like Lough's father."

CHAPTER 15 – THE MLP

It was early the next morning and Keltin was in the process of getting dressed when he heard a sudden, insistent knock on his door. He'd barely managed to open the latch before Harper had shoved his way inside, closing the door behind him.

"What's the matter?" asked Keltin.

"MLP officers downstairs. They're investigating last night's fight. They'll be up here any time now."

Keltin glanced at the pale light of morning coming from his window. "I'm surprised they're here so early."

"I'm not. That's why I was downstairs. I had a hunch they would come. Quickly, do you remember the story we discussed last night?"

Keltin's reply was interrupted by a harsh knock at his door. They exchanged a quick look, and Keltin quickly pulled on the last of his clothes.

"Just a moment," he called. "I'm getting dressed."

A harsh voice answered him.

"This is the Malpinion League of Protection! Open up!"

Harper opened the door as three large men entered the room, each one wearing the insignia of the MLP on his arm. Keltin turned to face them from where he stood next to his bed, keeping his hand close to the pillow where the tiny pocket pistol that Jessica had made for him lay hidden underneath.

"Can we help you gentlemen?" asked Harper.

One of the officers closed the door before turning to speak. He regarded Harper for less than a moment before turning his attention to Keltin.

"Are you Keltin Moore?" he asked.

"Yes."

"We'd like to ask you a few questions."

"About what?"

The man cocked his head to the side slightly, reminding Keltin of a winged strangler. "You needn't be so closed off. After all, this is not an official inquiry."

"Then maybe you should introduce yourself."

The man's thin lips curled in a sneering smile. "All right. My name is Yassel Panz. I am the Prefect of the League here in Carris, tasked with keeping peace and order."

Keltin gave a slight nod.

"Nice to meet you. I'm Keltin Moore."

"Oh yes, I've already heard about you. A legendary beast hunter from Riltvin. Please, take a seat."

Keltin sat on his bed as Panz took the only chair in the room, sitting with his back to the door and the two accompanying officers to either side of him. Harper stood in the far corner, all-but ignored by the MLP Prefect as he began his questioning.

"Tell me, Mr. Moore, what has brought you so far away from home?"

"I came to Krendaria to protect its northern farmlands from the seasonal influx of monsters."

"A noble and lucrative venture I'm sure. But, Mr. Moore, this is not Krendaria." Panz's voice was soft, but his eyes betrayed an edge to his questioning. "What brought you to Malpin, Mr. Moore?"

Keltin resisted the urge to glance towards Harper. As much as he would have preferred to have the newspaperman speak for the both of them, he realized that it would only increase Panz's suspicions if Keltin didn't speak for himself. Staring into the Prefect's searching eyes, he tried to speak as much truth as he dared.

"My contract with my employer ended once the last of the crops were brought in. Work in Riltvin is often light during this time of year for beast hunters, so I thought I'd try my luck in Malpin and see if I could find some work here."

"And how did you get across the closed border?"

Keltin braced himself as he plunged headlong into the lie.

"The border closed after I came across."

Panz arched an eyebrow. "And yet here you are, miles north of the border. How odd that your first thought was not to immediately attempt to return home."

Keltin shrugged, doing his best to look unperturbed. "As I said, my intention was to come to Malpin to seek out bounties. The fact that the border closed behind me had no bearing on that. Besides, I'd assumed that the closing of the border was to keep your own people in, not foreigners."

Panz's smile was predatory. "A closed border is not like a net, Mr. Moore, allowing some fish through while others remain caught. You may be ignorant of it, but let me assure you that you are indeed 'caught'."

Keltin's eyes narrowed. "Well, I suppose I'll just have to worry about that when I'm ready to go home."

"Be careful, Mr. Moore. You've already done enough to draw the attention of the MLP. If you attempt to illegally cross the border, you will be dealt with as any other lawbreaker. I'm sure you don't want that."

"Thank you for the warning. Was there anything else?"

Panz's eyebrows went up. "Are you ejecting me from your room?"

Keltin stood up. The two agents standing behind Panz tensed, but Keltin remained in place, fixing the Prefect with an icy stare.

"You said that this conversation is not a formal investigation. That being the case, I'm tired of you being here, so I'm going to politely ask you to leave."

Panz slowly rose to his feet, his expression turning

dangerously dark.

"Be careful, Mr. Moore. I can easily make this encounter very official."

Suddenly Harper spoke up. "If you do, may I just remind you that Mr. Moore and I are both citizens of Riltvin, and that his status as a national hero will likely turn any action you take here into an international incident. Consider that, Prefect, before you try throwing your legal weight around."

Panz gave a daggered look at Harper for a moment before turning back to Keltin.

"We'll see. In the meantime, let me give you some advice, Mr. Moore. Leave town. Tomorrow. Early. Go to Kerrtow. Your country has an embassy there. They can see about getting you back to where you belong."

"I'll keep that in mind," said Keltin.

"Good."

Panz started towards the door before hesitating. He turned slightly, giving Keltin a slit-eyed smile.

"By the way, do you remember a young man you encountered last night named Lough Karven?"

"I remember him."

"Well, you might be interested to know that we went to visit him before coming to see you. We wanted to ask for his side of things, see how he was doing after all of the tragedy his family has faced. Unfortunately, we found him in a deplorable state, and when he resisted us, we were forced to act in self-defense. Goodbye."

Panz turned and walked out of the room, followed by his two agents. Harper went to the door, closed it, and pressed his back against it with a heavy sigh.

"Well, that complicates things," he said softly.

Keltin didn't move. His hands were clenched and his breathing came in short, deep draughts. Harper crossed the room to him, bending his tall frame down slightly to look him directly in the eyes.

"Keltin, listen to me. This is not your fault. You couldn't have saved that boy."

Keltin pulled away and sat down on the bed. His stomach was in knots and he wondered if he would throw up. He covered his eyes with his hands and took in a deep, shuddering breath.

"I'm sorry," he said, his voice barely a whisper. "I told you I was no good at this sort of thing."

Harper sat next to him.

"It's all right. You've done admirably. You can't control what these people do, and there wasn't anything that you could have said that would have made that little interview go any better than it did. That Prefect knew what he was going to say to you before he even came in the room. He was just testing you to see if you might do something incredibly stupid. You didn't, so the best he could do was threaten you and leave."

"And after what happened to Lough, we know that he isn't bluffing."

Harper gave a somber sigh. "No, he's more than bluster, that's for certain. I'm sure that he suspects that you and I smuggled ourselves across the border, he just doesn't know why. I think he's hoping for one of two things. Either we leave in the morning and take our problems with us, or we stay and tip our hand as to what we're really up to."

"So what do we do?"

"For one thing, we'll have to move faster than I would have liked. I would have preferred for you to stay here at Jacoby's throughout the day while I went out asking questions. That way you'd be easy to find if someone were trying to contact you. As it is, we'll both have to spend what little time we have looking everywhere we can for the Brothers of Kerrtow. At least Panz gave us one day in town."

"He'll have us followed."

"Maybe. Then again, maybe we're a low priority for him. Lough was local and likely an ongoing problem. Last night was simply an excuse for removing him. As long as you and I are gone in the morning, I think Panz will be willing to overlook us."

Keltin wasn't convinced but realized there was little that he could do about it. He felt the whole situation spinning out of control and took only a little comfort in knowing that he would be out and doing something, anything, rather than just sitting around at Jacoby's.

"How should I try looking for the Brothers?" he asked. "I can't exactly start asking people on the street."

Harper chewed his cheek for a moment while he thought.

"You have a few friends who are Loopi, don't you?"

"Yes."

"All right, then perhaps you can go around town asking for a friend of theirs. Any Loopi will likely know something of the Brothers, and if we can convince them that we're a friend, then we'll be set."

"But I don't know of any Loopi friends they have."

"That's fine. Just pick one of them and say that they have kin here, and you're trying to find them. If you find someone that's helpful, they'll likely point you in the direction of any Loopi that's still in the area, and that's all we really need. Do you understand?"

"I think so." Keltin glanced at the growing light outside. "I suppose we'd better get started."

"Agreed. We'll meet up here tonight unless we find something. Good hunting, Mr. Moore."

Less than half an hour later Keltin was standing in the rain out on the streets of Carris, trying to decide how to begin. Perhaps he could start at some local shops, asking merchants if they knew of any acquaintances that Bor've'tai might have in the area. It seemed an awkward and flimsy lie, but with little time to come up with something better, he was prepared to fully commit to it.

He was about to step into a general store when he saw the back of a woman that seemed to have familiar dark, tightly curled hair. Immediately he turned and rushed after her. Pulling his hat low to shield himself from prying eyes as much as from the cold, drizzling rain, he hurried down the wooden walkway in the direction the woman had taken. He didn't see her on the street ahead of him, and began peering into each window he passed in case she had ducked inside somewhere. Finally, through the glass of a bakery window he saw the woman that he had been pursuing. Entering to the sound of a tinkling bell Keltin stepped up behind her. She faced away from him, so he edged to her side and risked a sideways glance at her.

His heart sank. It wasn't Elaine. She took a parcel from the baker and left without even noticing his reaction to her. Keltin cursed himself for a fool. Of course she wouldn't be out in the open like that. He'd let his heart do his tracking, and had only succeeded in wasting time. He had to focus. Treat this like a hunt. Think like a hunter. The baker turned his attention to Keltin.

"What can I get for you, sir?"

Keltin steeled himself and began his deception.

"I thought while I was in town I'd try to look up some of the kin of a friend of mine. They're supposed to live around here. My friend's name is Bor've'tai."

The baker seemed to shrink inside himself at the sound of the Loopi name. His eyes darted around the room at all of the other customers before shaking his head.

"Sorry sir, don't know that name."

It was clear that the man was uncomfortable, but Keltin didn't have time to waste. He pressed further.

"You may not know the name, but he may still have kin here. Where's the nearest Loopi? I could ask them."

Now the baker was truly unsettled, as were those customers within earshot.

"I'm sorry sir," said the man. "I can't help you. Have a good day."

The man turned to the next person in line to take their order. Keltin left the bakery, pausing to watch the gray raindrops falling from a leaden sky. He felt so helpless. A small part of him wished that he could simply drag someone into a back alley and force them to tell him where the Brothers could be found. Of course, even if he could do that, he never would, but the image of it made him feel just a little better as he entered the next open business and repeated his line of questioning, with a very similar result. For the rest of the morning he wandered the streets, going into every shop and eatery that was open, repeating his story and receiving the same evasive answers. Once, he spied Ross in a disreputable looking bar, but the two of them avoided eye contact and Keltin soon left. Nowhere did Keltin find a Loopi, or even hear of one in the neighboring farms.

By mid-afternoon, he'd been through the town twice with nothing to show for it, except for noticing that he was being followed. It wasn't always the same person, and Keltin wondered if perhaps there were multiple agents of the MLP taking turns at watching him. None were in uniform, and each maintained a distance that might have kept them unseen to someone whose senses had not been honed by long years of hunting beasts. Well, let them follow him. He had found nothing.

Defeated, Keltin slowly made his way back to the hotel, looking at every passerby in the vain hopes of spying a Loopi among the crowd. There were none, and he returned to his room at Jacoby's, looking out his window until evening fell and Harper arrived with his supper.

"Any good news?" asked the newspaperman.

"No. I tried your story everywhere, but all I achieved was getting followed by someone."

Harper tensed. "Do you know who?"

"No, but they're still out there. They're watching me through that store window down the street."

Harper came to his side and peered through the fading light.

"I don't know how you can even see them," he said.

Keltin shrugged and closed the window shutters. "You don't have to see something every moment to know it's there." He sat down to eat, not noticing the taste of his food or even what it was. "I assume you had similar results?" he asked as he chewed mechanically.

"I'm afraid so. This town is like a pinthar nut. Even if you could get the shell open, I'm not sure the prize inside would be worth it. People seem afraid to even look like they know anything. If I had a week, I might be able to find something. But in just one day…" Harper shook his head. "I'm sorry Keltin."

They finished their meal in silence then sat watching the flickering light of the single lantern in the room. Harper sighed and stood up.

"Well, we're going to have to leave in the morning. We'll regroup with Wendi, and wait to see if Ross was able to find something. If not, well, we'll just have to try something else."

"All right."

Harper hesitated, as if he were considering whether he should say something more before quietly leaving the room. Keltin prepared for bed and blew out the lantern, his mind weary with worry. He had barely gotten into bed before he began turning over restlessly. He had always been a light sleeper, and years of hunting beasts alone had only increased that. While he had gotten more accustomed to mundane nighttime noises from his time spent with Jaylocke and Bor've'tai, when he was alone or particularly stressed, his old habits returned with a vengeance. Every sound seemed amplified in his ears. The settling of the hotel, the tap of dripping shingles, the distant snoring of another guest. Each new sound added to the quiet bedlam.

Footsteps in the hallway joined the soft cacophony. It sounded like whoever was walking was also sensitive to sound, as they tried to walk slowly and quietly across the protesting old floorboards. Keltin lay counting footsteps as they got louder. Looking at the gap under his door, he saw the telltale flickering of a weak light grow brighter with the approaching steps. The sound approached his door, and Keltin waited for the steps to continue on, but they hesitated.

Keltin sat up. The light was flickering just outside his door. Someone was outside. Was it Harper? What couldn't wait until morning? Maybe Ross had come secretly to try to speak with him. Keltin thought of Panz. The Prefect had said that they would have until the morning to leave, but could he really trust anything that the man said? Had he sent someone in the night for him? Keltin got up silently, slipping the pocket pistol from under his pillow. There was the muffled chunking of a key placed into the door lock, and Keltin moved against the wall behind the door.

The lock clicked as the door swung open slowly. A figure stepped into the room, shielding their candle with their hand. From behind it was impossible to make out any features of the figure, but the rough outline was too short for Harper and not broad enough for Ross. Keltin wished that he had had time to create a decoy lump on his bed as the figure drew next to it. He had only seconds to act before the figure turned.

Keltin pounced forward, wrapping an arm around the stranger's neck while his other hand pressed the small muzzle of the pocket pistol against the man's temple. The stranger froze. Keltin tried to force the adrenaline from his mind as he struggled to think of what to do next.

"Who are you?" he whispered.

The man replied in a low, even voice.

"My name is Whelks. I am one of the Brothers, and have come on behalf of the Destovs."

Keltin's heart leapt within him, but suspicion forced him to be cautious.

"The Destovs? Who are they?"

Whelks gave a soft chuckle. "Miss Elaine was right. She thought you'd be too cautious to reveal yourself right away, and told me to ask you if the patches she sewed onto your coat have held together."

Keltin sagged with relief. He lowered the pistol, closed the door, and turned as Whelks lifted his hand away from his candle to reveal his face. It was older than Keltin expected, plainer, not one that would stand out on a busy street. The perfect face to blend into the background and hide a wealth of secrets. Keltin placed his pistol back into his pocket.

"Sorry."

Whelks gave him a half smile, made eerie by the shadows of

his candle.

"Don't be. I'd be disappointed if you were less cautious. We need to get going."

"Someone was following me earlier today. I may still be watched."

"You are, but we know where he is. Get dressed and packed. You're not coming back here."

CHAPTER 16 – CORNERED

Keltin began throwing on his clothes.

"We'll need to get Harper," he said as he laced his boots.

"I already woke him. He's getting ready. Incidentally, he tried to pull a gun on me too, but couldn't make it stick."

Keltin decided not to ask for details as he shouldered his pack and the Ripper, taking his rifle into his hands.

"Ready."

"Good. Follow me. And stay quiet."

They stepped back out into the hall. Moving to Harper's door, Whelks ran his fingers over the wood in a movement that was just loud enough to be heard. The newspaperman appeared and followed them without a word, reaching out to give Keltin's arm a squeeze as they quietly made their way downstairs. Whelks paused at the landing.

"Wait here," he whispered.

He disappeared around a corner for a few moments. Keltin and Harper waited in the darkness until he returned.

"Returning the key," Whelks said by way of explanation.

"Is Jacoby one of the Brothers as well?" asked Harper.

"No. He's just a heavy sleeper who doesn't hide his things very well. Follow me."

Keltin and Harper followed Whelks through the empty

170

sitting room and into the darkened kitchen. Threading their way past the large stove and preparing tables, they came to a small door leading out into a cold, dark alleyway. Whelks extinguished his candle and motioned for the others to keep close. Keltin followed the man into the night, weaving through narrow streets and crawling over rubbish bins and low fences. Eventually his sense of direction suggested to him that they were retracing some of their steps, and he wondered if Whelks did this to throw off unwanted followers or to prevent his two charges from memorizing the way.

Eventually they reached an unassuming warehouse with boarded up windows and the faint outline of graffiti on its walls. Whelks led them around to the back and gave a soft, complicated knock at a small door. It opened, and the three of them were ushered into the greater darkness within the building. Keltin felt Whelks's hand on his wrist as the Brother led him through the gloom. He paused, and Keltin heard the rustle of fabric and the creak of hinges.

"There are steps here," said Whelks, lowering Keltin's hand down to the floor. "Go to the bottom and stand to the side."

Keltin descended to find the smell of damp muskiness and sweat. His attuned ears detected breathing nearby, and his hand went into his pocket to find the tiny pistol resting there even as Harper and Whelks descending down to him. It wasn't until the hatch above them was closed that a match was struck, dispelling darkness in a small pool of light, revealing two additional figures. The first was a smallish man with a bushy brown beard and a pair of spectacles perched on his nose. The second was a Loopi with chocolate-brown fur and dark, piercing eyes. Something seemed off to Keltin about the Loopi, and it took a moment for him to realize just what it was. It was the eyes. Every Loopi that he had ever known had had an aura of stoic calm about them. Even Bor've'tai –who had described himself as being too emotional for one of his people— still radiated a spirit of quiet strength. But this Loopi standing before Keltin was not calm. Despite his stone-like posture, his eyes belied a burning intensity, a dangerous energy that reminded Keltin of a cornered animal. He was still watching the Loopi as the small, bespeckled man spoke to Whelks.

"I still don't agree with bringing these two here," he said, his voice high and nasally. "You should have led them to the outside of town and pointed them in the right direction. Or better yet, wait until they left and then meet them outside the city. This way is just too risky."

"You were outvoted, Quibly," said the Loopi, his voice flat and cold. "Don't embarrass yourself by showing your weakness in front of strangers."

"I can still speak my mind, Kor'sa'vor. You can't scare me."

The Loopi turned on the man, and Keltin saw Quibly shrink before the hulking form.

"Brave are you? Then why don't you come down in the shadows with me, instead of pretending that you don't know about any of us while you enjoy the sunlight every day?"

"Enough," said Whelks. "We discussed the risk of bringing these two here, and decided it was worth it due to the potential benefits to the cause."

"Then hurry up and get started," said Quibly, turning away from them and sitting at a table in the corner.

Whelks turned to Keltin and Harper.

"I apologize for our display. This is a small cell, and we've had little contact with the larger groups in the capital. We didn't know anything about the Destovs until they arrived in town under the supervision of a Brother from Kerrtow itself, who left almost immediately after arriving."

"Are the Destovs here in Carris then?" asked Keltin.

"No. With Panz and his officers on high alert, we felt it was better to turn them over to another cell in the country."

"Where?"

"A farm outside of town. I'll give you directions once we're done here. First, however, I wanted to discuss a proposition with you."

Keltin noticed Harper give him a warning glance.

"Mr. Destov didn't mention any additional business

172

between Keltin and the Brothers in his correspondence," he said. "Are you insinuating that your assistance has a hidden cost?"

"I suppose you would prefer we risk exposing ourselves just because you deserve our help," said Kor'sa'vor. "How shameful of us to ask for anything in return."

"Hear us out at least," said Whelks. "I think you can spare us that much. If you don't agree to help us, we'll tell you where the Destovs are and you can be on your way."

Harper didn't seem convinced, but he turned to Keltin.

"This is your endeavor. I'll leave it up to you."

Keltin turned to Whelks.

"We'll listen," he said. "But we won't promise anything beyond that."

"Fair enough. Now, you already know about the closing of the borders, but what you don't know is that the Vaughs are moving a large number of soldiers to the south to bolster the border guards. Among them will be Jolice Freck, a close advisor of Grik Pallow, the new Supreme Minister. Freck will be overseeing the deployment of the troops personally, and will be establishing his headquarters here in Carris."

"That sounds like confidential information," said Harper. "How did you find out about it?"

Whelks gave a sneering smile and jerked his chin towards Quibly in the corner. "We've got a man who works in the MLP office here in town. He had a chance to rifle through Panz's missives."

"You don't have to tell them everything," said Quibly. "What if they're captured?"

"Show some backbone." Whelks turned back to Keltin. "As I was saying, Panz has been especially vigilant in the execution of his duties in anticipation of Freck's arrival. I think that you've seen some of that already in the short time that you've been here."

The brash young face of Lough flashed in Keltin's mind before he could push the thought aside.

"So what does this have to do with us?" he asked.

"It's just you that we're interested in, Mr. Moore. Your abilities as a beast hunter are incredibly valuable. You're skilled at moving stealthily, learning the lay of the land, marksmanship… and beyond that, you've got a clear exit strategy. You can leave the country as soon as it's done."

"As soon as what's done?"

"We want you to kill Freck."

"No."

"There will be little personal risk. We've already—"

"I said no. I'm no assassin. I kill beasts, not people."

"Freck is a beast. You've met Panz already, and Freck is ten times worse. If you knew half of what he's been a party to since the Heterack Empowerment—"

"I don't care. I've told you no. Now tell me where the Destovs are."

Kor'sa'vor spoke up, his voice deceptively calm.

"And what if we decided not to tell you?"

Keltin turned to the Loopi slowly, meeting his dark-eyed gaze steadily.

"You don't want to do that," he said softly.

"Why not? You've already said that you don't kill people. Or do you think 'apes' aren't people?"

Keltin ignored the barb and watched the Loopi coldly. Harper spoke up, addressing his comments to Whelks.

"You said that you'd tell us where the Destovs are once we'd listened to you. Are you going to hold up your end of the bargain, or not?"

Whelks's voice was edged with steel. "I said that we would tell you once you'd heard us out. Which you haven't done. Besides, we don't take well to threats."

"Neither do we," said the newspaperman, "but we're not afraid to make them if we have to."

"And just what sort of threat do you think you can make?" said Whelks. "We're in the position of authority here. You need our information."

"We could turn you in to Panz."

There was a heart-beat's hesitation before Whelks's snide

reply.

"Why should he believe you?"

Harper shrugged. "I doubt Panz would need much of an excuse to make a few more arrests before Freck gets here, especially if it's of three would-be assassins."

"Talk like that won't see you live through the night."

"You didn't bring a beast hunter to this meeting. I did."

"This is getting out of hand!" said Quibly as he jumped up from his chair and rushed in front of Whelks, grabbing the taller man by the lapels. "Whelks, don't make this worse. We have to keep cool heads, remember? Cool heads!"

Whelks muttered something that Keltin couldn't make out as he was keeping his attention on Kor'sa'vor. The Loopi watched Keltin like a card player, not giving anything away, waiting for his opponent to make the first move. Keltin felt his body tense like a wound spring, waiting for the release of violence.

Quibly was right. Things had escalated too quickly. Tension and tempers were getting the best of them. Angry as he was at the actions of the Carris cell of the Brothers, Keltin couldn't let his pride get in the way of helping the Destovs.

He was about to say as much to the Brothers when there was a sudden shudder of rattling wood above them. Whelks and Quibly instantly silenced their whispered argument. The light was doused and they all stood in the darkness, listening. It came again, and there was no mistaking it. Somebody was knocking down the warehouse's front door. A third shuddering strike was followed by a crash and the tread of heavy footfalls above them. The floor creaked and protested as multiple heavy bodies filled the space directly above them. Keltin's hand went for his hand cannon, still loaded with wax rounds. Drawing the oversized revolver, he took a position near the bottom of the stairs.

A muffled voice drifted down to them through the floorboards.

"Area is clear, sir. There's nobody here."

"Search for secret doors." The voice was Panz's. "Nobody

has been observed leaving this building. They're here somewhere."

The sounds of overturned furniture filled the darkness. Keltin could sense rather than hear the others moving around him. He heard a nearby whisper, and felt someone drawing close to his place by the bottom of the stairs. The smell of muskiness suggested Kor'sa'vor, and Keltin moved away to avoid a collision with the Loopi. Suddenly there was a rattling stomp on the hatch door above them.

"Sir! I've found a door."

"Open it up! Pistols at the ready!"

Light spilled down the stairs as the door was flung open, revealing nothing but empty space as everyone had drawn back into the shadows, though Keltin could make out part of Kor'sa'vor's outline from where he stood near the stairs.

"Listen up down there!" called Panz. "We know you're there, and we have every member of the Carris MLP ready for you. Come into the light with your hands up and you'll survive the night. If we have to come down there, not a one of you will live through it."

Nobody moved. Keltin looked up at the floorboards and tried to gauge how many men were actually above them. Judging by the squeaking of the floor it certainly wasn't the entire local MLP force. Less than half a dozen, he estimated. He was debating whether a Reltac spinner could go through the floor and still stop a man without killing him when he heard footsteps on the stairs.

Turning his attention to the pool of light, he saw an officer come racing down the stairs –a nightstick in one hand and a pistol in the other— with another officer close on his heels holding a revolver and a lantern. The first officer was approaching the final steps when a long, hairy arm reached out of the darkness and plucked him like an apple from a tree, yanking him into the shadows. The second officer cried out and fired blindly, swinging his lantern wide to try to light the space around him. Suddenly there was a second gunshot from the darkness and the officer tumbled down the stairs. Whelks leapt into the pool of light provided by the fallen lantern. He took it up along with the man's pistol and rushed the stairs. He raced upward, his gun firing as fast as he could pull the trigger. Keltin heard several thumps of bodies above him joined with screams of pain and animal fear.

Seeing his opportunity, Keltin rushed towards the bottom of the stairs but was knocked aside as a heavy weight fell on him. Kor'sa'vor raced past him as Keltin struggled to free himself from the unexpected burden. He wrestled with the weight, struggling to roll it off of himself as gunshots continued to sound from upstairs. Finally he freed himself and turned over the weight to see that it was Whelks, a bullet hole in his face. Struggling to his feet, Keltin realized that the shooting had stopped. He hurried up the stairs, hand cannon at the ready, but found that the violence was already over with. All of the officers were on the ground silent, with the Loopi standing among them. Kor'sa'vor stood with a pistol looking like a toy in his large hand as blood ran down from a gunshot wound in his other arm. The Loopi was looking down at a prone figure that Keltin recognized as Panz.

Keltin quickly went to the fallen officers to remove their weapons but found that there was no need. Every one of them was dead. Turning one over, Keltin saw the killing shot that had done it. A blast in the top of the head. The man had been killed after he was already down. Looking up at Kor'sa'vor, he saw the Loopi staring at Panz, a slowly bleeding hole in the Prefect's face. The creak of footsteps signaled Quibly and Harper coming up the stairs. Harper was pale, and Quibly was visibly shaking.

"Why… why?" he said, looking at the dead bodies all around them. He stepped up to Kor'sa'vor's side, looking down at Panz.

"What have you done?" he whispered.

The Loopi didn't respond as he bent down and retrieved the guns from the officers, turned, and began to make his way out of the warehouse.

"Where are you going?" demanded Quibly. "You can't

leave me like this!"

Kor'sa'vor paused in the doorway. "Whelks is dead," he said. "The cell is dead. Do what you think best, Quibly."

The Loopi left. Keltin turned to Quibly as the shaking little man looked down at the body of his former employer. The Brother was clearly in shock. Keltin went and stood in front of him, blocking his view of Panz's body.

"Quibly, we can't stay here. We have to leave."

"Dead... they're all dead..."

Harper came to the man's side, his voice soft and gentle.

"Come on, Quibly. I'll help you. You just need to tell Mr. Moore where the Destovs are, and then we can take care of everything. All right?"

"The Destovs?" Quibly seemed far away, his voice traveling a great distance. "You go to the Harstev farm," he said. "It's east of here. Ask for Petrov. Tell him the crows have flown, and you have to make the sign."

"What sign?"

Quibly didn't answer.

"Quibly, what sign?"

"...what?"

"We don't have time for this," said Keltin. "He's told us enough for now. Let's get him out of here."

"You go," said Harper. "I'll get him to safety. You go to the Harstev farm."

"But—"

"Keltin, there isn't time. Someone will have reported those gunshots. Go tell Wendi what's happened then go after the Destovs. They may be in trouble. I'll find Ross, we'll pick up Wendi and Kuff, and follow you as soon as we can."

"I—"

"It's all right. Go!"

Harper turned and began to lead Quibly away via the small side entrance they'd come in through. Keltin hesitated for two heartbeats then turned and left through the front doorway. He was less than a dozen steps down the street when he heard approaching footsteps. Looking up, he saw two MLP officers approaching him, each with nightsticks and revolvers in their hands.

"Stop right there!"

Keltin stood his ground as the two men came to a stop in front of him.

"Put your weapons on the ground!" one of them shouted.

"That will take a moment," Keltin said as calmly as he could.

Keltin gauged the distance between himself and the two officers. Six steps, maybe seven. He could likely clear that distance and strike with the Ripper before one of them was able to fire his pistol, but it would be close, and there was still the second officer to contend with. He also had his hand cannon inside his open coat, hidden for the moment but easy enough to get to. Still, the men already had their revolvers out, and while Keltin was fast, he couldn't draw and shoot twice before they fired. Calculating the risk, he decided on a gamble.

Setting his rifle down on the ground, he stood back up and reached for the Ripper hanging on his shoulder. In a single motion he flung the weapon at the feet of the officers blade first. They both flinched, looking down and jumping back slightly to avoid the savage blades and hooks. It was just a brief moment, but it was all Keltin needed to draw his hand cannon out in rapid time. He didn't hesitate as he fired, blasting a wax round into the center of the first man's chest. The sound of air rushing from his lungs was like a bellows as he reeled backwards onto the ground. The second officer reacted in shock, hesitating for a moment before acting. He took too long. Keltin fired again, this time aiming for the man's elbow. He cried out and stumbled against a nearby lamppost as his gun fell from his limp fingers and clattered on the cobblestones. Keltin quickly retrieved both guns from the fallen officers before grabbing his fallen weapons and racing away. Behind him, he heard cries of alarm and confusion, but he didn't turn back as he raced through the darkened city streets, running with all his remaining strength until the last building was well out of sight.

CHAPTER 17 – SWEET REUNION

Keltin's eyes burned with fatigue as he sat with them shut by the campfire. He'd wanted to press on straight to the Harstev farm, but Wendi had suggested he take a moment to rest and he hadn't argued. He felt her sit next to him and smelled the hot cup of sweet broth in her hands.

"Would you like something to drink?"

"Thank you."

Keltin accepted the steaming mug and inhaled deeply as Wendi sat next to him silently. He'd told her enough of what had happened in the warehouse for her to know that things had gone badly, though he'd kept the details to himself. No need to share those.

Kuff rose from where he'd been drowsing by the campfire and approached him, assaulting him with foul breath and a great, toothy canine grin. Keltin rubbed the hound behind the ears, drained his cup, and stood.

"I need to go," he said. "Stay here until Ross and Harper return."

"All right," said Wendi. "Good luck. Be safe."

"You too."

Keltin tried to think positively as he struck out eastward. He finally knew where Elaine and her family was, and he was on his way. But all he could think about were the horrible sights and sounds of only hours before. His mind went back to the bodies he'd seen. The officers. Panz. Whelks. Strangers and people he'd hardly known, yet their deaths troubled him deeply. Was it his fault? Could he have done anything differently and prevented so much bloodshed? He had no answer, and the question only left him numb. He couldn't even summon enough anger to hate Kor'sa'vor for what he had done. It all just left him feeling sick. Sick, and ready to put it all behind him as quickly as possible.

After more than an hour of walking across country he decided it was safe enough to travel the road moving roughly in an eastward direction. There was little other traffic, and Keltin studied the countryside to try to distract himself from the horrors of the night before. The road was flanked by farmlands on both sides, recently harvested and lying bare in the late autumn air. How tranquil everything seemed in the country, as if the horror and tragedy of the Heterack Empowerment was only a bad dream, and this was the reality. For a brief, terrible moment, Keltin had a flash of the scenery in a very different way. He saw the harvested fields as battlefields, strewn with bodies and soaked with the blood of men who would have rather stayed home than go to war. Shuddering, Keltin forced the thoughts from his mind and kept walking.

It turned out that Quibly had neglected to say just how far from town the Harstev farm was, and it was late in the evening by the time Keltin had reached what a helpful neighbor had assured him was the correct farmhouse. With his travel lantern in hand, he pushed his weary legs up the beaten earth track leading to the home, searching for any sign of habitation. He saw no one outside, but the telltale burning lights inside the home hinted that someone was within. Pausing at the front door, he did his best to steady his heavy breathing and resist the urge to sit in the weathered chair on the front porch. Summoning what strength he had left, he gave a sharp knock on the cracked paint of the front door. No response. Keltin knocked again, and again. Finally, the door was cracked open and a male silhouette peered out at him, his features masked by the light behind him.

"Who are you?" it said. "I don't recognize you. Do you have business here?"

"My name is Keltin Moore, and the crows have flown."

"I don't know what you're talking about, friend."

Suddenly Keltin remembered something through his fog of exhaustion. Quibly had mentioned some sort of signal that was meant to accompany the secret phrase, but the shell-shocked clerk hadn't been able to demonstrate it for him. Keltin's exhaustion was saturated in frustration at the thought of coming this close and being held up by such a trivial detail. A desperate part of him was tempted to muscle his way past the man in the doorway and see if the Destovs were there for himself. Forbearance won out for the moment, and he tried an explanation.

"Listen, things went badly in town. We met with Whelks, Kor'sa'vor and Quibly and they were in the process of telling us where you are when Prefect Panz arrived with his officers. There was shooting, and Whelks died along with Panz and his men. I don't know where Kor'sa'vor is now, but my companion had Quibly in his care while I came here to check on you and the Destovs. Quibly is the one who gave me the key phrase, but he wasn't able to show me the signal that went with it."

The door opened slightly wider.

"Was this Quibly injured?"

"He was in shock, but otherwise fine."

The figure stood silently for a moment, and Keltin felt himself being studied for any sign of duplicity or deception.

"Rot. All right. Come in."

The man opened the door and Keltin gratefully stepped inside. The man shut the door and turned, revealing a face with intelligent eyes and a shock of graying hair with a matching beard.

"Are you Petrov, then?" asked Keltin.

"That's right. I'm sorry to hear about Whelks and the rest, though it's some consolation that that keb Panz is dead."

"There's more that you'll want to know."

Keltin described the events of the night before, detailing the meeting with the members of the Carris cell and the subsequent attack and escape. Petrov took special interest in the troops being sent south under the command of Freck, and asked Keltin for as many details as he could remember. When he had finished, Petrov sighed and shook his head.

"I'm sorry, Mr. Moore. The isolated nature of each cell of our organization ensures greater security for the group as a whole, but at the cost of a lack of central leadership or direction. I never would have tolerated the sort of strong-arm tactics that they tried to use to make you into their personal assassin, and I doubt the Brothers in Kerrtow itself would approve either. Still, the news of Freck and his troops is most troubling."

Petrov stared into space thoughtfully. Keltin blinked his heavy eye-lids, exhaustion and frustration warring within him.

"Are the Destov's here, then?"

"Hmm? Oh, yes. I'm sorry. I'm sure you're eager to see them. I think they may already be asleep, but I can check if you'd like."

"Please."

Petrov led Keltin into a sitting room dominated by a large fire and several overstuffed chairs before disappearing into the dark farmhouse. Keltin looked at one of the overstuffed chairs with longing but resisted the urge to sit. He went to the fire to remove his gloves and warm his hands. Shifting his shoulders, he realized that his befuddled mind had forgotten that he was still wearing his pack and equipment. He had finished laying out his gear by the fireplace and was removing his coat when Petrov returned.

"You said that you had other companions?" he asked.

"Yes, I have three more people traveling with me that should be on their way here. I'm not sure when they will arrive."

Petrov was giving a response when Keltin heard the light tread of swiftly approaching footsteps. He turned. She stood in the entryway, a shawl thrown around her shoulders and a long cotton dressing gown draped over the rest of her figure. Her dark hair was up in a mass of ringlets, framing her pale angelic face and sparkling blue eyes. Keltin looked into her eyes and felt relief and anxiety rush into him. Words flooded his mind, but he couldn't say any of them. He swallowed and took a step towards her, holding his hand out, terrified she wouldn't take it.

"Elaine, I'm sorry it took me so long to get here."

Elaine made a sound somewhere between a sob and a laugh as she threw herself forward, wrapping her arms around his neck and pressing her cheek against his chest.

"Oh Keltin!" she breathed. "You came! I knew you'd come. I knew it!"

She drew a shuddering breath, and Keltin found himself wrapping his arms around her, not daring to speak for fear that the moment might end. Petrov cleared his throat.

"We can discuss our plans in the morning," he said. "In the meantime, feel free to use the divan there for tonight. Goodnight."

Elaine pulled away as Petrov left the room. Her eyes fluttered from his face to the fire then down to his tattered coat.

"What's happened to your coat?" she asked.

"I was on a beast hunt this summer. It didn't go as planned."

Elaine's green eyes showed a sudden flash of concern.

"Were you hurt?" she asked.

"Nothing serious, though I did have to get some stitches in this arm."

Keltin was completely unprepared when Elaine took his arm gingerly and rolled up his sleeve to reveal the scar running along the outside edge of his forearm.

"Someone has done a good job of stitching this," she said quietly.

Keltin nodded, unwilling to pull his arm away from her. "The local doctor had attended university in Maplewood. I was lucky that he was able to get to it before any infection set in."

Elaine nodded, looking up from his arm into his eyes.

"I'm glad you're safe," she said, her sincerity like a blanket wrapping around Keltin's heart.

"And I'm glad that you're safe. Is the rest of your family all right? Are they here?"

"Yes, they're just upstairs. Oh! I should tell them that you're here. I'm sure that my mother and brothers will want to finally meet you. I'll be back."

She hurried away and Keltin listened to her light footsteps as they ascended the stairs and moved across the floorboards above him. He heard soft words being spoken, followed by two sets of steady footsteps as well as a series of bounding thumps that sounded like a pair of whip legs let loose in the upstairs. Something was said in a harsh tone, and soon four sets of footsteps made their way calmly to him as the Destov family entered the room.

Looking at Elaine's mother, it was clear where she had inherited her striking eyes and elegant features. The boys had taken more after their father, with curly dark hair and bright, inquisitive expressions. Mrs. Destov went to Keltin, extending a hand in a gesture that bespoke a lifetime of elegance and poise. Keltin felt like an clumsy oaf taking her hand and wasn't sure what he should do with it, but was relieved when she merely squeezed his fingers tightly between both her hands.

"Mr. Moore, we have prayed for your safety every day since we left Kerrtow. Thank you so much for coming to our aid."

Keltin felt his ears warm slightly. He cleared his throat and nodded.

"Of course. I'm only sorry I didn't get here sooner."

"Please don't trouble yourself over it. I can only imagine what trials you had to overcome to find us." Mrs. Destov sighed, casting a disappointed look at their surroundings. "I must admit, I had hoped that if we ever did meet, it would have been under much better circumstances. I'm afraid we have little means of entertaining you."

"We could teach him to play Swift, mother," said the smaller of the two boys.

"Hush, dear. Mr. Moore isn't interested in card games at a time like this."

Keltin dropped to one knee. Despite his lack of experience with children, he felt a sudden need to make his best effort here. He thought of Jaylocke's ready grin and friendly persona. Trying his best to emulate his friend, he gave the boy a slight smile.

"Perhaps you can teach me later. For now, why don't you tell me which brother you are?"

The boy smiled, showing dimples on his freckled cheeks. "I'm Derrick. I'm nine."

Keltin nodded and looked at the other boy.

"I'm Col." he said. "I'm twelve. Do you really hunt beasts?"

"That's right."

Col's eyes went wide. "Wow. That's so brave. How many beasts have you killed?"

"I haven't really kept track."

"More than a dozen?"

"I'd say so."

"More than a hundred?"

"A thousand?" put in Derrick.

"All right," said Elaine. "Let's give him some time. You'll both get plenty of opportunity to ask him all sorts of questions."

"Oh, I don't mi—"

Keltin was cut off by a sudden, uncontrollable yawn. He blinked owlishly and shook his head.

"Pardon me. I'm sorry."

"You're completely fine," said Mrs. Destov. "Come along, boys. I'm sure Mr. Moore is weary from the road. We can all speak more once he's had a chance to rest. Has Petrov found you a place to sleep?"

"Yes, I'll be down here by the fire."

"Good. Sleep well, Mr. Moore. I look forward to speaking

with you further in the morning."

Mrs. Destov turned and ushered her boys away. Elaine hesitated, giving Keltin a small smile.

"We can speak more in the morning," she said softly.

"All right. Good night."

"Good night, Keltin."

Elaine turned to go, joining her mother where she had lingered at the foot of the stairs to wait for her daughter. The two of them ascended out of sight as Keltin finished clearing off the divan in the sitting room. He undressed for bed by the light of the fireplace before lying down, pulling his tattered coat over him as a makeshift blanket. For a moment, he stared at the ceiling, thinking of the woman only a few feet directly above him. At last, he had found her. Regardless of whatever else may happen, he had found her, and somehow he would figure out a way to protect her and her family and reunite them with their father and husband. With that thought in mind, he allowed his heavy eyes to close, and for the first time in a long while, slipped into a heavy, dreamless slumber.

CHAPTER 18 – BALANCED RISK

Keltin awoke feeling warm and snug, his mind in a pleasant haze of ambiguity as he slowly came back to his senses. He rolled over and realized that he was not covered by his coat. Instead, a heavy quilt had been placed over him. Blinking in confusion, he sat up and looked around for his jacket, but didn't find it among his kit and gear at the foot of the divan. Rising to his feet, he padded across the wooden floors in search of anyone else that had awoken.

Stepping into a small library, he found Elaine, wrapped in a house shawl and still wearing her white cotton nightgown. Across her lap was his coat, her hands skillfully moving a needle and thread between a patch and a large tear. Keltin felt a surge of concern that Elaine had inadvertently found the letter that he had written to her while at the farmhouse in Krendaria. His eyes flew to a nearby table, finding the boxes of bullets and other items that had filled the coat's many pockets, but no envelope. Suddenly he remembered that he had placed the letter along with his other correspondence tucked safely away in the bottom of his pack. His sigh of relief must have been audible as Elaine glanced up with a slight start.

"I'm sorry," said Keltin. "I didn't mean to startle you."

"No, it's all right. I just didn't hear you."

There was a brief, awkward silence. Elaine turned the coat over and pointed out a dark green patch.

"I recognize this one. I did it for you while we were in my uncle's farmhouse."

"Yes. It's stayed on all this time."

Elaine shook her head as she held up the coat. "I'm afraid there's not very much I can do with it now. It's coming all to pieces. It will be more patch than coat soon."

Keltin could only nod as he felt a rush of words come to his mind. Words about all their letters since they'd last seen each other, words about his friends and her family, words about Angela, words about each other... They jumbled and tumbled through him without forming any cohesive phrases he could give voice to. He thought of retrieving his letter from his pack and bringing it to her, but for some reason he hesitated. The time just didn't seem right.

Elaine looked up at him.

"Are you all right?" she asked.

Keltin took a deep breath.

"I just... there is so much I've wanted to say... but now..."

Her answering smile was so gentle and kind that Keltin immediately felt that he didn't deserve it.

"I know. It's all right. There will be time. Do you know if Petrov has started the fire in the kitchen stove yet?"

"I don't know. I'll go check."

"Thank you."

Keltin found the kitchen and its cold, dark stove. Opening the hatch, he cleared a space among the ashes of previous fires, creating a small stack of kindling from the nearby wood box. One match was enough to breathe life into the dry tinder, and Keltin added fuel until he had a healthy blaze developing. Looking back into the wood box, he saw that it was nearly depleted and went outside in search of the wood pile.

The first light of dawn was in the sky as he found the stacked wood under an awning against the side of the farmhouse. Most of the pieces resembled quartered blocks, and were much too large for the kitchen stove. There was a wood ax and wedge lying on top of the stack, so he took it up and pulled out one of the intact rounds to use as a splitting stand. Soon he was lost in a comfortable routine of setting, chopping, stacking, and repeating. Time passed without Keltin noticing it as the morning sun rose, bringing color to his gray surroundings. Soon the cold in his joints had melted away as the heat of honest labor warmed him and brought damp sweat to his brow.

A slice of wood went flying farther than his chipping circle, and Keltin turned to retrieve it. Looking up, he was surprised to find that he had an audience. Col Destov stood under the eve of the house, hugging a coat to himself and watching him silently. Keltin straightened and called to the boy.

"Good morning," he said.

Col gave him a shy smile. "My sister sent me to get more wood for the stove. She says breakfast should be ready soon."

"All right. You can take it from that stack there."

Col gathered an armful of wood that seemed a little too ambitious to Keltin. He wondered if perhaps the boy was trying to impress him and smiled to himself at the thought as he set about finishing the wood he had left to do. Col carried away several more armfuls of wood before returning to continue watching Keltin quietly. Keltin chopped the last piece from the pile and stretched.

"Mr. Moore?"

"Yes?"

"Will you tell us some of the stories of your hunts today? Elaine's told us some of them, but I'm sure that you have many more."

Keltin smiled. "I suppose, though beast hunting isn't all glory and excitement."

"Oh I know. It can be hard and long, sometimes boring and sometimes frightening, even for someone like you. But you do it anyway."

Keltin looked at the youth in surprise.

"Where did you hear that?"

"My sister. She says that it's because you still do what you do even when you're tired or scared or lonely, that that's what makes you a real hero."

"She said that?"

Col nodded. "So, will you tell us some stories?"

"I promise. But first, let's go inside and see what's for breakfast."

The morning meal turned out to be sweet porridge and thick brown bread with marmalade spread. As soon as grace was said and the dishes began to be passed around, Keltin turned to Mrs. Destov.

"I've been wanting to ask how you made your trip here from Kerrtow. Mr. Destov wasn't able to give me many details of your escape plan."

"Have you heard from him recently? Is he all right?" she asked eagerly.

"I received a letter at the end of the harvest season in Krendaria. That's how I knew to come looking for you. He seemed fine, though he was painfully worried about you."

Mrs. Destov shook her head. "Poor Severn. I tried to get word to him that we were going to have to leave the house sooner than we thought, but by then it wasn't safe to send any sort of correspondence, even in code."

"Were you in danger in Kerrtow?"

Mrs. Destov's eyes flickered to her sons before answering. "I think we may have been, if we had stayed any longer than we did. As it was, we had to move fairly quickly once the Brothers came to us. We had intended to take the train, but the stations were too heavily patrolled. The Brothers provided us with a wagonette and driver which we loaded with just our dearest possessions and ourselves. We left all of our remaining goods to the Brothers as compensation, such as it was."

"Do you know if you were followed?"

"No, thankfully we were able to do most of our traveling at night."

"In the dark? That was a serious risk to take, even with a well-kept road."

"Actually, it wasn't as bad as you might think," said Petrov.

"The wagonette was formerly used as a shuttle between the train station in Kerrtow and the finer hotels in the city. Since many of its passengers required transportation after dark, the carriage was already equipped with two large travel lanterns that provided more than enough illumination for the driver to get them here before returning to the capital."

"Do you still have the wagonette here?"

"It's in the barn. We thought it would likely be needed again to make the rest of the journey. Speaking of which, have you considered what route you'll take to get out of Malpin?"

"I'm not familiar with the country in this area. Do you have a suggestion?"

"Perhaps. I'll know better once I get some news on the conditions at the border. I'm still very concerned about these reports of troops making their way south to secure it."

The rest of the meal passed with little conversation. Afterwards, they cleared the table and Petrov left to see to the needs of the farm as Keltin and the Destovs moved to the sitting room. Keltin fed some wood to the fire to ward off the chill then took a seat to find the Destov's all looking at him. Derrick tugged at his mother's sleeve.

"Now?" he pleaded.

Mrs. Destov shushed her son before turning to Keltin.

"Elaine has kept us well informed of your adventures from your letters, Mr. Moore. I'm sure my sons would be very interested to hear anything you might add to the tales, if you are amendable, of course."

"Well, I'm not sure what Elaine has already told you."

"Is it true that you fought a tusked giant all by yourself?" asked Col.

"Well, I did face a tusked giant in the Krendaria campaign, but I wasn't alone. I had plenty of help, including from your sister."

Elaine gave him a small smile. "Why don't you tell us something of your adventures hunting beasts recently? How was Krendaria this year? What sort of beasts did you see?"

Keltin obligingly described several of the beasts that he'd

encountered on Mr. Whitt's landholdings. The boys sat on the edge of their seats with wide eyes, eagerly devouring every detail of the stork-legged beast, whip leg, and armored leech. As he spoke, Keltin glanced at Elaine to see her smiling warmly at him and her siblings. He smiled back, and launched into a lengthy description of Lost Trap and the legendary Ghost that had plagued the prospectors along the Wylow river.

He was just getting to the final hunt for the monster when there was a sudden sharp knock on the front door. Everyone froze. Another knock sounded. Keltin rose slowly and went to his gear lying where he'd left it in the corner. Retrieving his hand cannon, he gave the Destovs a reassuring look before making his way to the door. As he prepared to open it, he heard a soft step behind him. Turning, he saw Elaine standing behind him with his hunting rifle in her hands. She nodded to him and he nodded back before turning to the door and opening it a crack, keeping his hand cannon out of sight. He took one look outside and then threw the door open with relief at the sight of Harper and the rest of his friends along with Quibly of the Brothers of Kerrtow.

"It's good to see you all safe," said Keltin. "I wasn't sure when to expect you."

"It took a little time to find Ross," said Harper. "You won't believe the dive he had ended up in."

"Is Petrov here?" asked Quibly.

"I think he's out in the fields," said Keltin.

"We need to find him. There's news that he needs to hear."

Soon all of the adults were sitting around the dining room table while the boys and Wendi played Swift in the sitting room. Quibly took a long drink of spirits that Petrov had provided for him and ran a shaking hand over his eyes.

"This is all like a bad dream," he muttered to himself. "Freck arrived in Carris just yesterday with his troops."

"I didn't think he was that close, based on what you said at the warehouse," said Keltin.

"Our information was incomplete. He was a full two days ahead of what we expected."

Quibly's head sank to his hands. Harper spoke up.

"There's more, I'm afraid. There was an assassination attempt on Freck's life soon after he arrived."

Keltin felt his stomach clench.

"Kor'sa'vor?"

"Yes. The Loopi fired from an upstairs window as the troops were parading down the street. They swarmed the building in seconds, but he'd already taken his own life by the time they reached him."

"Was Freck hit?" asked Petrov.

"He was, but not badly. He'll survive."

Petrov shook his head. "This couldn't have gone worse. Freck will take his revenge on the whole territory, and the propagandists will have a field day with the shooter being a Loopi."

There was a long silence. Keltin thought of the impulsive Loopi and his fiery eyes filled with life and anger. For a brief, fleeting moment he wondered if he shared some responsibility for the terrible turn of events for the people of Carris and the surrounding territory. If he had taken the task that Whelks and the others had asked of him…

No. Even if Freck were dead, someone else would have taken his place. Keltin was not responsible for the actions of Kor'sa'vor or the consequences that would follow. For better or worse, Keltin's time in Malpin had come to a close. All he could do now was focus on getting himself, the Destovs, and his friends out of the country before anything else happened. With that in mind, he turned to Harper.

"What about the troops? Have they been deployed yet?"

"I'm afraid so. Freck is convinced that there are more would-be assassins that are fleeing south to Krendaria. He had the soldiers force-marching through the night to the border. Even if we left now, they'd already be in place. It looks like the door behind us just got closed and locked."

"They can't cover all of the border at once." Keltin turned to Petrov. "Is there anywhere that the military hasn't been deployed to, or at least, hasn't established itself yet?"

Petrov shrugged. "I suppose there's the stretch running through Pike Forest, but that place is more dangerous than anywhere else."

"Why?"

"Pike Forest runs between south-eastern Malpin and north-eastern Krendaria. The Bent Knee River doesn't mark the border there, so it's always been a point of contention since the Three Forest War and the redrawing of the Malpin border. Whether out of a desire to make use of the area or out of simple spite, Malpin has used that forest as a breeding ground for more than a generation now."

"What do they breed there?"

"Sleevaks."

Harper shot Keltin a worried look. Keltin saw him but kept his focus on the table in front of him as he considered their options. If they went any other way, he'd have to deal with well-armed soldiers. Of course, some would say that a feral sleevak was worse than a man with a rifle, but Keltin saw the beasts as just another monstrous creature, one he had killed more than once in his life. Besides which, he had no compunctions about killing the boils, as opposed to soldiers who, for all he knew, were simply following the orders of a government that they resented but were otherwise unable to do anything about.

On the other hand, he had the Destovs to consider. While he knew that he could rely on Elaine to be a cool head and a steady aim, there was her mother and the two boys to consider. There was no telling how many sleevaks were in Pike Forest. Could he keep all of them away from those under his protection? Then again, he wasn't the only capable one in the group. Besides Elaine, there was Ross and Kuff, along with Wendi and Harper. Between them all, they could travel with some degree of boldness during the day and keep two-man watches in the night.

Keltin looked up to see all faces turned to him, waiting for his word. He turned to Petrov.

"How large is Pike Forest?"

"It would probably take you two-to three days traveling with the carriage to get to the border, if you knew the way."

Keltin nodded. "Then I think we should go that way."

"I don't think that's wise. I know that you have a moral objection to the possibility of taking human life, Mr. Moore, but that's not good enough to risk everyone's life in the breeding grounds of those monsters."

"Ross and I were both on the Krendarian campaign. We know how to travel through a forest full of beasts. And Harper, Wendi, and Elaine all have experience with beasts as well. If we travel quickly and carefully, we should be able to get through safely."

"I still don't think it's a good idea," said Petrov.

"Well, it's not my decision alone to make."

Keltin turned to Ross. The Krendarian hunter blew out his cheeks before answering.

"Well, Kuff has never faced a sleevak before, but Captain Tallow always used to say that a good hound can bring down any pair of those brainless boils. At any rate, he'd have a better chance against those monsters than a patrol of armed soldiers. I vote for Pike Forest."

"I can respect that," said Harper, "But I'm inclined to side with Petrov on this one. He has the connections and the network to potentially make our crossing at a military-controlled border much safer. I vote we try crossing somewhere else."

Keltin turned to Elaine and her mother. Mrs. Destov sighed and shook her head.

"This has all been so difficult. I know that each of you would do anything to help my family, and I am eternally grateful. But I fear that I have no experience in these matters, and would only complicate things by trying to guess at what decision would be best." She reached out and took the hand of her daughter sitting next to her, smiling sadly at Elaine as she continued. "My daughter has been such a strength to me since we left home. I trust her judgement, and will defer my vote to her."

Elaine squeezed her mother's hand before turning to the group. She met Petrov's eyes first. "Like my mother, I could never fully express my gratitude for your generosity and assistance since we arrived here." She then turned to Ross. "I don't know you sir, but I have known several other veterans of the Krendarian campaign, and I am convinced that only the very best of your profession would have survived those horrors. I thank you for your insightful input, just as I thank you for yours," she said, directing the latter statement to Harper.

Elaine then turned her brilliant eyes to Keltin. As she spoke, her words were loud enough for all to hear, but her whole being seemed focused solely on him.

"Keltin, you are the reason that I am here. Without you, I would have been lost in my uncle's farm just a year ago. And now, you've come here, ready to do whatever must be done to see my family reunited in a safe land. I believe with all my heart that you would sacrifice anything to see that happen. I know you would."

Keltin couldn't speak. His throat was tight. He swallowed and could only nod, slowly. Elaine continued, her eyes sparkling.

"Keltin, you know my heart. I have faith in you. I will follow you wherever you lead for as long as you will let me."

Keltin felt his heart pounding in his chest. He glanced at Mrs. Destov to find her still holding Elaine's hand with a proud smile directed to her daughter. Keltin took a deep breath and forced himself to acknowledge the rest of those gathered around the table.

"It's settled then," he said. "We will go through Pike Forest."

Petrov sighed. "Well, if you insist on going, I can at least write you a letter of introduction to our Brother in Velef. It's a small village just north of Pike Forest that caters to the sleevak breeders. He should be able to tell you the best route through the forest to the border."

"That's very courteous of you," said Mrs. Destov. "Thank

you."

"I wish I could do more for you, but circumstances are becoming more complicated all the time, and will likely only get worse. I suggest you leave soon. It's a few days' journey to Velef, even with the wagonette."

"I fear that it won't be large enough to carry all of us," said Mrs. Destov.

"Those of us who are able will take turns walking and driving," said Keltin. "It won't be very quick traveling, but with the wagonette's lanterns we should be able to do most of our traveling on the road after dark. Petrov, are we likely to run into any other traffic on the main roads in that direction?"

"I doubt it, aside from the odd parcel coach, you should be able to make the journey without meeting anyone as long as you hide during the day."

"Then I suggest we plan on leaving tonight after dark. Are we agreed?" He was met by a series of nods. "All right. In that case, we should all try to get some rest. It's going to be a long night."

Keltin was just getting up from the table to follow Elaine into the sitting room when Petrov pulled him aside.

"May I have a word in private, Mr. Moore?"

"Of course. What's the matter?"

"Come with me."

Petrov led Keltin up the stairs to the farmhouse's second floor. He walked to the end of the hallway and stopped in front of a closed bedroom door. Removing a key from his pocket, he unlocked the door and opened it, gesturing inside. Keltin was about to step inside before he realized that there was no room to stand. Every inch of floor-space was occupied with stacks of crates, packages, and boxes. Among the containers were a variety of other items, all of them exotic and fantastic. Keltin realized that he was looking at a treasure trove of art. He struggled to take in all that he saw. Canvases covered in glorious colors stood stacked together between great sculptures of wood, metal and stone, while every flat surface seemed covered with elegant, meticulously shaped figurines and jewelry. Turning to Petrov, he found the Brother of Kerrtow watching him carefully.

"I'm not sure how much you know about the Brothers of Kerrtow, Mr. Moore. Perhaps it's best that you know as little as possible, though I think the danger of you being apprehended by the government is fairly low now that you're going to Pike Forest. But this much I will tell you. We're in the business of rescuing more than people from this country. It is our solemn duty to preserve and protect the heritage of our Loopi neighbors and ancestors that the Vaughs would rather see silenced. This is one of many temporary safe-houses for some of these precious relics rescued from the museums and personal collections of our oppressors."

"Are you saying that you stole these?"

"Liberated. The original owners were driven from their homes and possessions. We may not be able to return everything to its rightful owners, but we can at least deny some of these treasures from those who took them."

"I see. I suppose I never really thought about preserving art at a time like this."

"Art is the embodiment of a culture's soul, Mr. Moore. Take it away, and the Vaughs will have destroyed more than the Loopi's way of life. They will have destroyed their heritage.

"I know that there's limited space in the wagonette, but I was hoping that you would take at least a small portion of this collection with you. We have contacts in Carvalen who can take the items off your hands, and you'll likely pass through the capital anyway on your way to Riltvin. I won't force you to do it, but even if you don't care about our cause, it would be a nice gesture of gratitude for what we've tried to do to help you and the Destovs."

"We'll take what we can spare the space for," said Keltin.

"Thank you. We'll have the pieces ready by the time you leave tonight."

"Just make sure you pack them securely. I suspect they're going to have a rough journey before this is all through."

CHAPTER 19 – ON THE RUN

Keltin suppressed a yawn and blinked rapidly to keep a clear picture of the road before him. He had never been more than an average driver, finding little need to handle horses in the heavily wooded hill country of Riltvin. His was hampered further by the darkness all around him, though he was grateful for the foresight of the Brothers in procuring a carriage with lights. The two massive, oil-fed lanterns contained brilliant reflectors that shone their light ahead onto the road directly in front of the pair of horses before him. It was slower going than driving during the day, but at least they had the road entirely to themselves.

"Keltin?"

He roused himself from his stupor of driving to look down at the dark silhouette walking alongside the wagonette that spoke with Harper's voice.

"I think it's my turn to drive."

"All right."

Keltin dropped down to the ground as the newspaperman took his place. He fell into step beside the coach, keeping his eyes on the road ahead to avoid tripping in the dark.

"Are you all right?"

Keltin was too weary to react with more than mild surprise

to hear Elaine's voice next to him in the darkness.

"I'm fine. How are you? Do you need to take a turn riding in the back with your mother and brothers?"

"I'm all right. I bought a pair of men's shoes before leaving Kerrtow. They're more comfortable than any of my own. How much longer do you think it will be before dawn?"

"A few hours. We'll find somewhere well off the road to make camp once there's some light."

Elaine was silent. Keltin wondered if perhaps she was nodding, or simply too tired to respond. They plodded along in silence for a time until she spoke again.

"I neglected to ask you how your beast hunting company is doing."

"Fairly well, so far. Jaylocke and Bor've'tai are managing it right now."

"You're getting a lot of business then?"

"A fair amount. Sometimes I think I used to get more work when I went off in search of bounties by hunting down rumors and stories of beasts, but maybe that's just the result of spending so much time traveling from one place to another that it felt like I was working more. There's a lot more sitting around with a home office."

"Well, it's been several months since you opened the office. Have you tracked your average income since starting the company and compared it to when you were out actively searching for bounties?"

"Not really, I've never been much of a record keeper."

"Mmm."

Keltin heard Elaine lose her footing slightly and immediately reached out into the darkness to steady her. One of his hands inadvertently touched her side, giving him a temporary thrill that drove away all of his fatigue. Her gloved hand took his and gave it a squeeze.

"Thank you." She released his hand and began speaking again. "Have you considered keeping someone out of the office to search for work while someone else stays at home to handle any jobs that come to you?"

"We're trying to. Jaylocke and Bor've'tai were off on a job while I stayed in the office until your father approached me about coming here."

"So Jaylocke and Bor've'tai are watching the office now?"

"I suppose so, unless they're on another job. I haven't heard from them in a while."

"Then perhaps you should consider having someone who isn't one of your hunters working in the office. That way you could have all of your hunters out hunting or searching for work without sacrificing any potential jobs that come to you."

Keltin shook his head. "I can't see the sense of hiring an employee just to sit around and wait in case a customer comes by."

"Perhaps you don't need them full-time, but it seems to me that you lose the benefit of having an office if there isn't someone there a few times a week for potential customers to come and speak with. Besides, you wouldn't have to pay someone just to sit around and wait. They could spend their time doing things like balancing the books, searching newspapers for work, or handling correspondence for the business and placing advertisements. Have you ever considered writing letters to past customers to thank them for their business?"

"I... no, I hadn't. I hadn't considered much of any of this. I suppose I don't have a head for business."

"Don't say that. You've managed to support yourself and still send help to your family for years. I only asked about those things because they were the sort of things that my father would talk about with the companies that he worked for as a solicitor. I was always fascinated by the workings of business. Come to think of it, I'm sure that he'd be willing to advise you when we get back to Riltvin, if you asked him."

"Perhaps. Or maybe I'll just ask his daughter."

Elaine didn't reply, but Keltin swore that if he could ever have felt someone smile without actually seeing it, then he certainly would have at that moment.

False dawn came steadily upon them. Inky blackness gave

way to the dim outline of blue-tinged farmlands around them. Once he could make out the outline of his hand against the ground, Keltin put out the call for everyone to start looking for a likely place to lay low during the day. They found an apple orchard that had already been picked clean of the year's harvest and showed more leaves on the ground than on its branches. Still, the neat rows and columns were dense enough to keep the wagonette out of sight of the road or any nearby farmhouses.

Finding a suitable place to make camp, Keltin helped Mrs. Destov and her sons out of the carriage, pausing for a moment to crouch down and check the long, thin wooden crate that had been stowed underneath the driver's seat of the wagonette. Petrov had said that it contained several paintings, some hardy metal figurines, and an ancient, ceremonial costume worn by a Sky Talker more than six centuries ago. Finding the precious cargo still safely secured, he stepped aside to allow the Destovs to climb under the cover of the wagonette to make their makeshift bed. Turning and making sure all was in order, he placed Ross and Kuff on the first watch and crawled into his own tent, trying to will his tired body into relaxation.

He woke without realizing that he'd been sleeping. He debated trying to go back to sleep, but was roused by the smell of salt pork cooking. Crawling from his tent, he found Wendi sitting by a fire with a large pan of the crackling strips of meat. Once the pork was crisp, she poured in some water and added dried beans and a few sprigs of cuth spice, mixing it all together into a stew that immediately made Keltin's mouth water. Retrieving his battered kettle, he settled in across from her, filling the kettle with water from their supply and setting it by the fire to heat.

"You still aren't much of a sleeper, are you?"

Keltin looked up to see Elaine rubbing her eyes and taking a seat next to Wendi. Keltin shrugged.

"I suppose not. Too many nights spent alone hunting. It takes quite a lot to get me to have a fair night's sleep."

Once he judged the water to be hot enough, Keltin flipped

up the top and poured in a small portion of the contents from a fabric bag in his pocket.

"What's that?" asked Elaine.

"Sweet broth. I got a taste for it in Lost Trap. It warms you on the inside and is more pleasant than just heated water."

Elaine nodded and turned her attention to Wendi as she sliced some small potatoes into the salt pork-and-bean stew.

"That smells positively intoxicating, Wendi."

The farm-girl blushed. "It was a favorite of my father's. He called it throw-together stew. It was one of the first things I learned to cook."

"Do you enjoy cooking?"

Wendi nodded. "It reminds me of my mother. She was always cooking. I learned all I could from her. I… still miss her sometimes."

"I'm sure she'd be very proud of how well you learned your lessons from her," said Mrs. Destov as she joined them. "This does smell wonderful, dear."

"Thank you, Ma'am. It's nearly ready."

Soon Wendi was scooping out generous portions of the stew into everyone's dishes. Keltin took his travel kettle from the fire and poured himself a cup of steaming broth.

"May I have some?" asked Elaine.

Keltin obligingly took her cup and poured for her. She cradled the broth between her hands and inhaled the steam for a moment before taking a sip and humming deep contentment.

"Mmm, that is good."

Keltin smiled, feeling a warmth that came from more than the broth and stew. Despite all their current hardships and what was still likely to come upon their journey, for the moment, sitting together by the campfire, it seemed that everyone was content, if not outright happy. Keltin finished his meal and scraped his pan clean before crawling back into his tent in another attempt to get some sleep, trying to focus on the good feelings of the moment and put from his mind what may yet be ahead of them.

* * *

Velef was little more than a village on the northern edge of Pike Forest. Seeing it from afar, Keltin immediately realized that their company would draw far too much attention in the small hamlet and decided that he and Harper would go on ahead to try to find Petrov's contact. Following the directions the Brother of Kerrtow had given them, they easily smelled the man's home long before they reaching it. Topping a rise, they saw the small hut completely surrounded by pig pens, each one stocked with the loud, smelly animals.

"Well, I'll say one thing about this fellow," said Harper as they made their way down a narrow track between two fences through the churned up mud. "He keeps a low profile."

"Just so long as he can help us."

Keltin spied a large man with a shock of greasy hair that may have been blond when it was clean. The man was carrying two slop buckets that had likely never been rinsed out since they had been made. Despite the man's soiled coveralls, Keltin could discern a powerful, barrel chested frame underneath the rough, dirty clothing. The man emptied the two pails into a pair of troughs before looking up and spying Keltin and Harper approaching. He paused, watching them approach with a laconic, almost lethargic bearing.

"Are you Wulp?" Keltin asked when he had gotten within earshot.

"That's right," said the man, his voice slightly slurry. "You in the market for sleevak bait? You don't seem the type. Maybe you want something to be eating yourself?"

"Maybe, but the crows have flown, and there are more important things to worry about first."

Keltin held out Petrov's letter. Wulp wiped his hands on his coveralls and took it. He read slowly, his bottom lip twitching as his eyes crawled slowly across the page. He looked up after a moment.

"So Petrov says I'm supposed to help you. What do you need? I could hide you here for a time if you want."

Keltin had a brief image of Mrs. Destov hiding amongst Wulp's hogs and shook his head.

"Thank you, but we're trying to get out of the country as quickly as possible. Petrov mentioned that you know a way through Pike Forest to the border."

Wulp shrugged. "That I do. There's a cart-trail that goes through the whole forest, but you wouldn't want to use that. Pike Forest has been set aside for sleevak breeding. Nobody goes in there but handlers and them that serve them."

"We'll manage. We've got two beast hunters among us."

Wulp snorted. "They'd better be plaguing good to trust your life to them."

"They are," put in Harper. "Keltin here is one of them."

"That so?" Wulp considered Keltin for a long moment before slowly nodding. "Maybe. Maybe you'll make it. If you're careful and quiet. And go quickly. Most of you may make it through."

"Anything you can tell us would be appreciated," said Keltin. "What are the sleevaks' habits? Are they naturally occurring here? I always thought that they were native to bogs and fens, not deep forest."

"They are. We still get the occasional feral from the Rumpton Fens up north. But they breed faster down here. Easier conditions, less competition."

"What about the seasonal migration of beasts from Malpin to Krendaria? Does that affect your sleevaks here?"

Wulp gave a gap-toothed grin. "Even migrating beasts circle Pike Forest. Only men and Heteracks are fool enough to go into the sleevaks' home. As to their habits, they hunt and move in packs. We breed them that way. If one of the matriarchs starts getting too big, we cull her. Sleevaks need to learn that the handlers are the ones in charge."

"How big are the packs?"

"Seven or eight head. Much more than that, and they can't hunt enough to keep them all fed." Wulp got a thoughtful expression as he rubbed his palm against a month's worth of stubble on his chin. "How many did you say were traveling with you?"

"I didn't say. Better you only know as much as you need to, right?"

Wulp shrugged. "I suppose so, though I'm a loyal Brother. I don't squeal. Well then, I suppose you're traveling on foot?"

"Most of us are, but we've got a wagonette as well."

"You'll have to use the cart-trail then. I can lead you to the head of it, if you prefer."

"Can you give us directions for once we're on the trail? I imagine it winds around a fair bit through the forest."

"It's a twisting road for certain, but traveling it is simple enough. It's like a great tattered feather, one central vein with lesser strands going off to the left or right. But if you always choose the south-bound track, you'll eventually come to a stop right at the boundary fence."

"Fence? We knew that the Malpinion army had been deployed to the border, but we hadn't heard anything about a fence being built."

"The fence south of Pike Forest is an old one, built back when it was first decided that it would be used for breeding sleevaks. Krendaria and Malpin actually built it together, if you can believe it. I think Malpin didn't want Krendaria stealing our sleevaks, and Krendaria didn't want them wandering down and killing their livestock."

"Will it take much work to get through the fence?"

Wulp shrugged. "It was built to keep sleevaks in, not people. A good pair of cutters should open it up. I'll give you a pair if you'll take a spool of wire and promise to close it back up again behind you. You might be able to cut and run, but I've got a living to make."

"That's fine. I wouldn't wish those hexed monsters on anyone south of the fence."

"In that case, I suppose that's all I can do for you. Unless you need some supplies. I don't have much, but I could give you some meat. You want some pork?"

Harper made a face. "It's not the same stuff that you feed the sleevaks, is it?"

"And why not?" said Wulp, his face screwing up in an indignant scowl. "My hogs are strong and healthy, and if you're worried about them being unclean, well, you're eating the inside, not the outside, aren't you?"

Keltin noticed Harper looking a little green as he glanced at a nearby hog rolling in a thick mixture of mud and defecation. Keltin turned back to Wulp with a pleasant smile.

"That makes perfect sense to me. Why don't I send my friend into the village to buy some supplies and I'll stay here and help you butcher one of your hogs."

"Alright."

Wulp gave Harper one last dirty look then turned and walked away. Keltin spoke softly to the newspaperman.

"You go on ahead. I'll stay here and make sure our meat is kept clean."

Harper gave Keltin a relieved look. "Thank you, though that fellow seems awfully stubborn. What if he insists that something is fit for humans when it really isn't?"

Keltin shrugged. "We'll take it anyway. It'd be bad manners to refuse, wouldn't it? Besides, if we don't like it, we can always feed it to the sleevaks."

"That's not very reassuring," said the newspaperman as he turned and began threading his way back out of the muck and mud.

CHAPTER 20 – PIKE FOREST

Keltin looked over his shoulder as the last sign of Velef disappeared behind the densely growing trees. Turning, he focused on the trail through the forest. It was fairly well-kept, with the clear marks of recent traffic from wide-wheeled wagons. Keltin was grateful that the wagonette seemed to be able to handle the trail well, though he didn't like the idea of other traffic keeping it well-maintained. Still, Wulp had assured him that nobody would be using it for at least a few days, and that they would be long gone before anyone encountered them, if all went according to plan.

Soon they reached a tall, blade-wire fence that stretched across the trail and disappeared into the dark woods to either side of them. Keltin called a halt.

"What is it?" asked Harper from the driver's seat of the wagonette. "Did you see something?"

"No, but I think we should all know just what to expect from here on in."

"Can't this wait until we're safely camped for the night?" asked Mrs. Destov. "I don't like us speaking out here in the open."

"There's no-one else here," Keltin explained. "Besides, once we pass this fence, there won't be any place to camp safely until we're through to the other side."

"How should we proceed, Keltin?" asked Elaine.

"Well, the horses should be able to travel for several hours at a time with short rests. If we push them hard, Wulp said that we should be able to pass through Pike Forest in about two days. In that time, I'm certain we'll encounter sleevaks. There will be no avoiding them and everyone will need to do all that they can to help keep each other safe."

He went to his pack and withdrew the pair of pistols that he'd taken from the MLP officers he'd faced in Carris.

"Now, for arms, I have my rifle and hand-cannon, Harper has a rifle, Ross has his scattergun, and we have these two pistols. We should have plenty of ammunition for the rifles, scattergun, and hand cannon, but these have just six shots a piece, once those are out, they're done. Beyond that, we have Kuff of course, as well as the Ripper and a pair of hunting knives. I say we start by giving the two pistols to Wendi and Elaine, then we can redistribute weapons as needed as we move on."

"What about me?" said Col. "I can help!"

"Hush," said Mrs. Destov. "Mr. Moore is not playing. This is very serious."

"But I want to help. How will I protect everyone without a weapon?"

Keltin looked at Col. The boy was close to the same age that Keltin had been when he had first accompanied his father on a beast hunt. Looking into young eyes full of determination, Keltin quickly made a decision.

"Come here, Col." Keltin unbuckled his belt and slid his sheathed Lawrie hunting knife free. He handed it to the boy. "Take this so that you can protect your mother and brother."

Col took the knife with a small frown. "I had hoped to get a gun."

Keltin chuckled softly. "Maybe one day. But first, you need to learn to respect and use that knife. Remember, it could save your life, so take care of it. All right?"

Col pulled the knife free to examine its long, razor edge for a moment. He slipped it back into the sheath and gave Keltin a somber nod. "All right. I will."

"Good." Keltin turned back to the group. "We'll keep a double watch whenever we stop to rest. If you need to speak, do it quietly. If you see a sleevak, let Ross or I know. Do not fire on it unless it's attacking. Does everyone understand?" He was met with solemn silence. "All right. I suggest everyone check their gear and ready themselves before we continue."

As the rest of the company made their final preparations, Keltin made his way a short distance from the group. Sinking to his knees, he took a deep breath and said a silent prayer. He expressed gratitude that they had made it this far, and asked for safety as they continued. He was considering what more he might say when he heard a rustle of fallen autumn leaves. Keltin's eyes snapped opened as he reached for the hand-cannon at his hip. He had the large pistol half-drawn before he realized that it was somebody approaching him, not something.

"Keltin?"

It was Elaine.

"Yes? Is something wrong?"

"No, I just… I just thought that I might join you."

"Oh… yes, all right. If you want to."

Elaine knelt down next to him. Keltin hesitated for a moment. He'd gotten very used to offering his prayers in silence, even when Jaylocke was around, out of respect for their differing faiths. He cleared his throat and began again, this time out loud.

"Dear Father in Heaven, I'm grateful that we've gotten this far. We shouldn't have to worry about the Malpinion government from here on. But I'm worried. There's only a few of us that have experience with beasts, and I don't know if we'll be able to protect everyone. Please help me. What should I do? How can I keep everyone safe?"

Keltin hesitated, trying to think of something more to say. After a moment, he gave up and closed his prayer. He was about to rise up off the ground when Elaine suddenly began praying, her voice soft and clear in the darkness.

"Dear Lord of All, I ask for a special blessing upon Keltin. He bears a heavy burden as he cares for the rest of us. Please comfort him. We need him. Give him the guidance that he needs to keep himself and the rest of us safe. Help those of us that he is protecting to be strong and obedient to whatever he counsels. Amen."

Keltin opened his eyes and looked at Elaine. She gave him a gentle smile as she reached out and took his hand.

"We're ready now," she said.

"I hope so," said Keltin as they stood and returned to the others hand-in-hand.

She gave his hand a final squeeze before leaving his side to join her family on the wagonette. Once everyone seemed prepared, Keltin stepped up to the blade-wire fence, peering through the sharpened metal to look for any sign of a sleevak. Seeing none, he reached into his pocket and withdrew the key that Wulp had loaned him. The padlock was large but simple, and popped open easily as Keltin turned the key. He pulled the gate open to allow Harper to drive the wagonette through. Waiting for the last of their company to pass by, Keltin then locked the gate again and hid the key at the base of the fence. Turning, he pulled his rifle off his shoulder, took his position at the front of the group, and proceeded to lead them into the forest.

It started to rain less than an hour's journey through the forest. Raindrops fell gently though the trees as they reached to the sky with bare branches. Keltin was grateful as the rainwater soaked the carpet of leaves underfoot. The wet leaves made less noise than dry ones would have as they traveled, and while it would have been easiest to see the trail if it were completely clear, the well-worn ruts became more pronounced as the leaves grew heavy and wet, filling in the deep tracks of wagon wheels and churned earth from mules and horses.

Unfortunately, the constant pattering of the rain mixed with the groaning of the wagonette wheels and the creaking of the harnesses made it almost impossible to try listening for any sign of sleevaks nearby. Instead, Keltin scanned the forest for any sign of movement. His eyes darted from tree to tree, searching every bush and thicket for the telltale sign of the beasts. The task became harder as a gentle breeze began to pick up, stirring the bare branches and causing a hundred false alarms within Keltin's mind. The gentle breeze had turned into a series of gusts by the time they had stopped for a mid-morning rest. Ross pulled Keltin aside to whisper softly to him as the others shared cold roast pork and travel bread.

"If this wind gets much worse, it may start bringing down some branches."

"I know," said Keltin. "We're going to have to keep a careful watch on the trail for anything that comes down in our way."

Ross nodded, his eyes scanning the surrounding trees.

"I haven't seen any sign of the boils yet. Have you?"

"Not yet. Has Kuff caught a scent?"

"He's acting like it, but I can't get him to give me a direction."

"Well, keep an eye out. Those things are definitely out there."

The first attack came less than an hour later. They had just begun to press on when Wendi suddenly cried out.

"Over there!"

Keltin spun around, trying to find Wendi to see where she was pointing even as the rest of the group began shouting and pointing in various directions. It took a moment for Keltin to realize that something was coming from the forest on the other side of the wagonette. Cursing under his breath, he began racing around to get a clear view of what was going on. Through the corner of his eye, Keltin saw Harper jump to his feet in the back of the wagonette and fire into the forest with his long rifle. The newspaperman fired again and again, as all the while Keltin felt as if his pumping legs were pushing through molasses.

Finally rounding the wagonette, he pulled his rifle into his shoulder and examined the scene before him. It was a single sleevak, looking much the worse-for-wear. Blood poured from two fresh bullet holes in its flanks as it stumbled forward, one of its stubby legs dragging along with a nasty looking injury just above the knee joint. Its staggering, stumbling gait made an aimed shot easier than it otherwise would have been, and Keltin sent a Reltac Spinner through the back of the beast's skull and onward into the forest behind it. The beast shuddered to a halt. Keltin hoisted himself up onto the bed of the wagonette to spin around and check for any other sign of movement, but the forest was still.

"Looks like it was just the one," said Harper at his side.

"It seems that way, but keep an eye out. I'm going to take a closer look at this one."

The sleevak lay twitching on the ground as Keltin approached it. He could clearly see that several of the beast's injuries were days old, and had likely been inflicted by others of its kind. Ross came up to Keltin's side and looked down at the carcass before them.

"Looks like a pariah that got driven from a group," he muttered. "Could be a female that wanted to take over the matriarchy and was cast out."

"Maybe. This could also be the old matriarch that was cast out. Some of these other scars are old."

Ross shook his head and spat. "I wish we knew more about how these things act in the wild. It could have made this trip much easier."

"You're right, but it doesn't do us any good now. We've got just two days left, and then we'll be out of here. We just have to keep our heads until then."

* * *

Dusk was beginning to fall when Keltin noticed Wendi stumble a third time as she walked along in front of the wagonette. Reluctantly, he called a halt and suggested that they make camp for the night. As he pulled his pack off his back and unlashed his tent and bedroll, he allowed himself a cautiously optimistic outlook on their journey thus far. The lone sleevak attack had been the only sighting for the day. There had been multiple false alarms, and Ross insisted that Kuff was acting like something was still close by. Still, while Keltin would certainly continue to be cautious, he'd learned long ago the dangers of becoming too tense on a hunt. Jumping at shadows was the realm of prey animals, and it was very important to remember and project to both his companions and the lurking beasts that he was not prey.

As they sat around the cooking fire waiting for their evening meal, Keltin took the opportunity to study the faces of his companions. Ross' expression was calm but alert, while Kuff lay by his side in what would have seemed a composed, relaxed posture except for the rapid breathing that belied his heightened attention to their surroundings. Harper was somber, staring moodily into the fire, while Wendi showed clear signs of fatigue as she stirred the pot in the cooking pit by the fire. Keltin made a mental note to suggest she take another turn on the wagonette as either a driver or passenger once they headed out again in the morning.

Turning to the Destovs, he was impressed by their stoic strength despite their hardships. Mrs. Destov held Derrick close to her, while Col sat just far enough away from his mother to feel independent as he studied the leather laces of the sheath covering Keltin's Lawrie hunting knife. Turning his gaze to Elaine, Keltin found that she was looking back at him. She gave him a slight smile, and he returned it. In her eyes he saw the same determination that had kept her alive for all those weeks in a farmhouse surrounded by beasts. Keltin looked into those eyes and realized that of all those gathered around him, it was she that he felt he could rely on the most, and while he never would have wished her to be in their current predicament, he was grateful that she was with him.

With that in mind, he addressed the group in a voice just loud enough to be heard as they began eating, outlining his plan for the night's watches. He and Harper would take the first and most difficult shift, followed by Wendi and Kuff taking the relatively easiest turn in the middle. The third and final watch would be handled by Ross and Elaine, the two members of the company that Keltin had the most confidence in.

After supper, Keltin went to the wagonette and removed the reflectors from the two large lanterns, bathing the area in a pale, yellow light. Harper took his position by the campfire to keep it going while Keltin climbed up into the driver's seat to have the highest vantage point possible. Turning, he watched as Elaine and Col spread the woolen ground cover out under the wagonette that would protect the Destovs' quilts from the cold, wet earth. She straightened and looked up to see Keltin watching her. She gave him a grim smile.

"It's going to be hard getting any sleep tonight," she said.

"Do your best. I'm counting on you for the third shift."

"I'll be ready. Goodnight Keltin."

"Goodnight."

She crouched down and crawled under the wagonette as Keltin turned his attention on the rest of the camp. As the last of the company bedded down for the night, he exchanged a brief nod with Harper before turning to begin his watch. He positioned himself so that he wasn't facing the light from the fire or the two lanterns, letting his eyes adjust as much as possible to the gloomy night. The rain had stopped, and with the horses sleeping on their feet and the camp still, Keltin was able to train his ears for anything that might be lurking beyond the range of light from the lanterns and campfire.

Time passed slowly. He resisted the urge to check his pocket watch, knowing that less time had passed than it felt like. He stretched his shoulders and neck and rubbed his fingers together. It was a luxury of movement he wasn't able to take advantage of during a stand hunt, where the most important thing for him to do was to stay as perfectly still as possible. Then again, there was usually far less personal danger involved with a stand hunt than keeping watch over a campsite. Sitting out in the open, bathed in light, he felt terribly exposed, and was keenly aware of how vulnerable his sleeping companions were around him.

Eventually, Keltin broke down and withdrew his watch from his pocket. Popping open the old, scuffed brass clasp, he checked the hour and found that his shift was already more than half over. It was a small relief, though he would likely not get any sleep after lying back down. He was debating letting Wendi and Kuff sleep a little longer when he heard a rustling behind him.

Everything seemed to slow down like a nightmare moving at half-speed. Keltin turned as if submerged in pitch, raising his rifle to his shoulder with seemingly agonizing slowness. His eyes were temporarily blinded by the light of the campfire and lanterns. Even his eyelids felt slow as they tried to blink away the sunspots that filled up the campsite. A sudden, harsh scream came from somewhere behind the flashing red and green lights dominating his vision. He forced himself to look slightly to the side so that he could make out what was happening in his peripheral vision.

A sleevak was on top of Harper. A second one moved through the camp, as sounds of slavering monsters seemed to come from all sides. Keltin spun his rifle in the direction of the sleevak that was running through the camp, not trusting his adjusting vision to fire at the beast attacking Harper. Keltin advanced the chamber to a Capshire Shatter Round and fired in the direction he thought the beast was in. He was rewarded with a squeal of animal pain and fired a Haurizer Smasher at the sound.

As his vision cleared, he was able to take in the scene better. There were four sleevaks. One was on Harper, another was thrashing in the dirt just a few feet from the wagonette, the victim of Keltin's two lucky shots. The third and fourth were free and rushing towards the rest of the company. Everyone was awake and scrambling to defend themselves. Kuff was up like a bolt of lightning and tackled the third beast as it ran, knocking it over and rolling together in a frantic heap until they were both beyond the lanterns' light. There was a gunshot from under Keltin's feet and he knew that Elaine was firing upon the fourth beast.

He turned his attention to Harper. The sleevak was still on top of him, thrashing and biting with its long fangs. Keltin had three rounds left. A Reltac Spinner, a Capshire Shatter Round, and an Alpenion round filled with belferin acid. The Spinner might go through and hit Harper, and the shrapnel from the exploding Capshire could do the same. Keltin fired the acid round into the beast's spine between its shoulder blades. He regretted having already used his Smasher round, as it would have likely severed the spinal cord and paralyzed the monster. Still, the sudden, intense burning of the acid caused the beast to freeze and clench its muscles, arching upward and giving Keltin a clear shot. He fired a Reltac Spinner through the monster's exposed throat. The beast collapsed on top of Harper.

A quick survey of the camp showed that the immediate threat was over. Elaine and Wendi had put down the two other beasts in the camp, and Ross had gone off to support his hound. Keltin jumped down from the wagonette and raced to Harper. Grabbing the beast on top of him, Keltin flipped it over onto its back. The man it revealed underneath was in terrible shape with blood flowing from multiple wounds, including one long, angry cut across his left eye. Harper groaned and tried to sit up but Keltin dropped to his knees and pushed him back down.

"Stay still," he said firmly. "You're going to be all right."

Keltin pulled aside the man's clothes to see just how severe the wounds were. Several of the gashes were deep and weeping blood, but none of them seemed any deeper than the outer muscle layer.

Keltin looked up and saw several of the others approaching him. Col was among them.

"Get back!" Keltin yelled, pointing a hand covered in Harper's blood at the boy. "Don't come over here!"

Mrs. Destov immediately turned and steered her son back to the wagonette as Elaine rushed to Keltin's side. She made a small choking sound at the sight of Harper's injuries, but she drew in a shuddering breath and dropped to her knees beside him.

"What do you need me to do?" she asked quietly.

"Keep him calm. I've got bandages in my pack, though we may need more. We've got to get pressure on these wounds to keep him from bleeding out."

"Should we stitch them closed?"

"No. Don't sew him up too soon. You could lock in contamination and introduce infection that way."

Keltin got up and rushed to his pack. Ross appeared at his side as he rummaged through his kit.

"I've got bindings in my gear as well," he said. "Let me and Elaine take care of it. I've got experience with this sort of thing. With all this blood around, we need you back on watch."

"All right," said Keltin, passing the bandages over to the tamarrin hound trainer.

He took up his rifle and went to the wagonette resuming his place at the driver seat. Wendi came up to him hesitantly.

"What can I do, Mr. Moore?"

"Take up a watch position next to the others. We need to keep several lookouts in case the smell of blood draws any more of the boils to us."

Wendi nodded and went to stand near enough to Ross and Elaine to watch over them without having to see Harper. Mrs. Destov tentatively spoke to Keltin from the back of the carriage.

"Do you think your friend will survive?" she asked quietly.

"I don't know. First we have to stop the bleeding."

"And after that?"

Keltin took a deep breath and shook his head. "We'll have to strike camp and travel through the night. If there's any chance of saving him at all, it won't be here in the forest. We have to get him to civilization quickly."

"Of course. I'll help the boys get ready."

Keltin spared the briefest of looks towards her as she efficiently began directing her two boys to help her strike the camp before turning back to his watch, praying fervently that they wouldn't be too late for Harper.

CHAPTER 21 – LAST RESORT

Keltin rubbed his eyes and face with the palm of his hand. He inhaled the steam of his sweet broth and sipped it, willing the hot brew to imbue him with some desperately needed energy. It had been a long night of traveling after the attack. Hardly anyone had been able to sleep by riding in the back of the wagonette with Harper, and everyone was showing clear signs of exhaustion. At dawn, they'd paused long enough for a small cooking fire to be lit so that they could get something warm into them before pressing on.

Draining his cup, Keltin stowed it in his pack and checked to see if the rest of the group was ready to go. Elaine had taken over the task of driving the wagonette, and while her eyes were red, she gave him a brave, tight-lipped smiled. Ross and Kuff took a position in front of the wagonette, while Keltin placed himself behind it as the rearguard. He told himself that if they could only get through the day that they would be out of the forest by nightfall. At least, that was what he fervently prayed for as they began moving down the trail.

The wind, which had fallen off somewhat in the late night, had picked up markedly with the coming of dawn. The trees creaked and groaned as they twisted and leaned away from the severe gusts rocking through their bare branches. Keltin turned up the collar of his coat against the chill breeze as it whipped around him. Despite his weariness, he jumped every time a branch was broken off and fell with a crash nearby. Several times, they were forced to stop and wait while Ross and Wendi pulled branches out of the trail as Keltin watched for sleevaks.

It was late in the morning when Keltin noticed Elaine turning in the driver seat and waving to him. He quickened his pace to catch up to her.

"What's wrong?" he said. "Do you see something?"

"No, but I think we need to rest the horses."

Keltin sighed, but nodded.

"All right. We'll rest, but only for a short time. We need to keep moving as much as we can."

Elaine nodded and reined in the horses as Keltin went back behind the wagonette. He found a log near the side of the trail and took a seat, watching for signs of bestial movement among the blustery forest. After a moment Elaine approached him and sat down next to him.

"How are you holding up?" he asked, his eyes on the forest.

"I'm all right. I'm not much of a driver, but they're good horses. Still, I worry about controlling them if sleevaks attack again."

"Just keep a tight hand on them. If they bolt, they could turn the carriage over."

"I'll do my best."

"I know. How's Harper?"

"He's in a lot of pain. Don't tell my mother, but Mr. Ross has been giving him sips from a flask of spirits that he had."

"I'm going to check on him."

"I think he finally managed to get to sleep."

"I'll be careful not to wake him."

Keltin found Harper lying on the narrow floor of the wagonette between the two benches positioned over the wheels and facing each other. Sitting on one of the benches, Keltin looked down at the newspaperman. His dressings were soiled, though most of the bleeding seemed to have stopped for the time being. The hardest thing to see was the dark, dried blood on the strip of cloth tied over his left eye. Keltin was certain that even if Harper survived the rest of their journey, his eye was lost.

Keltin was just getting up to leave when Harper's good eye opened. He stared at the sky with an unfocused gaze for a moment before turning to Keltin.

"I'm sorry," said Keltin. "I didn't mean to wake you."

"I wasn't asleep."

Harper's voice was barely more than a whisper. Keltin leaned down to hear him better. "How's the pain?"

"Like a soul in hell." Harper fixed Keltin was a somber gaze. "How did my eye look?"

Keltin hesitated. Harper feebly waved his hand.

"Don't bother trying to lie. We both know you're no good at it. Listen, I know you're all driving the horses slower than you could because of me. Don't bother. You need to get out of this plaguing forest. And if you need to leave me behind—"

"Don't talk rot," said Keltin. "We're not leaving you."

"I'd rather die knowing that it helped keep the rest of you safe."

"Well it wouldn't. We're traveling as fast as we can right now, and you're not doing anything but taking up some space in the wagonette. Leaving you behind wouldn't accomplish anything but getting you killed and upsetting Wendi and the boys."

Harper blinked his good eye in shock at the blunt words. Keltin gave him the ghost of a smile.

"Remember, I'm a bad liar, so you know it's all true. Just hold on until we get to Krendaria. Then we can work together to come up with some embellished story about how you nobly saved us all at great personal risk."

Harper made a sound between a chuckle and a groan as he gave a tight-lipped smiled.

"You just worry about the sleevaks, Mr. Moore, and let me handle the embellished stories."

"It's a deal."

Harper sucked in air through his teeth as a spasm of pain

hit him. He let it pass, then opened his good eye again. When he spoke, his voice was even softer than before.

"Tell the truth, Keltin. Do you think we'll make it out of this forest?"

Keltin looked up at the rest of the company, somewhere between sleeping on their feet and keeping an eye on the trees. He looked back at Harper.

"We're in the middle of a twisted fete, I can't deny that. But Wulp said that it was only two days' journey through Pike Forest. We're almost through. We just have to keep pushing. With luck, we'll be on the other side of the fence before sundown."

* * *

Keltin stumbled and quietly cursed himself. It was getting dark, and they still hadn't reached the end of the forest. Worse, they were all desperately tired. Mrs. Destov and her sons had gotten back onto the wagonette more than an hour before, and Elaine had followed soon after. Even Ross had given up, climbing onto the driver's seat to take the reins and allow Wendi to rest her head on his shoulder, leaving just Kuff to trail along behind the carriage at Keltin's side. Keltin trudged stubbornly on, but he had to admit that he was losing steam. His eyes kept drifting to the forest floor instead of the shadowed trees around them, and his feet kept dragging and catching on branches and roots.

"Keltin?"

Keltin looked up with a start without realizing that he had been staring at the ground again. Elaine was sitting in the back of the wagonette, watching him with clear concern.

"Why don't you take a turn riding with us? You're the only one who hasn't yet."

"I'll be all right. I'm used to walking."

Elaine fixed Keltin with a plaintive expression.

"Keltin, please, you need to rest, if only for a moment. We need you."

Keltin sighed. "All right. But only so that I can keep watch from the wagonette, and only until I'm rested."

Elaine opened the backdoor and reached down to help Keltin jump up into the moving carriage. He turned around, trying to find a spot for himself in the cramped conditions. Harper lay on the floor between the two bench seats while Elaine and her family sat above him, all of them keeping their feet up on the seats to avoid stepping on the poor injured man below them. Keltin carefully stepped over Harper to sit on the left-side bench seat next to Col with Elaine sitting opposite him. He admitted to himself that it felt incredibly good to be off his feet as he set his pack down next to him. He set down the Ripper and was about to rest his rifle next to it when something occurred to him.

"How many shots do you have left in that pistol?" he whispered across to Elaine.

"Just one."

"Here."

Keltin handed her his rifle.

"Don't you need it?"

"I have this," he said, pulling his hand-cannon from its holster. "Besides, you're the only one here besides me that's used my rifle before. Do you remember how to work the chamber?"

"I think so. What do you have it loaded with?"

"Two Spinners, two Haurizer Smashers, and a belferin acid round. You may want to go all Smashers though. If anything attacks us, it'll likely be coming straight towards you, and that bony head-frill will cover most of the vitals."

"Will a Smasher round break through the bones of its skull?"

"Maybe, if you hit the right spot. Don't worry about it though. Just aim for the head. Even if it doesn't penetrate the skull, the impact of the Smasher should stun it enough for us to get away from it as long as we keep moving."

"All right. I'll do that."

Keltin reached into his pocket and handed her his last box

of Haurizer Smashers. Popping open the chamber of his hand cannon, he considered briefly what to load it with. After a moment's thought, he went with a combination of Reltac Spinners and Capshire Shatter Rounds. Clicking the chamber back into place, he turned to watch the shadows of trees drifting by.

The rain and wind had finally died off, leaving a sky filled with the tattered remnants of clouds and winking stars. The silver light of a three-quarter moon painted everything in shades of gray and black, with no color at all beyond the golden warmth from the lanterns. Keltin blinked his eyes rapidly, trying to discern between actual movement and the hallucinations of his exhausted mind. His thoughts drifted, meandering from the feel of the cushioned seats to the blood seeping from Harper's wounds to the smell of Wendi's cooking. Everything blurred together in a jostled, disturbing haze as the carriage bumped and rumbled through the night.

Keltin found himself somewhere between dreaming and imagining, struggling to tell the difference between what was real and what wasn't. Twice, he decided that he needed to get back up and start walking again, just to shake the heavy malaise upon him. Both times, he only gradually realized that he hadn't moved from his spot on the bench. He thought he heard voices too. Whispered conversations between Wendi and Ross, then Elaine and one of her brothers. He couldn't tell which one. There was only the sound of voices, no discernable words or phrases that he could pick out.

"There!"

The voice was Col's. Keltin felt himself nod in pleased satisfaction for identifying it, followed by annoyance when the voice came again.

"There! Right there! Look!"

A gunshot rang out in the night. Keltin came awake gasping for air to fuel his drowsy mind. He opened his eyes and looked around frantically, trying to make sense of what was happening. Elaine was braced against the railing on her side of the carriage, firing his rifle into the night. Col was up and pointing by her side, his hunting knife bare in his hand, as Wendi struggled to turn Harper's rifle around from where she'd had it propped against the seat. Suddenly she screamed as a sleevak appeared out of the darkness and threw itself onto one of the horses. The terrified animal screeched and reared up in the harness, causing the carriage to veer violently to the side. Keltin tried to aim for the beast on the horse but was unable to get a clear shot. Ross tossed the reins in Wendi's direction and blasted the sleevak clinging to the horse with his scattergun. Unfortunately, Wendi hadn't realized that Ross had tried to give her the reins as they fell down out of reach. With no driver, the two terrified horses bolted, sending the carriage careening through the forest at a reckless speed.

Keltin tried to make his way to the front of the wagonette to help, but was blocked by the Destovs all standing up in the center of the carriage bed, trying to stay away from the sides without standing on top of Harper. In a desperate attempt to get around them, Keltin jumped up onto the left side bench. He struggled to keep his balance as the carriage bumped and swayed on the winding trail, focusing on putting one foot in front of the other to inch his way forward.

"Mr. Moore! There!"

Keltin turned to where Col was pointing and saw a sleevak launch itself up and cling to the railing on his side of the coach. Keltin fired a blast from the hand cannon into the beast's face. The creature's skull bulged out as the Capshire Shatter Round blew apart the monster's brain, knocking it backwards and leaving it somewhere behind the carriage. The wagonette gave another sudden lurch. Keltin felt his balance give way and instinctively took a step forward to steady himself, but instead of the firm running board around the outer edge, he encountered only air. For a moment he was weightless, then he felt his left side collide with the wagonette and suddenly he was on the ground. He immediately rolled and started to stand when a stabbing pain erupted from his ankle. He crashed back down to earth and realized that he had hurt himself badly in the tumble.

Looking up, he saw that the red tinted trailing lights of the carriage's twin lanterns were already quickly fading from view. He called out, but in a moment they were gone, leaving Keltin alone in the dark night. Nearby he heard the sound of sleevaks. Clutching his hand-cannon, he forced himself into a sitting position and tried to force his eyes to adjust to the gloom. He was able to make out the dim outlines of trees and bushes, but nothing more.

Something struck him from behind. Keltin fell forward and instinctively covered the back of his head with his free hand as he tried to get the hand-cannon into firing position over his shoulder. The sleevak thrashed and tore at his coat, tossing Keltin around like a boxer's practice bag. Keltin fired his pistol but the shots went wide as he felt jaws snap shut around his arm. He cried out in pain, struggling to adjust his aim before the beast's claws found purchase in his flesh.

Suddenly the weight on top of him was gone as the pressure around his arm disappeared. Looking up from the leafy ground, Keltin saw Kuff's silhouette striking the sleevak like a train engine, launching them both into a rolling knot of savage fighting. It was too dark for Keltin to risk a shot into the melee. He turned and began to crawl off of the trail, seeking some small measure of cover. His probing hands found an exposed root and followed it to the base of a large tree. Turning, he pushed himself against the trunk, unable to contain a cry of pain as he moved and shifted his injured ankle around to get into position. With his back against the tree, he turned back to the darkness with his revolver in his good hand, ready for whatever may come.

The sounds of fighting kept coming from Kuff and the sleevak somewhere in front of him. He could see movement, but didn't dare fire. Keltin tried to remember the command to draw Kuff closer so that he could see better and help the hound. He was still trying to remember it when he suddenly heard a hiss from his left side. Keltin readied himself, but the beast didn't attack him. Kuff yelped horribly as the second sleevak joined the fight.

"Kuff!" Keltin cried. "Here! Come here!"

Keltin screamed at the top of his lungs, trying to draw the hound to him so he could help, but it was useless. Even if Kuff wanted to heed his command, he wouldn't be able to. The hound was in a desperate fight for his life. Keltin cursed the sleevaks, hurling every foul oath he could think of at the monsters to draw them to him, but nothing worked. His voice went hoarse, leaving nothing but the sound of savage fighting and Kuff's plaintive sounds of pain and defiant barking. Eventually, the horrid noises faded into faint whimpering and mewling. One way or another, Kuff's fight with the sleevaks was over.

"Kuff? Kuff, come here."

Nothing stirred. Keltin leaned back against the tree. Adrenaline drained from his blood and Keltin's body roared with pain in its absence. His leg felt like it was crushed under a boulder, while his arm and side burned like flaming pitch. The wind pulled the clouds away from the moon and revealed more of the silver-tinged forest around him. Keltin looked where Kuff had fought the sleevaks. He saw bodies. Bloody, torn, mutilated. Among them, he saw one that lay sprawled and helpless with a long feathered tail.

"Kuff!"

Keltin's throat ached as he called out to the hound. Kuff didn't move. Keltin tried to sit up but fell back in agony. His vision blurred for a moment, and he closed his eyes, sucking in deep breaths as he tried to gain control over his senses. Opening his eyes again, he was confronted by the sight of a sleevak up on its feet, moving slowly towards him. He couldn't tell if the beast had been there before or had recently arrived. The light was too poor to see if it was injured. It crawled forward slowly, either from injuries or from cautiousness of the death surrounding it. The sleevak paused, seemingly surveying the scene.

Keltin lifted his hand-cannon and pulled the trigger. Click. He tried to move his free hand to his coat to find more ammunition, but his arm wasn't working right. How badly had the sleevak injured it? There wasn't time to consider as the beast in front of him continued slowly towards him. He dropped the hand cannon in his lap and used his good hand to fumble for his coat, but it was gone. The sleevak that had pounced on him had managed to tear the tattered, patchwork garment apart completely, leaving nothing but sleeves and shreds left on him.

Keltin reached for his hunting knife, remembering too late that he'd given it to Col. Looking up at the approaching beast, Keltin's heart pounded heavily in his chest. He was unarmed, wounded, and totally helpless. Memories mocked him of all the times he'd had people react in awe and fear at his impressive array of weaponry. His custom-made hunting rifle, the Ripper, the hand-cannon, his Lawrie hunting knife... how proud he had felt wearing them like badges of honor, to say nothing of the...

Pocket pistol! Keltin dug in his vest pocket and felt the small shape of the tiny firearm. He drew it out, feeling like a child facing a giant with a toy. The single Haurizer Popper in the chamber had no stopping power for a beast the size of the sleevak. His only chance was a precise shot, just a single chance to hit a moving target only slightly larger than the round itself. Second eye from the left, straight to the brain.

Keltin had to improve his chances. The sleevak was only yards from him now. He took the hand cannon in his off-hand, gripping it by the chamber as he wrapped what was left of his coat around his hand and arm. He was just finishing when the sleevak lunged forward. Keltin thrust out the hand cannon towards the gapping jaws. The gun and his hand disappeared between the fangs as the sturdy steel propped the jaws open. The man-sized creature threw itself upon him, and Keltin used all his remaining strength to wrestle the pocket pistol into position. Directly in front of the eye. One of the claws caught his thigh and tore downwards. He pulled the trigger even as he screamed.

The report of the pocket pistol was lost in the screams and cries of Keltin and the sleevak. He reached down for the foreleg clawing his leg and pulled it up and away. He struggled and pushed against the beast, trying to free his hand from its jaws and legs. Slowly, a realization seeped through the haze of his desperation. The sleevak wasn't fighting back. Keltin paused. Silence and stillness. The Haurizer Popper had found its mark. Keltin collapsed back against the tree, the sleevak still on top of him. The forest grew dark, though he didn't know if it was clouds covering the moon again or his own vision fading. A distant part of his brain told him that he must be in shock as he felt himself trembling uncontrollably. Somehow he managed to extricate his hand from the sleevak's jaws and shoved the beast over. He smelled blood everywhere and wondered how much of it was his own. He tried to get up, but his body convulsed painfully and he sat back. He closed his eyes and laid his head back against the solid tree behind him.

"Keltin!"

Forcing his eyes open again, Keltin saw Elaine racing towards him bathed in the golden light of a lantern in her hand, his rifle held firmly in the other. She threw herself on the ground next to him, tears streaming down her cheeks as she sobbed. She set aside the lantern and rifle and reached out to him, her hands fluttering with uncertainty at the sight of his injuries. Her fingers found his face, and she drew close to him.

"Are you all right?" she whispered desperately. "Tell me you're all right."

Keltin coughed softly and met her glistening eyes.

"I think I twisted my ankle," he rasped.

Elaine gave him a stunned look for a moment. Then she laughed, which quickly turned back into sobbing. She drew her face just an inch away from his.

"I thought I would die without you," she whispered, and kissed him deeply.

There was an anguished cry, and they both looked to see Wendi and Ross kneeling next to Kuff. Wendi was sobbing as Ross carefully examined his hound.

"He saved my life," Keltin said softly. "He gave his life for me."

Ross said something to Wendi, and they had a hurried conversation. Wendi got up and rushed to Keltin's side as Elaine began pulling aside his clothes to examine his wounds.

"Keltin! We were so worried. Are you all right?"

"He's cut in several places," said Elaine. "We need to stop the bleeding. And he's not able to walk right now. Is Kuff…"

"He's alive. If we can get him to a town, we may be able to save him."

Keltin shook his head. "There's no telling how far we still have to go before we're out of this hexed forest."

Elaine smiled through her tears.

"But Keltin, we're already there! When the horses bolted, they took us right to the perimeter fence. It's only a few minutes' walk away."

"Then help me up. We'll get to the other side of the fence and then treat our wounds."

"Just as soon as I get these bound," said Elaine, using the tatters of Keltin's jacket to bind his wounds.

Wendi ran off and returned a short time later driving the wagonette. Elaine and Ross had finished binding Keltin and Kuff's injuries by that time, and together with Wendi and Mrs. Destov they managed to get them both into the wagonette on the two bench seats above Harper. As soon as they were settled, Ross started up the exhausted horses as the rest of the company fell in step beside the carriage.

Keltin looked down from his perch to see Elaine dabbing at her eyes with her sleeve as her brother Col walked alongside her.

"Can I show him now?" he said in a soft voice.

Elaine wiped at her eyes and smiled.

"Yes, Col. Go ahead."

Col took her place next to the wagonette and called up to Keltin.

"Mr. Moore, I'm glad that you're all right. I wanted to show you something."

Col held out Keltin's hunting knife. In the light of the carriage's lanterns it was easy to see the red stain on the blade.

"I used this on a beast, Mr. Moore. One of them was climbing up the side of the wagonette, and I slashed it with your knife. Mother says that I must have killed it all on my own, but I think Elaine was the one who did. But I did help."

Keltin gritted his teeth as the wagonette jostled around and managed a gamely smile.

"Good work," he said. "But remember, you need to keep your weapon clean. Remember, you never know when a weapon, any weapon, may save your life."

"I'll remember," said Col. "I promise."

CHAPTER 22 – IN RECOVERY

Keltin tried in vain to find a comfortable position in his hotel room bed. It seemed as if no combination or configuration of pillows and blankets could compensate for the maddening need to remain bedridden. It all seemed so unnecessary. After all, the town doctor had said that he had only sprained his ankle, and the bite and claw wounds he'd suffered had been relatively minor with little signs of infection. Still, he'd been confined to bed in the local hotel until the next train bound for Carvalen made it to their secluded town in the north of Krendaria.

At least he had company. Harper lay in a nearby bed, propped up by pillows so that he could more easily write in the notebook on his knees. Keltin took the opportunity to examine his friend. He'd come through a little more roughly than Keltin had, but would survive in fairly good health, except for his eye. Harper would wear a patch for the rest of his life, news that he had born stoically since receiving it, only saying that it would mean his days of undercover journalism had likely come to an end.

Harper looked up to see Keltin watching him. He gave a wan smile and lifted his notebook.

"At least this gives me a chance to get a head-start on my

next piece," he said.

"I bet I can guess what it will be about."

"Maybe. I don't share my work before it's done, though I predict that you'll probably say that I exaggerated most of it."

"I don't doubt it. Just be sure to mention your part in all of this. We couldn't have made it without you."

"That's kind of you to say, but I know that you all sacrificed a great deal to see that I made it back in one piece. Mostly. I want you to know something. When we get back to Collinsworth, if you ever need anything from me, you just let me know. I may never make much of a beast hunter, but I can find all sorts of ways to make myself useful. If nothing else, I can give you 'first look' at any reports of beast attacks that come to the desks of the Gazette."

"I appreciate that. And you know that you can rely on me if you need anything."

"I know Keltin. Trust me, I know."

There was a soft knock on the door.

"Come in."

Ross stepped inside and closed the door behind him.

"Well, how are you two feeling? Well enough to travel?"

"We should be," said Keltin. "Did you get the tickets?"

"I did. Krendaria North Line, it should take you all to Carvalen. You can get another train from there to Collinsworth."

"What sort of price did you manage for the horses and wagonette?" asked Harper.

"Fair, I'd say. Neither were in the best shape after that plaguing forest. But it was more than enough to cover the train tickets, and I gave the rest to Mrs. Destov." He turned to Keltin. "By the way, I had a fellow from the Brothers come to me asking whether we had any gifts from Malpin for him."

"Was everything in good condition for him?" asked Keltin.

"He seemed satisfied with it, and said how grateful he was."

"I'm glad. Despite what happened in Carris, the Brothers did do a great deal for us and the Destovs. It was only right that we try to repay them a little."

"How's Kuff doing?" asked Harper.

Ross sighed and shook his head.

"He'll live, but he'll never hunt again. One of his legs was too bad to keep. He'll have to learn to walk with three now."

"He fought those sleevaks to protect me," said Keltin. "I'm so sorry, Ross."

"He's alive because of you. That's what important."

Harper cleared his throat uncomfortably. "Then you're not going to... well..."

"No. Kuff has the strength of his mother in him, I'll not waste that bloodline on an early injury. I'll take him home with me. He'll make a fine stud."

"I'm glad to hear it, though I'll miss that big lout. I won't know what to do with all of my meals just to myself from now on."

"Well," said Ross, "I suppose this is as good a time as any to say my farewells."

"You're not going to see us off to the train station?"

"I don't like long goodbyes." He extended a hand to the newspaperman. "I was glad to know you, Harper. Safe travels back to Collinsworth." They shook hands and Ross came to Keltin's bedside. "It was good to hunt with you again, Mr. Moore. Good luck with your business."

"Thank you, Ross. If you ever need work, come look me up."

"I appreciate that, but I'm a Krendarian man, and I won't leave my country just because it's in poor straits. Maybe I'll petition the government to start another company of tamarrin hound trainers. I think Captain Tallow would approve of that."

"I'm sure he would, and you'd make a fine successor to him. Take care."

"You too. I think the ladies were hoping to visit you sometime this afternoon. Would you like me to let them know that you're able to see them now?"

"Of course. Thank you again, Ross."

The tamarrin hound trainer left them. Soon, another knock sounded from the door.

"Come in."

Keltin tried to sit up as Wendi, Elaine, and her mother entered the room. Mrs. Destov quickly raised her hand.

"Please don't bother on our account, Mr. Moore," she said. "By all means, stay comfortable."

Elaine immediately went to Keltin's side.

"How are you feeling?" she asked.

"Tired of being in bed, but otherwise I'm fine."

Keltin gave her a smile that he hoped showed none of his inner uncertainty. They hadn't had a chance to say anything to each other of their shared kiss in Pike Forest, and Keltin had begun to wonder if they ever would. Forcing his mind from Elaine for the moment, he turned his attention to Mrs. Destov.

"Ross told us that everything has been taken care of for the trip."

"Yes indeed, as long as you are sure that you're able to travel."

"I can travel. I'm very ready to go home."

"I'm glad. It's been too long since the children have seen their father." Her face fell as her eyes drifted away from him. "Although, it will be difficult starting all over again. We were able to bring so little with us, and we know no one where we are going."

"Don't worry, Mother," said Elaine. "We'll make a new home for ourselves."

Mrs. Destov gave a brave smile.

"Of course. And we will be among good friends. Mr. Moore, Mr. Harper, and of course our dear Wendi."

Keltin blinked, turning to the young woman. "What's this? You're not staying with Ross?"

Wendi shook her head and gave a shy smile. "Actually, Mrs. Destov has offered to take me with them and hire me on to do the cooking once they're established somewhere."

"I'm surprised Ross didn't mention that."

"I think that he's trying to pretend that it doesn't bother him," she said with a sad expression. "I feel bad for him."

"He has his own life, dear," said Mrs. Destov. "I know he's

come to see you as the daughter he never had, but he knows that it's only proper that you should find your own way in life. I know that I will dearly love to have you nearby."

"Well, I'm glad for you, Wendi," said Harper. "It sounds like all has ended very happily for everyone involved, all things considered."

"I agree. But, we must allow you both to have your rest. Come along, Wendi, Elaine, there's still packing to be done before we catch our train this evening."

Elaine gave Keltin a parting smile and left along with Wendi and her mother. Harper set aside his notebook and almost immediately began to softly snore. Keltin laid back on his pillow. He wasn't sure he'd be able to sleep through the newspaperman's snoring, but for once, he didn't mind not being able to sleep. Just knowing everyone was safe for the moment was enough, and he let himself relax, watching the sunlight through the window and waiting for evening to fall.

EPILOGUE – GOLDEN MOMENTS

"You know something, Keltin? When you clean up a bit, you're not half-bad looking."

Keltin grimaced into the mirror.

"I hope you're right, because I feel like a fop."

"Oh no," said Jaylocke with a grin from where he lounged on the bed. "You're not wearing nearly enough face powder to be a fop."

"Thank you."

Keltin fidgeted with his cravat. He was fairly certain that he was wearing his outfit correctly, but it still looked wrong on him. He tugged self-consciously at his high collar as Bor've'tai appeared in the mirror behind him.

"How are you feeling, Keltin?"

"I'll be all right as long as I can keep from adjusting this thing during the ceremony."

"Then you feel ready to give away your sister?"

Keltin clenched his jaw. "I don't like hearing it said quite that way."

"Forgive me. I only meant to ask how it felt to know that she will soon be getting married. Of course, she'll always be your sister."

"I know. I suppose I'm all right. Isaac did ask my

permission, and I gave it. I think he'll make her happy. Don't you?"

The Loopi nodded. "When I look in their eyes, I see a deep love between them. For my part, I think Isaac will take good care of Mary."

"He'd better," said Jaylocke. "I certainly wouldn't want to see what was left of the fellow if Keltin ever heard of him mistreating his sister."

"Don't be morbid, Jaylocke. This is a happy day."

"I am happy. Can't you tell?"

"To me, you look like you always do."

"Well there you are." Jaylocke frowned slightly as he turned to Keltin. "I am sorry that you weren't able to see your mother. It's a shame that she wasn't feeling well enough to stay for the wedding and had to go back to Harringtown."

Keltin nodded without answering. He'd spoken to Mary about their mother and her convenient departure before being forced to see her estranged son. Keltin had told Mary that as much as it would hurt him, he was willing to avoid the wedding if it meant that Mary could have her mother there, but she would have none of it. She wanted him to present her at the wedding in their father's place. If their mother couldn't put aside her stubborn pride, then she would only hurt herself. Keltin tried to remind himself of that, but the ache was still there. Looking up, he saw Bor've'tai watching him with the same deep, penetrating eyes he always seemed to have whenever Keltin was feeling troubled. The Loopi placed a large hand on Keltin's shoulder, and they shared a warm smile.

A knock came from the door. Jaylocke jumped up from the bed and answered it to reveal one of the Whitts' maidservants.

"Mr. Moore?"

Keltin left his cravat alone and turned from the mirror.

"Yes? Is it time?"

"Not yet, sir. But the Destov family wish to see you briefly before the ceremony begins, if you are able."

"Of course. Where are they?"

"They're gathered together in the library. Shall I escort

you?"

"Yes please. I'm still not very good at finding my way around the house." Keltin turned to his friends. "Will you two be all right?"

"Don't worry about us," said Bor've'tai. "We'll see you at the ceremony."

Keltin nodded and followed the maid out of the room and downstairs. The Whitts had made a fantastic effort to evoke a spring-time wedding despite the gently falling snow outside. Silken flowers and green holy boughs festooned the bannisters and side tables as expensive wall drapings bathed the great house in warm shades of pale rose and lavender. Keltin passed by the ballroom and glanced inside at the location for the ceremony itself. A staging area had been set up at one end where Father Rafferty sat serenely waiting to act as the officiator. Guests and family members had already begun to gather in the assembled chairs, and Keltin waved to a few of his family before turning and following the maid to the library.

Stepping inside, he found Mr. and Mrs. Destov along with their children. All of them were dressed for the wedding, but there was one of them that captured Keltin's entire attention. When Keltin had first seen Elaine, she'd already been trapped for weeks in a farmhouse surrounded by beasts . Later, when he'd found her at the Harstev farm, she'd been living on the run for days, after which they had spent most of their time together roughing it across the countryside. But now he saw her in the resplendent glory of a young woman of elegance and refinement. Her dark hair was up in a cascade of curls, and her gown shimmered in shades of gold and white, showing off her elegant shoulders and sculpted arms. When she saw him she smiled, and he felt himself go light-headed. He barely heard or saw Mr. Destov approach him and shake his hand enthusiastically.

"It's good to see you as always, Mr. Moore," he said. "Congratulations on this blessed day. You must be very proud."

Keltin struggled to find his voice, his eyes still beholding nothing but Elaine.

"Thank you," he murmured. "I'm very happy for Mary."

"And how handsome you look," said Mrs. Destov. "Truly, you'd look a catch for any of the young girls we knew back home. Don't you think so, Elaine?"

Elaine's cheeks reddened slightly as her smile deepened.

"I do, mother. I truly do."

Mr. and Mrs. Destov chattered away pleasantly about the upcoming ceremony, seemingly oblivious to Keltin and Elaine's silent staring. Or, perhaps, they noticed it and didn't mind. Keltin wasn't sure which, and frankly couldn't be bothered to figure it out at the moment. He was torn back to reality by young Derrick tugging on his mother's arm.

"Mother, can we give it to him now?"

Mrs. Destov smiled. "Of course, but I think Elaine would like to give it to him."

"But I want to give it to him."

"Hush dear."

Elaine turned and picked up a package from a nearby table. She floated to Keltin and handed it to him.

"This is from all of us," she said.

Keltin opened the box. Inside, he saw a flash of rich brown. Reaching in, he pulled out a long, magnificent leather duster coat. Running his hand over the leather, he could feel that while it was glorious to look at, the hide had been specially treated to be uncommonly sturdy and resistant to damage. The coat reached below his knees, and even had a detachable inner lining for colder weather. Elaine's eyes glowed as she watch him examining it.

"We made sure to find one with plenty of deep pockets," she said. "It should also repel snow and rain, as well as being tougher than regular leather. I do hope the fit is right."

"Try it on!" said Derrick.

"It doesn't go with his clothes," said Col.

"He can still try it on."

Keltin turned the jacket around and slid it over his arms. The fit was perfect. He adjusted the sleeves and turned to the

241

Destov family. They smiled at him. He felt his throat tighten.

"Thank you," he said. "It's the finest piece of clothing I've ever owned."

"It's only a token of how we all feel," said Mr. Destov. "If not for you, our family would have remained separated, perhaps forever. If you ever need anything from us, you need only ask."

"And we expect you to come and visit us as often as you can," put in Mrs. Destov. "We'll be finding a home in Collinsworth so that Mr. Destov can see to Mr. Whitt's investments from there. That's where your company is, isn't it Mr. Moore? I insist that you come to our home as often as you can once we all return there."

"It would be my greatest pleasure."

There was a gentle knock at the door. Keltin turned to see the same maidservant again.

"Pardon me, but Mrs. Whitt says that it's almost time, and that Mr. Moore should take his place."

"Of course," said Mrs. Destov. "Come along everyone, let's go take our seats."

Keltin quickly removed his new coat as the Destovs filed past him. Elaine paused, placing a hand on his arm and leaning close to him.

"There will be a dance after the ceremony," she said softly. "I would love it if you asked me to accompany you to it."

Keltin swallowed. "I'm not much of a dancer."

"I'll teach you. Will you say yes?"

Keltin nodded. "Nothing would make me happier."

Elaine gave him a radiant smile and followed her family to the ballroom. Keltin set aside his new coat and followed the maid, his mind reeling. The Destovs would be in Collinsworth. Elaine would be in Collinsworth. And he had a standing invitation to visit their home. He realized that he was grinning like a fool, and didn't bother hiding it.

The maid stopped him and indicated where he should stand and wait. After a moment, a door opened, and Mary stepped out. She was beautiful in pure white, her cheeks flushed and her eyes shining. Keltin smiled at her and held out his arm. She took it as he turned and led her into the ballroom to the sound of soft music and a collective sigh of joy from their friends and family.

ABOUT THE AUTHOR

Lindsay Schopfer is the award-winning author of *The Adventures of Keltin Moore*, a series of steampunk-flavored fantasy novels about a professional monster hunter. His second Keltin Moore novel, *Into the North*, won first place in the OZMA Award for Fantasy as part of the Chanticleer International Book Awards. He also wrote the sci-fi survivalist novel *Lost Under Two Moons* and the short story collection Magic, Mystery and Mirth. Lindsay's workshops and master classes on the craft of writing are top-rated in writing conferences across the Pacific Northwest. Currently, he teaches creative writing at South Puget Sound Community College.

www.lindsayschopfer.com

Made in the USA
Columbia, SC
01 October 2021